The Winter War

The Winter War

*Translated from the Swedish
by Tiina Nunnally*

Philip Teir

W F HOWES LTD

This large print edition published in 2015 by
W F Howes Ltd
Unit 4, Rearsby Business Park, Gaddesby Lane,
Rearsby, Leicester LE7 4YH

1 3 5 7 9 10 8 6 4 2

First published in the Swedish in 2015
by Serpent's Tail

A CIP catalogue record for this book is available
from the British Library

ISBN 978 1 51000 974 5

Typeset by Palimpsest Book Production Limited,
Falkirk, Stirlingshire

And yet those trivial matters were not without significance in life, because life consists of trivial matters.

August Strindberg

NOVEMBER TO DECEMBER

CHAPTER 1

The first mistake that Max and Katriina made that winter – and they would make many mistakes before their divorce – was to deep-freeze their grandchildren's hamster.

The whole thing was an accident. Max happened to step on the hamster. He felt something soft moving under his foot, he heard an awful, strange squeak from the floor, and then it was too late. Blixten, who was only six months old, ended up in a plastic bag in the very back of the freezer.

That was enough to make their elder daughter, Helen, refuse to speak to them for two whole weeks. But when Max thought about it, he wondered whether the problems hadn't actually started earlier, back in November.

It had been a remarkably mild autumn. Töölö Bay sighed in the damp November fog as joggers huffed and puffed their way past. On a Friday towards the end of the month, Max and Katriina were invited to dinner by the Keskinens. Katriina was quickly drawn into the festivities while Max – just as he'd expected – was seated next to her boss.

Wivan Winckelmann was a short woman in her sixties with a horrible voice whose sole purpose seemed to be to seize hold of Max's nerves and squeeze them tight. She was an upper-echelon executive within the Helsinki and Nyland medical district, a woman with tremendous influence in the entire public sector. She was married to a rabbit-like, bald-headed man named Pertti, who always seemed to stand a metre behind her, as if he found Wivan to be an effective shield against the malevolent demands of the world.

The Keskinens lived in one of the new neighbourhoods in Nordsjö, in a flat straight out of a modern Finnish film: clinical, white and sterile, a flat in which Max imagined a serial killer would feel right at home. Previously they'd lived in an old Art Nouveau-style building on Fredriksgatan. Max had liked the Keskinens better when they'd lived in their former flat. It was the sort of residence that could be bought during the recession in the 1990s, which was exactly what they'd done. Like Max, Risto Keskinen had done well during those crisis years. They both worked in professions that had not been negatively affected by the bad times. On the contrary: while the rest of Finland sank into an economic malaise causing massive unemployment, Risto and Max had both prospered in their respective fields. The crisis seemed to increase the demand for the type of societal diagnoses that were Max's speciality within the field of sociology. And Risto, who was a psychiatrist, had been fully occupied with patients who came to him in the wake of the recession, bringing divorces and personal tragedies with them.

Max exchanged air kisses with Tuula Keskinen, who then disappeared further into the flat, linking arms with Katriina and carrying a gin and tonic in one hand.

Katriina and Max hadn't said a single word to each other in the taxi. Max had merely stared out of the window, enjoying the sensation of motion and the smooth ride as it raced along Sturegatan while the rain fell like glossy confetti. It had been raining all week, a gentle and pleasant rain that coloured the tree trunks black and brought a constant chill to everyone's cheeks.

The dark season had arrived early this year. Max had spent the entire autumn working on a manuscript with a March deadline that was approaching at a nerve-racking speed. Whenever he glanced out of the window of his office in the afternoon, he was always surprised to see how short the days were.

That same autumn their younger daughter, Eva, had moved to London, and Katriina had sunk into what she herself called a 'depression', although Max thought this was simply a self-absorbed description of what happened to all parents when their children got older. By turning this transition into a personal crisis, Katriina was able to use it for her own dramatic purposes.

5

Three months earlier, when they had driven Eva to the airport, Katriina had talked on and on – as she always did – about what Eva should do after her year in London, what opportunities might be open to her, how she should arrange her life and how much money she needed to save each month if she managed to get a job. She had also mentioned, as one possibility, that Eva could resume her abandoned studies in Helsinki, and maybe even study for her Masters exams.

'Do you know what? I really don't want to think about that, Mum. Not everybody wants to plan their life down to the smallest detail,' Eva said from the back seat of the car where she was texting on her mobile phone. She'd spent the whole summer living at home with them because she'd given up her flat when she was accepted at the art school in London. She claimed she needed to save money, even though she'd never tried to find a summer job. She was twenty-nine and had whiled away the summer lying on the balcony getting a suntan and drinking wine.

'Okay, okay, I'm just saying that it'd be good if you had some sort of plan.'

'But I do have a plan. I'm going to study art. And hopefully I'll be dating a lot of hot British guys. That's enough for me. Do you know how hard it is to get into this field?'

'I know, I know, and we're so proud of you.'

Max had tried to keep out of it. He really was very proud of Eva. Katriina and Eva often argued about things that Max found totally incomprehensible, but he assumed it was because they were so alike. They both possessed a certain proprietary view of the world. He realised that Eva had inherited this tendency from Katriina, but he had no idea where his wife might have come by it. He found it to be one of those personality traits that was easy enough to admire in theory, but much more difficult to live with. For as long as he'd known Katriina, she'd never once hesitated if there was something she wanted.

Tonight he'd said to Katriina that maybe she shouldn't be calling Eva every week, that maybe their daughter should be allowed to establish her own life in London. That had led Katriina to yell at him because he'd made plans to play tennis two hours before the dinner party at Risto and Tuula's place. Then he'd said that maybe she shouldn't be drinking so much wine on an empty stomach, and she responded by saying that she wouldn't need to drink if he spent more time with her.

And they'd continued on like that until Max slammed the door and went out in the rain to go over to the indoor tennis courts. He'd played like a fiend, irritably and without finesse, and by the time he got back home and stepped into the front hall, his mood was even worse. In the end, they'd caught a cab to the Keskinens' party, although without exchanging a word during the entire drive.

Max didn't have a driving licence. When they met thirty years ago, Katriina had admired him for refusing to join the ranks of car owners. Nowadays she ridiculed him for the very same reason. She claimed that for all these years his decision had been more a question of indolence and stinginess than any concern for the environment.

They arrived twenty minutes late, just in time to join everyone else at the dinner table. Max sat down, noticing that he either knew or at least recognised most of the other guests: Wivan and Pertti; Tuula and Risto, who nodded a greeting as he walked around the table, pouring everyone a vodka; and several of Katriina's work colleagues accompanied by their respective spouses.

Also seated at the table was a Norwegian couple who had been to their home for dinner on a couple of occasions. The husband's name was John, and Max recalled that he was a man of few words, but a highly likeable expert on international trade law. At the far end of the table sat Stefan and Gun-Maj, a Finland–Swedish couple who had sold all their possessions when they retired. They now devoted their time to travelling throughout the Far East and organising expensive meditation courses for other middle-aged Finnish couples who wanted to get out of the rat race. Stefan was always suntanned and leathery and Max could smell a trace of incense from across the table.

Max said hello to the two guests seated on either side of him, and Wivan immediately started up a conversation.

'I saw the interview you gave in the latest issue of *Anna*. I said to Pertti yesterday: "Look, there's Max!" Didn't I say that?'

Pertti, who was sitting a few places away, nodded, although it was highly likely that he had no idea what his wife had just said. He was simply programmed to agree with her in all situations. Wivan turned again to Max as she handed him a tray of beets. Her bracelet clinked against the silver tray.

'No, you must be thinking of my colleague,' said Max.

'But it said "a sociologist from Helsinki University". Surely there can't be other sociologists named Max Paul?'

He handed the tray of beets to the next person.

'Well, actually, there are two of us in the department. It's funny, but people often get us confused.'

For a few seconds Wivan didn't reply, then she laughed nervously. Max glanced in Katriina's direction, but she refused to meet his eye. She had obviously decided to ignore him for the rest of the evening. He looked at her wine glass and noticed that it was already half empty, even though Risto had just filled it.

'I'm serious. It wasn't me,' he said, turning again to Wivan.

She stopped laughing and gave him a confused look. In a manner of speaking, Max meant what he said. The person who had been interviewed in *Anna* was not him – it was a personality that he

9

assumed for the benefit of the media in particular kinds of situations, like when a women's magazine called him up and wanted a quick one-liner or two. The questions often had to do with family life or sex, and it was true that Max had done a lot of research on those topics, but they were by no means his primary field of expertise. Yet the more interviews he did, the more journalists called, wanting to speak to the 'sex professor'.

Max had promised himself he'd stop answering those kinds of questions, since sociology in Finland had begun to have a reputation as a discipline obsessed with sex. But he was frankly too lazy and polite to say no, and it was much easier to give a few quick answers than not to respond at all. On this particular occasion the interviewer had been a young woman, probably around twenty-five, who phoned him at the department just as he was sitting in front of the *Helsingin Sanomat* website and writing something for a discussion forum.

The reporter began by introducing herself – Max didn't catch her name – and then told him that she was calling from the magazine *Anna*.

'I was wondering whether you'd consider answering a few questions for an article that I'm writing about today's ideal housewife.'

'Sure, go ahead,' Max told her, his attention still focussed on the discussion forum. Lately it had been taking up more and more of his time. There were a couple of contributors who often popped up in the same discussions as Max. They'd been having fervent conversations for several months now about everything from Islam to the way in which the city of Helsinki was handling the expansion of the subway system to the west. Max knew that he shouldn't really get involved in debates on the Internet. The feeling of instant satisfaction at crushing an opponent's argument was spoiled by the fact that it never ended – there were always new contributors who entered the conversation from some tangent, or who tried to sabotage the discussion by deliberately provoking the others. It was like trying to win on a slot machine, always taking one step forward and two steps back, and it was equally addictive. Sometimes he found himself sitting at home at two in the morning, participating in discussions about the biological differences between men and women, attempting to inject a scientific perspective, even though he was well aware that the people he was arguing with might be secondary-school students.

The woman on the phone started asking her questions.

'Okay, well, first of all . . . some people say that we're witnessing a new conservative trend right now, and that women who were born in the eighties are embracing the traditional ideals of the fifties. TV programmes like *Mad Men* are an example of this. What's your opinion?'

The ideal housewife? That was simple. Max didn't need to think about it for long.

'It's difficult to say without taking the statistics

into account. If we look at recent decades, the figures show that, on the contrary, people are getting married later, and the number of people who live together without marrying is steadily growing. Women also have careers and are no longer relegated to the kitchen.'

'And yet it's said that there's a trend—'

'You can say there's a trend, but that doesn't mean there is one, from a purely statistical point of view.'

He closed his browser.

'Yes, but my article is about the new ideal housewife. Could you say a little about that? I mean, right now, for example, there's a huge interest in cooking. Why do you think that is?'

'People need to eat.'

The woman on the phone laughed politely.

'Sure, but could you say something about trends? I mean, the fact that more young women today seem to want to stay at home and have children earlier.'

This was a trend that Max had actually seen first-hand. His older daughter, Helen, had married young and soon after had children – he was inclined to interpret this as her way of rebelling against her parents. But it didn't look as if Eva had any plans to follow in her sister's footsteps.

'Is that really what they want?' asked Max.

'Well, er . . . I don't have the figures at hand, but there's a lot of talk about the new ideal housewife . . . more and more magazines are writing about it, and there are lots of new publications that are marketed specifically for young mothers . . .'

Max wasn't stupid. He understood how these types of articles got written. All they needed was a couple of statements that appealed to the imagination and – most important of all – one so-called case, an interviewee who confirmed the thesis that the reporter was trying to push. Best of all was if they could get a media-hungry expert like Max to confirm the hypothesis. He thought that he really ought to decline to comment, but instead he decided to give her what she wanted. He leaned back in his chair, speaking slowly, so that she'd have time to take notes.

'Okay, if we look at marriage from a purely historical point of view, it has always been linked to the state of the marketplace. For a long time we used to say that grain prices affected the number of marriages; that was almost a statistical axiom even in the 1800s. Do you follow me?'

'Uh-huh,' she replied. He could hear the clack of her computer keyboard.

'Today we have an extremely high standard of living in the Western world – so people don't need to marry simply in order to support themselves. And this change applies to women in particular. But marriage is an ancient tradition. Human beings have always entered into marriage in some form or another, in all cultures. Marriage is a very hardy enterprise. Today young people may get married because they view it as an integral part of establishing their identity. It may no longer have anything to do with a sense of security, but instead involve a kind of role-playing, a necessary rite of passage to adulthood in an era when the teenage years are being extended in absurdum. Or, as you say, a trend. Those of us who were young in the seventies were intent on breaking away from marriage because it was viewed as outdated and passé. Our parents represented the old patriarchal model, and we wanted equality. So, to answer your question: the overriding trend is probably that marriage has lost its force as a societal institution. It has never been easier to get a divorce than it is today. Maybe that's also why it's easier to get married.'

Max never knew where he was headed once he started talking, but he thought that this theory, improvised on the spur of the moment, sounded quite plausible.

When the text was later published, his comments had been reduced to three sentences. The journalist had also put words into his mouth. This is what it said:

> The sociologist Max Paul, whose specialism is researching sex practices, also believes that we're experiencing a boom in which many more young people want to get married:
>
> 'Marriage is part of our basic nature, it exists in all cultures. For young people

today, marriage is a way of signifying that they've become adults, and it's easy to get married.'

Wivan Winckelmann was still waiting for Max to explain further the reason for the confusion of names in his department. He was just about to say something when he heard someone clearing his throat at the other end of the table. Risto was preparing to sing a drinking song. Risto was a notorious boozer, tall and solidly built, with a circle of grey hair around his head. He could drink ten shots of vodka at one sitting and still show no signs of intoxication. He loved to take control of a room. Max wondered if this was a characteristic of psychiatrists. During the week they were forced to sit in silence and listen, so they became hyper-social when the weekend finally arrived.

The mood at the dinner table gradually grew more intense and boisterous. Everybody was laughing at a long, drawn-out story that Stefan was telling at the other end of the table, but those guests who were seated near Max couldn't hear anything, which caused Wivan to keep asking the person on her left to repeat what Stefan had said. It was obvious that the story lost much of its impact in the few metres from Stefan's seat to Wivan's. The longer the story went on, the more bewildered she looked. Max glanced at Katriina. She was listening to Stefan, but he could see she had that glassy look in her eyes that she often had

15

by this time of the evening. It meant that she wasn't really paying attention.

When the dinner was over, Katriina went out on the balcony to have a smoke with Tuula. It was still raining. Max went over to a corner of the living room and glanced at his watch. We should be getting home, he thought. As soon as Katriina came back inside, he'd ask her to get her things.

Until then, all he could do was stand in the corner and pretend to be enjoying himself. The other guests were now scattered about the flat, some still sitting at the table while others occupied the sofa.

Max was leafing through a book when Stefan suddenly appeared at his side. They had known each other since the seventies. Stefan had worked as a journalist and travelled a lot, to anti-nuclear power conferences in Japan and Geneva, covering them for *Fredsposten* and *Ny Tid* – writing articles that Max had never felt the urge to read – and he'd been involved in protests against NATO and European missiles in the early eighties. But these days he talked mostly about the small islands that he visited in Southeast Asia, places with names like Koh Phangan and Pulau Pinang. Max barely even had a chance to say hello before Stefan launched into a monologue about yoga.

'It's more than just yoga, you know, it has to do with a way of looking at life. I mean, I've always been involved in moral questions, just like you are, but at the end of the day – ever since I learned to breathe properly – I realised that the journey has to start from within. Don't you agree?'

Max nodded. 'Absolutely.'

'Just let me know if you want to join us and give it a try sometime. I can offer you a simple course in the basics. Free of charge, of course.'

Max promised to think about it, and Stefan looked pleased.

'I'll just tell you one thing: flexibility. You have no idea what the human body is capable of with a little training. Even at our age.'

Max didn't care to be reminded of his age.

'You mean that you get more agile?'

'Not only that. You learn to breathe, and your blood circulation improves. You learn to feel every movement in your body. You get more sensual – it's as simple as that.'

'Sounds amazing,' said Max.

'You're damn right,' said Stefan, nodding towards Gun-Maj, who was standing a few metres away. She gave him a wave that Max considered excessively flirtatious. Max wondered how often they had sex. Probably more often than he and . . .

He left the thought unfinished when he noticed Katriina coming back inside.

She was listening to Wivan, and it looked like they were talking shop, since Katriina kept nodding impatiently, as if the whole discussion was something she wanted to put aside as quickly as possible.

Max saw Risto appear, bringing new glasses for both of them, which he promptly filled.

An hour later they were sitting in a taxi, speaking to each other for the first time since the argument they'd had before leaving home.

'Can you explain to me why we spend any time with those people?' said Max.

Katriina was staring straight ahead. She was drunk – tonight maybe more than usual – and at first Max wondered whether she'd even heard what he said.

After a moment she told him, 'Because people spend time with each other, Max. It's perfectly normal.'

She sounded tired and resigned. Max should have stopped there, but he couldn't resist. He'd had a whisky with Stefan and was feeling rowdy.

'Sure, but I'm talking about those specific people. We have nothing in common with them. Okay, maybe with Risto and Tuula, but not all the others . . . Take Stefan, for example. I swear, if he starts telling me one more time about some fucking peninsula off Borneo, I'm going to strangle him. Do you know what he said to me tonight? That I should start doing yoga so I'd have a better sex life.'

Katriina giggled.

'For a man who spends his time researching the subject, you're surprisingly sceptical about everything that has to do with sex,' she said, putting her hand between his legs.

Max glanced at the cab driver, wondering if he'd noticed. The driver was in his forties. He's probably been driving in Helsinki long enough to have seen just about everything, thought Max. Then he tried looking at himself and Katriina from the driver's perspective: yet another unhappy, spoiled, middle-aged couple who hate each other and start bickering the moment they get in the cab.

'Why do people have such a hard time understanding that my research has nothing to do with sex? I only published *one* study on it, and that was almost twenty years ago.'

'A study that set the course for your whole career. You really should be more grateful,' said Katriina.

'I'm just saying that this is the last time I'm going to one of these dinner parties,' he told her, without much conviction. He knew it wasn't true. In a couple of weeks they'd probably be on their way home in a cab once again, having attended yet another party at the home of some friends.

For a moment neither of them spoke. Suddenly Katriina asked her husband: 'Do you know if Eva has a boyfriend?'

Max was staring out of the window. 'How should I know?'

'It's just that I'm worried about her.'

Max laughed.

'Why are you laughing?'

'Because she said the very same thing about you.'

'About me?'

'Yes, she said she was worried about you. "Dad,

19

I think Mum is depressed." Why do you have to tell her all your troubles? Why does she need to hear about your problems?'

'I don't tell her my problems!'

'So explain to me, why is it that you're depressed?'

'Just because I like to phone my children, it doesn't have to be something pathological. When did you talk to her?'

'I don't know. Day before yesterday.'

'She called you?'

'Called me? Yes, she did.'

He knew this was going to upset Katriina. Eva never called her. But that wasn't so strange, since she knew that her mother would phone sooner or later.

They didn't speak for the rest of the taxi ride. But once they got home and were brushing their teeth, Max went over to Katriina to explain things further. He hated not being allowed to make his point. She would simply fall silent and go and hide in the bathroom. But she pushed him away.

'I don't want to hear it. I'm tired and I'm going to bed.'

For an hour he sat on the living-room sofa in the dark, looking out at the rain. He poured himself a whisky, and then another, and when he'd finished his second drink he got up to fetch his computer from his study and bring it back to the sofa. He opened the *Helsingin Sanomat* website and looked for the latest comment threads. Max had an overwhelming urge to write some provocative entry, to step beyond the conventions of good taste. At this time of night, there were no moderators censoring what people said. But what should he write?

He opened a discussion, tested a few ideas, wrote a few lines and then erased them. He decided to link to a text that he'd written – if nothing else, it would allow him to find out what people thought about him. He found a thread that had to do with cutbacks in home-help support and decided that would do fine. He chose a different user name than his regular one and wrote: 'If women started working earlier, this would be beneficial to their families as well as to the Finnish economy in general. The new "ideal housewife fad" is a ticking time-bomb. Here's an article on the subject by the sociologist Max Paul.' He entered the link to an article about the biggest demographic groups and refreshed his browser. The article was about the fact that in a few years there would be a hundred working Finns for approximately every sixty-five retirees and children.

There probably weren't many people awake at this hour. He sat in front of the computer for fifteen minutes, waiting for somebody to write a response, but nothing happened. So he switched off the computer, put his whisky glass in the sink, and went into Eva's old room to go to bed.

But he couldn't sleep. He was annoyed because he wanted to talk more but there was no one to listen.

After half an hour he got up, made his way through the dark flat to the living room, and once again turned on his computer. A few comments had come in. A couple of them seemed sensible enough, but Max's eyes instantly fell on one remark in particular:

'Hello. Who cares what that sex professor thinks anyway?'

CHAPTER 2

At three thirty in the morning Katriina woke up and couldn't get back to sleep. Over the past few years her insomnia had grown worse, and lately she would awaken at this exact time and lie in bed thinking about everything that needed to be done that day and the next, about what might happen in her life during the coming six months, as well as in the lives of her children, and about how she ought to view what had gone on during the year so far. Often – since the early morning hours seemed endless – these chains of free association would cause her to ruminate about her whole life, her parents, her childhood, and how little she actually remembered about it all.

Katriina had enjoyed the evening at Risto and Tuula's place, even though she wasn't happy to be seated next to Risto. That must have been his idea. He'd been flirting with her ever since they'd first met, and she was surprised that Tuula never seemed to notice. He deliberately touched her hair every time he stood up or walked past. And the longer the evening went on, the more familiar he became.

But Tuula, as usual, was totally preoccupied with talking about her children. Last night she'd been upset because she had recently found something that she called a 'hash pipe' in her youngest son's backpack.

'And do you know what the worst thing is? The worst thing is that he lied. He lied right to my face.'

Tuula's expression had revealed a combination of alarm and fascination, as if she'd already rehearsed this particular revelation earlier in the day, while she was preparing for the dinner. Katriina had listened, trying to insert a few words of advice whenever she could. Tuula's son was fifteen, so it probably wasn't a huge shock that he would be experimenting with drugs and tobacco; most teenagers undoubtedly did the same. Katriina herself could recall throwing up all over Kaivopuisto Park in the late seventies.

'And you know how Risto is. He refuses to take this sort of thing seriously. Says it's just a phase, and wants us to pretend nothing's going on. But I beg to differ. One day it's a hash pipe and the next day it's heroin needles. Or those designer drugs that all the kids are into right now. I read an article about it . . . They order them online and take them so they can study for exams.'

Katriina couldn't remember the whole conversation, since she had focussed most of her attention on her wine glass. She had a feeling that she'd said something along the lines of how they hadn't been the most angelic of kids either and that her own daughters had probably tried one thing and another when they were in their teens.

'But you should see his friends, Katriina! You should see them! Their shoes are as big as yachts, they stink from sweat and God knows what else, and all they do is sit in front of their computers or hunched over their phones, giving off that smell of horny teenagers, belching and farting. I mean, do you realise what I have to put up with?'

And Katriina had said that she understood. As parents they were rather like travelling salesmen, telling anecdotes about their children's lives.

She had decided to go bed as soon as she and Max got home. If there was one thing she detested, it was a long, drawn-out nightmarish argument filled with derogatory accusations. It was just like sex: not worth all the commotion.

Katriina viewed marriage as a form of reciprocal tyranny, like living in a highly functional totalitarian state. There weren't many options, but as long as you kept to yourself and didn't challenge the status quo, it worked fine.

Being married to Max was like floating on a raft in a comfortable climate and occasionally going ashore without realising that you had been missing civilisation. In the proper mood he could be wonderful and generous, but over the past few years she'd also learned to appreciate her solitude, a sense of simply drifting aimlessly, without constantly yearning for the sight of a harbour.

Now she lay in bed, listening to Max snoring in Eva's room. He must be lying on his back, with his mouth open slightly and his head tipped back, exhausted after staying up late in front of his computer, as usual. He thought she didn't know that he slipped out of bed at night, but she always woke up whenever he left to go into the living room.

Why had they started arguing?

Oh, that's right. She was hungry. Max had come into the kitchen barely two hours before the dinner party, wearing his work-out clothes. Katriina had glanced at her watch and saw that it was five thirty. Then he'd asked if she'd phoned Eva again, as if she wasn't allowed to call her own daughter.

'Are you planning to go out to play tennis now?' Katriina had asked, wanting to keep the conversation focussed on what was important: the fact that they were about to go out for dinner.

She'd been looking forward to this opportunity to socialise. It had been weeks since she and Max had done anything together. She was already picturing the gin and tonic that Tuula would hand her the minute they went through the door, how Tuula would compliment her on her new dress and shoes, how they would enter the living room and sit down. And how Katriina would report on the plans she had for the new kitchen and how Tuula would nod with interest, maybe recommending a builder they could trust to redo their kitchen. (Tuula's sense for interior decorating had resulted in their home being showcased in a four-page article in *Avotakka*.) But, as usual, Max had come home late from his tennis game, since he never thought he needed to make any special effort when it came to his wife's friends.

Katriina listened for a moment. The rain had stopped. She got up and went into the living room. Edvard, their dog, was asleep on the sofa. She continued on to the kitchen and opened the refrigerator.

The shelves were crowded with partially open packages of butter, glass jars containing beets and pickles, a few tinned goods. There was some duck paté on a porcelain plate (when had she made that?), a half-full bottle of sparkling water, a plate of mashed potatoes, little bottles of veal and chicken and chanterelle sauce, several jars of sun dried tomatoes, pesto, mint marmalade, dijon mustard and blackcurrant jam. She couldn't remember when she'd last cleaned out the fridge.

She took out the duck paté and lifted up the plastic to smell it. Seemed okay. She spread some of the paté on a small piece of bread. Edvard woke up, ran into the room, and immediately leapt on to the table. She put a dab of paté on her finger and offered it to him. He sniffed at the reddish-brown lump for a moment and then devoured it with a light nibble. She thought about what Wivan had told her, that she would have to do a lot of travelling in the spring. Katriina had travelled a great deal over the past ten years, but it was starting to get old. Where she had previously seen excitement, she now saw only logistical problems.

The kitchen had been put in seventeen years ago, custom-designed for their flat. The carpentry work had been done by three Estonian brothers who had recently started up a family business. Max had heard about them from one of his tennis partners. He gave them a call and received an offer that sounded reasonable. Then one day the three men had shown up and started tearing apart the old kitchen without consulting either Max or Katriina about any of the details. It took only a couple of hours for them to demolish the existing kitchen completely, but after that the work proceeded at a much slower pace. The pile of cigarette butts grew on the dust-covered concrete floor until Katriina finally pointed at the butts and told the men they could no longer smoke inside. Apparently the brothers understood what she wanted, because they resorted to standing on the balcony to have a smoke, and consequently the work went on at half the speed.

When the kitchen was finally finished two months later, she was generally quite pleased. It was custom-made and well designed, and the primary material was a lovely, reddish oak, which had a timeless quality to it. The kitchen was impressive without being the least bit ostentatious.

'You can say what you like about Estonian workmen, but the ones who redid our kitchen were extremely meticulous,' Katriina usually said whenever the subject came up.

Now, even in the dim light of November, anyone could see that the kitchen had passed its expiry date. The surface of the wood had multiple stains and grease spots. The cupboards really should have been regularly polished and oiled, but nothing had been done to them in all the years the family had lived in the flat. Some of the cupboard doors had loose hinges or refused to close fully, and the fridge – which had once been shiny white and modern, with an ice machine in the door and a container for bottles – had yellowed and was starting to make strange coughing noises. They never used the ice machine any more. One night it had stopped working after sending a flood of water cascading across the parquet floor in the hall.

'There's really nothing wrong with this kitchen. It just needs a little freshening up. No kitchen redesign lasts longer than fifteen years, not even a Puustelli Brothers kitchen.' That was what Max had said when she'd broached the subject recently, and that was the extent of his comments.

When Katriina mentioned the matter of the kitchen to her children, they both agreed that she should have it redone.

'You'll make Mum happy if you get the kitchen redone,' their older daughter, Helen, had said when she was visiting one weekend. Helen was

29

the sensible one, and Max usually followed her advice.

'Well, maybe. But I need to do it my way. If I let her take charge, who knows how the costs will skyrocket. It's so easy for companies like that to tack on a thousand euros here, another thousand there, and for no good reason.'

'But what kind of cost overruns are we really talking about? Two thousand euros here or there won't matter much in the big scheme of things when you consider that the kitchen is going to last fifteen or twenty years.'

Katriina could hear from Helen's voice that she was truly trying to coax her father into agreeing. She thought it was nice to know that at least the children were on her side.

Eva agreed with Helen. She'd been staying with her parents during the summer, and she had a ready opinion about everything. To such an extent, in fact, that Katriina's patience had been tested daily.

'Besides, it's not just about the kitchen, Dad. It's about your marriage. You can't let this kitchen dispute turn into a weapon she uses against you. You need to choose your battles wisely, and think a bit more strategically.'

Eva always said exactly what she thought, and Katriina had the feeling that in this case her opinion had more to do with trying to provoke a reaction rather than taking her mother's side in the matter. Eva was slender and blonde. She had the self-confidence and easy disdain of a person who has always been told how beautiful she is. Katriina would never say this to anyone (not even Tuula), but sometimes she had the feeling that Eva looked down on her, as if she couldn't really accept that Katriina was her mother. That might be normal behaviour for a teenager. But a twenty-nine-year-old?

Katriina had paid attention to what her daughters said. And she had come up with her own idea of how the new kitchen should look: all white and shiny, no open shelves, and very modern, to an almost exaggerated degree. Cupboard doors that would roll and slide as if they were straight out of the interior of some science-fiction space ship. When she pictured her new kitchen in her mind, she also saw a life that was simple and white, white, white. Orderly and tidy. A life with perfect solutions to everything.

Katriina noticed that the food she'd eaten had made her tired. She went back to the bedroom and set the alarm clock for eight. Helen and the children were coming to visit later in the morning, and even if she couldn't sleep, she did need to get a few hours of rest.

CHAPTER 3

The flat was filled with the sound of the grandchildren and of Katriina exclaiming loudly: 'Oh, how wonderful!' 'Did you make that yourself?' 'What a lovely dress you have on!' All the voices seemed to be coming from a life that was happening someplace else. Through the window Max could see that it had to be past nine, maybe closer to ten in the morning. Something about the dazzling light outside told him that the rain had turned to snow during the night.

He must have forgotten that Helen was coming to visit today. Katriina hadn't mentioned it, but then she'd hardly said a word to him last night.

He lay in bed, thinking about a theory that had come to him in his sleep. What Katriina didn't know, what she had no clue about, was that Max had actually given their kitchen a lot of thought over the past year. Max hated the word 'integrated'. It seemed to be some sort of mantra that he kept hearing everywhere lately. Integrated, wireless, everything was supposed to be hidden away. In the future only blank surfaces would exist; everything was a potential touch screen. In Max's opinion, the whole world was being transformed into a gallery. That was why he had a hard time accepting that Katriina wanted to order a clinical-looking kitchen from an interior design firm.

A home was meant to be comfortable; it should slowly fill with things that you loved, and with which you had some relationship. Max despised the whole modern building tradition, which involved throwing out all things old and human, and replacing them with severe, clean lines. Essentially, he thought that a home was a living organism. Why did so much of contemporary design require all sense of life to be erased? Why couldn't people live in pleasant and beautiful settings? Why did everybody have to be forced into the same box-like structures, the same industrially produced mould, the same – and this was precisely what he meant – clinical laboratory surroundings? They were utterly without soul, and there was no reason for that. Today you could no longer see where consumerism ended and someone's personal living space began. Everything was supposed to look like a hotel lobby or like the Keskinens' socio-pathic flat in Nordsjö.

Max had a theory that a lot of people based their aesthetic ideal on things that they'd encountered as children. For him, it was obvious that his ideas about Beauty with a capital 'B' stemmed from his childhood in Österbotten: the snug cottages, the red-painted buildings with white trim, the furni-ture handcrafted by uncles on both sides of his family for wedding gifts and Christmas presents. Furniture that had a history, that might have travelled across the Atlantic and could say something about people's lives and hardships. It was impossible to establish any sort of relationship with a piece of furniture from IKEA; it held no surprises, no hidden inscriptions. And it had no story to tell, except possibly about the Chinese children who had toiled from morning to night making all the components.

Max also thought that certain experiences of beauty were comprised of something that lay deep inside the evolutionary coded consciousness of human beings. A study done in the nineties had shown that people all over the world tended to like the same kind of landscape, a landscape that largely resembled the savannahs where the human race first developed millions of years ago.

His train of thought was interrupted when his granddaughter Amanda suddenly came running into the room and jumped on to the bed to give him a hug. The annoyed feeling that he'd had only a few seconds earlier surged up inside him to be mixed with a feeling of gratitude and . . . what was it? Happiness? Amanda was an intelligent nine-year-old who seemed to love the world with a solemn passion. She hugged and petted him, whispering in his ear, 'Grandpa, I love you,' which always made Max melt, as if newly in love. This, if anything, thought Max, has to be an example of universal beauty. A grandchild's smile.

'Grandpa?'

'Yes?'

'You know what?'

'What, sweetheart?'

Amanda sounded excited. She looked him in the eye. 'Grandma says that you promised to do something with us today.'

'I did?'

'Yes! You're going swimming with us.'

'I am?'

'Well, Grandma says that you don't have anything more important to do today.'

'Did she say that?'

'She says that you think you have to work, but you'll have much more fun with us.'

Max thought it wasn't such a dumb idea, after all. He had no desire to tackle his manuscript today.

'Grandpa?'

'Yes?'

Now Amanda sounded worried. 'Do we have to take Lukas with us?'

'You don't want him to come along?'

'No. He'll just start whining because he thinks it's too cold. And he's not allowed in the big swimming pool.'

'I think he'll have to come too.'

Amanda sat up straight on the bed and peered at Max. 'Grandpa?'

'Yes?'

'Don't get upset, but your mouth smells yucky.'

Amanda made a big show of holding her nose. Max instantly closed his mouth, but he was also touched by her words: 'Don't get upset.' He felt a lump in his throat.

'That's because I haven't had time to brush my teeth yet. Hop down so I can go and do it. I need to get dressed and then I'll be ready to go.'

Amanda ran out to the hall. Max got up, noticing at once how sluggish his whole body felt. Sometimes it could take an hour before all the machinery started functioning as it should. He went into the bathroom and brushed his teeth as he stood under the shower, doing a thorough job of it, brushing for several minutes to rid himself of the feeling that he smelled like an old man. He loved the anonymity that his grandchildren gave him – to them he was merely Grandpa. At least until the day when they discovered how to Google.

When he went into the living room he kissed his daughter on the forehead and asked: 'Did Christian come with you?'

Helen lowered her eyes for a moment, as if hesitating over what to say. 'Uh-huh. He must be looking for a parking place. You're looking a little pale.'

'I'm fine. I just didn't sleep very well.'

Max had no intention of admitting that he'd been up late, sitting in front of the computer again. He realised that if he went to the swimming pool with the grandkids, the argument with Katriina – if it really was an argument – would be forgotten.

The fact that Katriina had suggested he take them swimming was, in his view, practically a gesture of reconciliation on her part.

Katriina went into the kitchen and he followed. Her blonde hair was pulled back in a loose ponytail. Under normal circumstances he might have hugged her from behind, but today he settled for placing his hand on her shoulder.

'Apparently I'm going swimming,' he said.

She was silent for a moment. Then she said, 'Fine, fine. Could you take the dog for a walk first?'

'Are you pissed off about something?'

'Pissed off? I'm not pissed off. But the dog needs to go out. I took him out briefly early this morning, and now it looks as though he has to pee. Why don't you take Amanda along to keep you company?'

As Max and Amanda stepped outdoors, he was struck by how the whole world had been transformed. The sun was shining and the air was very clear, so clear that he almost felt dizzy, a sober Finnish landscape that spoke directly to him, saying things like: pull yourself together, look sharp, today is the first day of the rest of your life!

They walked towards Töölö Bay, with Edvard happily running ahead alongside the buildings. Edvard was a West Highland white terrier, named after the nineteenth-century sociologist Edvard Westermarck, who had consumed Max's thoughts

37

over the past several years. The book he was writing was supposed to be the first real biography of Westermarck.

They stopped at the traffic light on Mannerheimvägen and waited for a tram to pass. Amanda was wearing a black winter jacket and a cap meant to resemble the head of a koala, ears and all.

The Sparbank wharf was visible across the water on the other side of Töölö Bay. Max's office was on Kajsaniemi. Aside from a few trips abroad – first to Berkeley in the late seventies, then a brief stay in Oxford during the eighties, and another visit to Berkeley when the girls were little – he'd worked in the same two city neighbourhoods during his entire career as a researcher.

Max Paul was a sociology professor at the University of Helsinki. He'd held the post for fifteen years, giving guest lectures, writing books and articles, contributing to research projects, participating in an intellectual talk show in the nineties (called *The Brain Trust*), and attending various international conferences. He had at most five or six years left on the job before he retired. In the nineties he'd published a study about Finnish sexual habits (as part of FINSEX, a larger research project), and for a few years he did nothing but travel around speaking about the statistics related to the sexual practices of Finns. Helen and Eva were both teenagers at the time. Helen, in particular, had to endure the sting of notoriety when her classmates saw Max speaking on TV about the Finns' relaxed attitude towards anal sex. One day she came home crying because a friend had seen a headline in which Max was dubbed 'The Sex Doctor'. He'd had to explain that his work involved serious research and headlines like that never presented a proper image of sociology as a scientific discipline.

In three weeks Max would turn sixty.

When he was younger he'd never worried about time running out. Back then it seemed endless. Now it felt like the ten years between fifty and sixty had vanished in the blink of an eye. There was plenty of research showing that people experienced time as moving faster the older they got, and Max had definitely felt the effect of this phenomenon over the past few years. It was also said that it was possible to counter this feeling by giving your brain new experiences. One theory was that the brain registered new experiences more strongly than those that were repeated, which would explain why everyone could remember their first kiss, but not the thousandth. Yet this was a theory with rather problematic implications: what should a person do in order to constantly experience new things? Was that why Stefan and Gun-Maj took their yoga trips? To create new memories for themselves and in that way slow down time?

Max decided that he and Amanda should walk around the bay and go up to Fågelsången. From there they went across the bridge and headed towards Tokoistranden. Amanda kept up a lively chatter, jumping from one topic to another. ('You know what food I hate the most? Fish with slimy gravy. We ALWAYS have that at school.' 'Grandpa, do you think some people never brush their hair?') Max quickly noticed that it was enough to murmur a simple 'hmm,' and Amanda would be satisfied that he was paying attention. She seemed as preoccupied with her own thoughts as he was with his.

He'd started at the university in the autumn of 1970, when sociology was all the rage. People flocked to the courses. Marx was everyone's professed idol, and the lectures were open to anyone who wanted to attend. Women students who came to the seminars would breastfeed their infants as they debated working conditions in the Finnish steel industry.

For Max it was an exciting and eye-opening time; he was swept up in leftist politics – and who wasn't? – but he always found the partying more fun than the rhetoric. In the February of his first year as a university student, a week-long strike was organised, beginning at the sociology department. Max was assigned to the picket line, and he recalled how narrow-minded some of his fellow students seemed to be ('We will never accept a sociology that takes precedence over the class struggle!'). They actually seemed to believe in a revolution, and a lot of them dropped out because it was only a matter of time before the university came under

Marxist rule. They reminded him of those religious fanatics who eagerly await the end of the world.

Having grown up in Österbotten, with roots in the rural district of Kristinestad, Max had a hard time understanding his fellow students from Helsinki. Even though they talked about the labour theory of value and social alienation, many of them lived in flats they had inherited, thanks to the very societal structures they were protesting.

Max, on the other hand, had taken lodgings with a family in Rödbergen, with a reduction in rent because he helped take care of the family's only child. Many of his peers from Österbotten lived in student housing on Rautalampivägen in Vallgård, but he rarely visited them. He hadn't come to Helsinki to spend time with other Österbotten natives, whose first language was Swedish. He was determined to learn to speak fluent Finnish as fast as possible. For the first six months he was forced to resort to his old high-school Finnish grammar book to figure out what to say every time he went into town.

His parents, Ebba and Vidar, came to visit him in Helsinki only once while he was at the university. He remembered it as an uncomfortable weekend, with his father constantly grumbling about how expensive everything was. He met them at the train station. They had decided to stay at the hotel in the nearby Sokos building, since they didn't want to walk too far. One of the first things his father did after disembarking from the train was to comment on a dark-skinned man he saw on Mikaelsgatan. ('I didn't know you had Negroes here in Helsinki!')

Max recalled how nervous his mother was about meeting the family he was living with. She'd phoned him ahead of time to ask what sort of gift she ought to bring and how much she should spend. He had assured her that a gift wasn't necessary, and that the family might not even be home when they visited, but she insisted. So after they had checked into their hotel room, she took a hideous painting out of her suitcase – the kind of artwork that was popular back then (this was in 1971), presumably done by some local artist in Kristinestad, using pine cones and corks that had been spray-painted.

Now that Max thought back on the matter, he found the whole thing rather touching, but at the time he was furious, since he was painfully aware that his parents belonged to a different era – maybe even a different century. It was obvious that they didn't fit in with the milieu that he'd now made his own. He was afraid that they'd drag him back down, into their musty old world.

Ebba wanted to go to a play, and Max's only experience with the city's theatre scene was through the student productions that were staged in connection with various political movements. But he found out that Lilla Teatern was showing a revue by Claes Andersson and Johan Bargum, and so they'd bought tickets.

His mother enjoyed the show immensely, mostly because she'd never gone to the theatre in Helsinki before, while Max's father had responded with grudging silence. For the rest of the evening he'd downed one glass of brandy after another, muttering 'utterly shameless' and 'no respect'.

Vidar was a big admirer of Marshal Mannerheim. Some of his family members had been imprisoned by the Reds, and Vidar himself had fought in Finland's Continuation War, which lasted from 1941 to 1944. In one of the play's scenes, Mannerheim had been ridiculed when an actor pasted a picture of his face on a horse's body and then whipped the horse.

Before his parents boarded the train to head back home on Sunday, all three of them had stood on the platform, staring at the ground. Max's mother had asked him if he'd met a 'nice girl', and Max had replied evasively.

They didn't come back to Helsinki until Max received his doctoral degree eight years later, in 1979. By then his father's alcoholism had escalated to such an extent that his mother and his sister Elisabeth had to devote all their energy to keeping the man upright. His university years had marked one of the happiest periods in Max's life, and he wasn't about to allow his father to ruin things. Not only had he finished his dissertation, which he'd written in one fell swoop, but he'd met Katriina at the university, and they were planning to get married very soon. Max was too much in love to be political about marriage. Katriina was from a Helsinki family, with roots in Russia, and Max had been dazzled with a sense of history – by the fact that her ancestry could be traced back to Czarist times, possibly even further. Compared to her, he felt like a real country bumpkin.

The Sparbank wharf looked like a mirage of granite up ahead, and Max thought that if they could find a café, they might stop and rest for a while.

Over the past few years the field of sociology had become particularly exciting because the neurosciences had made huge advances, supplemented by evolutionary psychology. For Max this was especially rewarding, because ever since the eighties poststructuralism had threatened to turn all research into relativistic blind fumbling, only to be followed by the prevalence of feminist studies. Today it seemed that the only research receiving funding had to do with equality, gender and cohabitation.

Max was fascinated by how brain research was able to contribute to so many of the age-old philosophical conundrums, such as the debate about reason versus emotion, or Freud's theories about the id and the ego. At the same time, there was a risk – especially on the part of the media – of reducing neurological research to metaphysical assertions. The brain was described as an organ with its own will. 'The human brain likes equality and justice!' was a statement that Max had recently read in an article. The author made reference to yet another American research group that had done a study focussing on the reward centre in the brain. Of course the brain didn't 'like' anything. That was a meaningless contention, just like all the talk about how a person was governed either by the left or the right side of his brain.

At the moment Max thought he was using his left brain too much. As he was paying for his coffee and Amanda's juice, a dark-haired woman in her thirties suddenly appeared at his side and began staring at him. She looked vaguely familiar, but he couldn't place her.

'Hi,' she said. Try as he might, Max couldn't recall who she was. Was she one of his daughters' friends? Or a former student?

'Do you remember me?'

Something in Max's brain refused to make the connection. He looked at her without speaking, unable to figure out how he knew her.

'I can understand why you might not recognise me. Laura Lampela. You were my advisor at a continuing education programme years ago. I studied sociology for a while, actually only a semester and a half.'

Suddenly it came to Max: this was Laura, that hippie girl. He had helped her with a term paper that had something to do with . . . He couldn't remember exactly, but he had a feeling it had to do with alcoholism. Or was it consumerism? It must have been almost ten years ago.

'Of course I remember you. Nice to see you again, Laura! This is Edvard and Amanda.'

'Hi, Edvard and Amanda! But you don't really remember me, do you? I wrote a paper about the restaurant business and employees' attitudes towards alcohol.'

'Right. Right,' said Max. 'Well, uh . . . here's our coffee and juice. It was good seeing you, Laura.'

He looked around the café for a table. Every one of them seemed to be taken. Laura noticed that he was looking for somewhere to sit down.

'It's really crowded, since it's Saturday. You can share my table if you like. I'll be leaving soon.'

Max picked up his coffee in one hand, holding the dog's lead in the other, and headed for her table. Amanda picked up her juice, giving Laura a suspicious look. After Max sat down, he didn't know whether he should start up a conversation or not, but before he could decide, Laura began talking.

'I have to make a confession,' she said. Her hair was very dark and thick. She didn't look anything like he remembered. It wasn't just the fact that she was older – she looked more professional and no longer wore hippie clothes. Instead, she had on attractive black jeans and a black tunic.

He cast a quick glance around the café. Did the other people think he was sitting here with his daughters, or with his young wife and child?

'Sorry, what did you say?'

'I said that I have to make a confession. You

46

know that interview you did that was published in *Anna*? That was me. I didn't want to tell you who I was when I phoned, because I was a little embarrassed.'

She tucked a strand of hair behind her ear. Max looked at Amanda. She was listening attentively, waiting to hear more.

'I thought the whole topic was ludicrous, but since that was the article I was writing . . . well, I suddenly thought about you. There was so much talk about that sex study back then. So that's why I called you.'

'That was you?' Max said.

'Uh-huh. I'm sorry. You're not angry, are you?'

'Angry? Why should I be angry with you?'

'When I saw how drastically they edited your replies, I asked them to remove my name from the by-line. This kind of thing happens occasionally, so then I use a pseudonym. I'm actually a serious journalist, otherwise.'

'Is that right?'

Max thought she must mean some kind of news reporting.

'So, I mean, if you'd ever agree to it, I'd like to do a proper feature article on you. A personal profile. I sometimes write for the *Helsingin Sanomat*.'

'You do?'

'On a freelance basis, of course. I'll try to interest the editor. But aren't you writing a book?'

Max thought about the 1,500-page document in his computer. All those scattered notes about

Westermarck, all the material that in some miraculous way still had to be shaped into a book.

'I'm afraid I am. Although I'm a bit behind schedule.'

'That doesn't matter. You used to be everywhere – I mean back in the nineties. I always watched *The Brains Trust* when I was a teenager. We could do an article along those lines, you know: "Where Is He Now?" That sort of thing.'

Max didn't like the sound of that. As if he'd been forgotten and someone had been forced to look him up. He would have preferred a more dignified comeback.

'I'm not really sure . . .'

'Don't you have a birthday coming up soon?'

'Why?'

'Sometimes they do features about people around their birthday.'

Amanda had lost interest. She'd finished her juice and was now offering Edvard what was left of the biscuits they'd eaten as she tugged at Max's arm.

'We'll go in a minute,' he told her. Then, turning to Laura, he said, 'Actually, in three weeks I turn sixty.'

'That's perfect!' said Laura. Max wondered why she was so enthusiastic. She acted as if he really was somebody important.

'Grandpa?'

He looked at Amanda. She clearly thought it was time to go.

'Here, I'll write down my number,' he said to Laura.

'And I'll talk to my boss. I can't promise anything, but I think this could work.'

'If it happens, it happens,' said Max as he stood up and called to Edvard, noting a happy tone in his own voice that surprised him.

When they got home, Edvard ran to the living room and jumped on to Helen's lap, making her spring to her feet with a muted shriek, since his paws were covered in mud. Amanda came rushing in after him.

'Grandpa is going to be interviewed for the *Helsingin Sanomat*!'

Max hung up the dog's lead and then joined the others in the living room. Helen and Katriina were sitting on the sofa. Christian still hadn't made an appearance.

'Where's Christian?'

'He went into town. To Clas Ohlson's hardware store and a few other places,' Helen explained.

Max liked his son-in-law. He was the kind of person who could make complicated things seem simple. He could build and renovate a house, which was something that Max had never had time to learn. Christian was also unmistakably a Finland–Swede in the typical Helsinki style: well-mannered, always willing to help, and so polite as to be slightly boring.

Now Helen asked her father: 'What's this

49

Amanda has been telling us? She says you're going to be interviewed?'

Max looked at Katriina. 'That's right. By a former student. Apparently she now works at the *Helsingin Sanomat*. Or maybe she said she's a freelancer,' replied Max, his eyes still fixed on Katriina, who nodded.

'That sounds risky.'

'Well, anyway. I guess she's working as a journalist now. She said that she wanted to do a feature article about me. It's not a big deal. And it might not even happen. But an article because I'm turning sixty.'

Edvard ran from one person to the other, greeting each of them in turn. Then he lay down in front of the door to Eva's old room to keep an eye on all of them.

Katriina looked at Max. 'Helen and I want to go into town, so you get to take care of Lukas and Amanda. Did Edvard pee?' she asked.

'And took a dump,' said Max.

CHAPTER 4

When Eva was seven years old she'd almost drowned near the family's summer cottage in Sideby. She'd learned to swim in the spring, and she'd gone out into the water without thinking that it was a whole different matter to swim in the sea, where there were rocks and high waves, than in the community heated swimming pool on Topeliusgatan. After swimming twenty metres she could no longer touch the bottom with her feet, and she panicked. The beach was on a small bay, and a strong wind was blowing in from the sea. It was cold (since it was still only June), and the waves were bigger than she'd thought. They came towards her like dark, threatening swells, and she suddenly felt that she'd lost all strength to fight back, that something was pulling her towards the bottom and she was about to go under. Her big sister Helen was somewhere up on the rocks, but Eva couldn't turn around. And when she tried to yell, not a sound came out.

But the strange thing was that the panicked feeling changed into something else. She thought:

so this is how I'm going to die. The realisation wasn't frightening but fascinating.

And when she accepted that she was going to die, she suddenly felt completely calm. She looked up at the sky and let her body fall back. Her body had gone numb, so the water no longer felt as cold as before, and Eva thought that she could see millions of different colours. Was this how it felt to drown?

The moment was shattered when Helen shouted that it was time to eat. Eva pretended not to hear, but then Helen, who was standing on the rocks, jumped in, and Eva noticed that her feet could touch the bottom after all.

She never told anyone what happened – not that day, and not afterwards, either. Maybe she hadn't been on the verge of drowning, but she'd definitely learned something: to die, to disappear entirely, was not something that she needed to fear.

She thought that was the reason why she was rarely afraid of failing, of making the wrong choice, or of ending up in unexpected situations. And that had led her to make some drastic decisions. For instance, she'd broken off her engagement to Alexander after four years, just as they were starting to talk about having a baby. Eva had done what men had been doing all through history: she told him that she was going out for a while, and then she never went back.

It was also Eva's fearlessness that had driven her to move to London, more or less on a whim, with no real plans other than to study art for a year.

Now she was lying in bed in her flat in Bethnal Green, pondering whether to drop the course and try to find a job instead. Her period was late, but she didn't know why. She suspected that it was due to a general stressed-out feeling.

It was the end of November and the course had been running for two months. The air was still warm enough to sit outside in the afternoon, and Eva often went to Weavers Fields, a nearby park, to sit on a bench and read. Or she would go to Brick Lane and stroll through the flea markets there. She enjoyed people-watching, and in London there were plenty of people to watch. Young pseudo-hippies sitting in cafés with backpacks, frowning as they read Hemingway; stylish couples in their eighties roaming through the art museums wearing matching tweed jackets; British children in school uniforms walking in perfectly straight lines through busy streets; bankers outside pubs drinking on Friday afternoons; the multicultural vibrancy of the city itself. Eva liked the anonymity of London and the feeling that no one demanded anything of her. She could wander aimlessly for hours, from one area to another.

The university was on the northwest side of London, a forty-five-minute trip on the Tube from her flat. Usually she didn't have any lectures to attend until ten in the morning, so she would get up at eight, eat a quick sandwich and catch the

Tube, provided that it was running. Sometimes she was forced to make her way by means of a combination of buses and Tube lines.

Her flatmate, Natalia, was often in the kitchen when she got up. Natalia worked at the London Stock Exchange. She was a highly social and extroverted person, which had turned out to be very practical when Eva arrived in London not knowing a soul. She'd found the flat through an advert. Natalia had opened the door in a cloud of perfume, with her brown hair gathered in a perfect knot. She was a large woman, not fat but curvy, and over the past two months Eva had seen how men would turn around to look at Natalia whenever they went to a pub. Eva had inherited her mother's blonde hair and her father's scrawniness – she'd always thought that she looked very ordinary compared to her sister Helen, and she'd never really got used to the fact that people clearly regarded her as, if not beautiful, at least genetically interesting.

That was more or less how Malik, her tutor, had expressed it after they'd slept together for the first time.

'You could be a fashion model,' he'd told her. 'You have that slightly cool and androgynous look about you that's so "in" right now. Seriously. I mean, don't take it the wrong way. I like it.'

'Don't be ridiculous,' Eva had told him, turning over in bed with the feeling that she was much too old for that type of flattery. She'd actually caused a stir on the streets of Paris when she'd gone there as a teenager with her mother. Men had wanted to take her picture, claiming to be the owners of model agencies. But that was probably something that happened to all Scandinavian girls. Her first boyfriend had broken up with her because he thought she was too bony.

After Malik started spending the night at Eva's flat, they often didn't fall asleep until two in the morning. When she woke up, she would feel tired and not especially motivated to go to class. Sometimes he'd have his car with him, and they would drive to the university together. Last night Malik had stayed at home, saying that he needed to correct papers. Eva had teased him, offering to help.

He got annoyed and told her dismissively, 'It's okay that we're in a relationship. We're both adults. But I take my work seriously, and you need to understand that it's a point of honour for me. My work takes priority over sex.'

She hadn't said another word. She didn't really know what sort of relationship she had with Malik. She couldn't remember ever hearing him call her his lover, or anything else, for that matter.

Eva had arrived in London in mid-August. It was still hot and sticky, and it seemed as though everyone had fled the city. Families with children were on holiday, the schools were empty, and the only people she met when she walked through Shoreditch were badly paid thirty-year-olds who had come from elsewhere and had uncertain career prospects. People in the same situation as Eva. Every time she went to a party – and in the beginning she often went to parties with Natalia – she would meet people with similar stories: arts graduates trying to make their way as freelancers; academics temporarily waiting tables in cafés; students with enormous debts; Australian IT guys working in the financial sector (they were the only ones who appeared to have any money, and Natalia seemed to know them all); young people with advanced degrees in hopeless fields like comparative literature and aesthetics. All of them were making do with improvised living situations; many had wealthy parents. Most had already finished their education. When Eva said that she was studying art, nobody seemed especially impressed.

She'd finished her BA in art history at Helsinki University after five years of indolent studying and then toyed with the idea of continuing for a Masters, but she realised that she lacked the incentive to do so.

It was on impulse that she'd applied to study fine art in London. She was almost certain that she wouldn't be accepted, since she had no practical experience. But she wrote an essay on the concept of beauty from a Darwinian perspective (she borrowed a quote from one of her father's articles: 'The aesthetic relativism of our era still cannot explain the universal and cross-cultural pleasures which we all enjoy on a daily basis') and dug out a few illustrations that she'd done during her last year in secondary school. She also made several new, fresh illustrations – dark watercolours inspired by the cave paintings in Lascaux. Painting them had been fun, and the results were significantly more provocative than she'd counted on, with different combinations of genitals and truncated body parts. In June she found out that she'd been accepted, which apparently hadn't come as a surprise to anyone else in the family.

'I've always known that you'd be an artist,' her father had said when she phoned to tell him the news. It was as though he'd just been waiting all along for her to make this decision.

'Why didn't you ever say anything?'

'I didn't want to influence you. You need to do what interests you most, and not what I think you should do.'

The classes started in September. During the first week there were two orientation days for foreign postgraduate students, and on Wednesday the lectures began. Eva showed up for the first lecture ten minutes early and found the room practically deserted. Only two other students were present – a guy and a young woman. Eva guessed they were probably a couple. She nodded to them as she came in, then took out her mobile to surf, trying to look busy.

There were very few chairs. The students were apparently supposed to sit on cushions and small

Oriental rugs in the room with bare whitewashed walls. The classrooms seemed new, although they were in an old building that Eva surmised was from the mid-nineteenth century. This part of town was called Hendon, and the campus consisted of both modern architecture and old stone buildings. At nine fifteen the doors were closed. Eva had found a place for herself in a corner of the room.

Malik Martin was a tall, broad-shouldered man in his forties. He had dark curly hair which was thinning at the back. He looked as if he worked out on a regular basis. He wore a tight cotton shirt with short sleeves stretched over his hairy arms.

'Before we begin, there are a few things that you need to know about my classes,' he said as he walked around the room, making everyone turn their head to look at him.

'Some of you may be here because you want to be the next Damien Hirst, because you've heard that London has the most dynamic art scene in the world. And you think you can make money here. In that case, let me spare you both time and effort: you can't. Or let's put it this way: ninety-nine per cent of you can't.'

Malik glared at them in a way that was presumably meant to signal a combination of authority and mystery, but Eva thought he looked a little shifty, like an estate agent.

'Another thing: there are certain words that I

never want to hear in my classroom. "Beauty" is one of them. "Sublime" is another. "Masterpiece" is a third. These are words used by people who think of art in an emotional way. They're words that belong to the romantic tradition, which admires the solitary genius and believes in essential values. But the last time I checked, this was the twenty-first century. The purpose of art is to explore the key cultural and social ideas of its time. If you want to create emotions and pleasure, you can go to Hollywood for that. What I want you to do here is to find your own voice.'

Eva felt her cheeks flush. Her essay on the application had been filled with words such as 'sublime' and 'beauty'.

There was a wide range in age among her classmates. Before they started, Malik wanted all the students to introduce themselves. Many seemed to have an impressive array of accomplishments. One person had already had his work exhibited in a gallery, another had a degree from Oxford. A young woman mentioned that she viewed this course as a means for her to get into Goldsmiths' famed art course. Eva knew that many of England's most successful contemporary artists had attended that college, and some of them had won the Turner Prize.

When it was Eva's turn, she briefly explained that she came from Finland and had moved to London a month earlier.

'And what is it that appeals to you?' asked Malik

Martin, running his hand through his black hair. Everyone's eyes were fixed on her.

'What appeals to me?' she repeated.

Malik nodded.

'I don't know . . . I guess I like the High Romantic period.'

Several guys in another corner of the room started to laugh. Another guy, a bit delicate-looking and sporting a moustache, looked at her with interest. Some of the female students were texting on their mobiles.

'Anything else?'

The truth was that Eva had very little interest in contemporary art. In her opinion it was often based on simple ideas that acquired importance merely through association with a specific gallery or museum. She had no idea what sort of work she intended to create.

'Well, it really doesn't matter what any of you think or know. You're here to forget about all of that,' said Malik, as he moved to the front of the room and took up position there.

'You've probably heard that my teaching method is a little unusual. I don't give any tests, and we won't be studying periods of cultural history according to some fixed chronology. Instead, each week for the next ten weeks we're going to discuss a specific work created by one of you. For each class, one student will be asked to prepare a work. And that's why we really need to get going. I expect you to start working immediately. Today we'll begin by discussing a particular work of art that I'm hoping you'll find exciting.'

In the afternoon, when Eva joined some of the students at a nearby pub, she got to hear all about Malik Martin. Everybody sat there eagerly talking about how exciting the class was going to be, and several times they mentioned someone named 'Sarah'. When Eva asked who Sarah was, a skinny young woman sitting next to her explained.

'That's his wife. She's almost as legendary as Malik. She owns an art gallery in Bethnal Green. Apparently they have an open marriage, or at least that's what people say. Malik's got something of a reputation.'

'That's right. He likes to sleep with young female artists,' said another student.

'Male artists too,' added the skinny young woman.

'I see,' said Eva.

She felt a slight tingling in her stomach, yet she was surprised at how comfortable the whole situation felt – sitting here with the other students and being able to say that she was studying art in London. Was it really that easy? She realised that she was the one who would have to give substance to that simple statement. She thought the others seemed very self-confident, and she had a hard time determining what they might think of her. Even though she didn't feel that she had her 'own voice', did that really matter? Wasn't that why she was here? To find it?

The class had ended with a video of an art installation. It showed a glass of water sitting on a shelf on a wall. Nothing happened, and yet they watched it for close to ten minutes.

Afterwards Malik handed out a sort of Q & A form that apparently went with the video, with the artist answering questions about the work. He claimed that the glass of water actually represented an oak tree.

Q: Do you mean that the glass of water is a symbol of an oak tree?

A: No. It's not a symbol. I've changed the physical substance of the glass of water into that of an oak tree.

Eva thought the whole thing seemed like an exercise that might be presented in a secondary-school philosophy class. But she didn't say a word, hoping that someone else would do the talking.

'So how would you interpret this? What do you think about it?' asked Malik. He was standing in the middle of the room, giving them an earnest, child-like look – the same look that Eva had seen on the faces of boyfriends when they played some new tune that they thought would impress her.

'No opinions? Come on, people, you're not here to sit in silence, are you?'

A wiry guy with reddish-brown hair and freckles cautiously raised his hand. He was wearing a

T-shirt that said 'Lipstick Lesbian', and he was as thin as his shirt.

'Yes, Mr Parr?'

'I think it's brilliant. At first you just see the glass of water and you think, like, okay, it has to do with life, meaning it's deep symbolism, with the water as a basic element. But then the artist, like, comes in and just fucks you over, because it's not a glass of water, it's not a symbol, it's a tree. So this is just as much about our preconceived ideas about how to interpret a work of art as it is about the work itself.'

Malik Martin raised his eyebrows. 'Uh-huh. Uh-huh. And what does that mean?'

'I don't know, or rather, I assume it's what it says here on the paper. "That to understand the classification of oak as a specific oak is not the same as understanding and experiencing a glass of water as an oak."'

'What else? Anyone?'

Malik looked around at the other students.

When Eva had studied art history, they'd sometimes used this kind of exercise in class. They could spend several class hours discussing what art was, and who determined what it was.

She raised her hand.

'Yes?' said Malik.

She looked around the room. 'Well, as I see it, the idea behind this work of art is to show how art is about trust. The spectator's trust in the artist's perspective. If the artist says that the glass of water is an oak tree, we have to believe him or her.'

Malik's expression revealed nothing about what his reaction might be to what she'd said. Instead, he moved to the middle of the room and said, 'Interesting. And what's your own opinion? Do you trust the artist?'

She hesitated. She'd learned that there was no right or wrong in this sort of discussion – and that resorting to personal preferences when it came to conceptual art was like using Hitler to win an argument. The point wasn't whether a specific work of art was good or bad. The point was whether it was interesting.

'It makes me think about Descartes. I mean, it's dealing with similar questions, isn't it? "Does the table exist – in reality?" et cetera. Although I don't think this particular text is very well written.'

'I'm sorry you don't think so,' said Malik Martin. 'The critics had a completely different view when Michael Craig-Martin first showed this artwork in 1973. Later a theatre piece was even made from it.'

'From this one work?' asked Eva.

'Absolutely. Picture it: what's happening here is just like in the theatre. The transformation from one thing to another. It's exactly what you're saying. Theatre is totally based on trust. The actor trans-forms himself into a character in the play, and we believe it, because that's part of the contract. Descartes is an excellent comparison. He asked himself: how we can believe that the table actually exists? And what was his answer? That we can't. We can only trust in the subject. This work of art shows how strong the subject's power is over the perceived reality. If we choose to believe the artist, then anything is possible. It's about *surrendering yourself*, as some wise person once expressed it.'

Eva blushed. Her reply was brief. 'But the actors don't just stand on the stage without doing anything. They move about and speak their lines. It's not the same with the glass of water, which is completely motionless.'

'Don't be so sure about that,' said Malik.

Now one of the young women students turned to face the others in the room. She had an eighties-style Cyndi Lauper hairdo, and her arms were covered with tattoos.

'Isn't it a little like the Duchamps pissoir? I mean, taking a totally ordinary object and calling it art?'

The guy in the Lipstick Lesbian T-shirt protested. 'We're not seriously going to talk about the Duchamps pissoir, are we? That was fucking ninety years ago.'

The young woman looked surprised, but Malik didn't reply. He abruptly clapped his hands and announced that the class was over. Eva stood up, noticing how stiff her joints were. Her brain also felt like it had gone numb, the same feeling she got if she hadn't eaten all day and just drank coffee – a huge echoing whiteness.

CHAPTER 5

Gradually, Eva's studies gathered momentum. She enjoyed showing up at the university every day and spending half her time just talking about various topics. Malik was a strong supporter of the idea that discussions were the most important part of these study years, and he thought they ought to proceed organically, without being steered by any preconceived notions about how art criticism should be formulated. Each student was assigned a place in a studio and was allowed full use of the school's art supplies, which were included in the tuition fees.

Certain factions soon crystallised. Some students were skilled at drawing and often could produce remarkable results very quickly. Eva belonged to this group. She'd always been good at drawing, and she had developed her own style, which she stuck to faithfully, especially early in the autumn, when she wanted to impress the others without taking any big risks.

The problem with these skilful drawings was that they swiftly became quite repetitive. For instance, Eva soon learned that Laurie, a young woman

66

with a freckled face and open expression that always reflected the mood of the group, liked to paint big, bright pictures that used a lot of paint and canvas. But almost all her paintings looked the same, flirting vaguely with the early modernist style, with everything blotchy and deliberately slapdash. Yet in places it was possible to *glimpse* a proper painting. This was the exact opposite of Ben's work. He spent his time making vector systems on Adobe Illustrator, which he then printed out and transformed into small, extremely detailed laser-printed pieces with titles like 'Reasons My Girlfriend Won't Fuck Me' and 'Experiences From My Four Years as an Involuntary Teenage Virgin'.

There were also sculptors, photographers and students who focussed on performance art. A quiet but interesting guy named Russ stood out from the others because he didn't shower his work with a bunch of conceptual bullshit but simply dedicated himself to his painting. Plus he painted in oils, which meant that he was always cloaked in a strong, but not entirely unpleasant, odour of oil and turpentine. His paintings were almost never done when they were supposed to be shown, so the discussions often ended with him promising to show more the next time it was his turn to present work to the class.

Malik Martin made an effort to offer everyone critiques, moving from one work of art to another, and sometimes handing out stern words. 'Good

God, Russ, is that your own pile of shit that you're trying to convey?' But the real core of his instruction was focussed on the weekly sessions when they all got together to discuss one another's work.

The first weeks were marked by a certain cautiousness in the group. No one dared criticise anyone else. Instead, they used adjectives like 'interesting' or 'exciting'. Another standard phrase was quickly adopted: 'I understand it much better now that you've explained the actual process involved.' Eva thought this was just another way of saying that the artwork was more interesting as an idea than it was in reality.

She felt that they rarely had time to do anything properly. They were always scrambling to create the next work, but when she pointed this out to Malik, he merely said that they weren't there to 'paint some fucking Renaissance masterpiece', but to form an initial, basic concept of themselves as artists.

During a recent class session they'd discussed Ben's small triptychs. He'd produced the actual pattern on the computer and then changed it into a screen print, which he highlighted using neon-pink and cyan-blue on three square canvases. When he talked about the work, he gave the impression that there was some sort of intricate numerological system behind the geometric figures in the painting, but the interpretation was made even more obscure by the fact that he'd titled the work 'Afghanistan'.

'I think it's exciting,' said Laurie, who was always generous with her comments and the one who broke the ice if no one else wanted to say anything. But her remarks were meaningless because she always liked everything the other students did.

The rest of the class sat in silence on their cushions and rugs. Most of them brought coffee and something to eat to these critique sessions. The student with the Cyndi Lauper hairdo – her name was Margot – had brought a bottle of wine, and since Malik didn't object when she opened it, some of the guys had asked her for a glass.

Now Malik was walking around the room, waiting for someone to say something. 'Doesn't anybody have an opinion about Ben's work?'

Margot looked at it and decided to venture a remark. 'I think it's nice. The colours are nice, and the composition is too. But I'm not really sure I understand the title. What does this have to do with Afghanistan?'

'Ben, care to comment?' asked Malik.

Ben shook his head. 'Preferably not. I don't want to steer the interpretation. Do I have to?'

'You're entitled to refuse to comment. But what if I put the question like this: would you describe this as a political work of art?'

Again, Ben shook his head. 'I don't think it makes any difference what I say. I'm not the one who determines that.'

Eva had a feeling that a lot of students in the class were making art that looked like art – meaning they had a definite idea about how art should look and function. Certain ideas and topics were considered to be 'important', and a proper inter- pretation was supposed to sound a certain way. So that was what served as the starting point for their work. Ben seemed totally uninterested in participating in the expected discussion.

No one said a word.

'I could tell you what I think, but what I think doesn't matter. Come on, folks!' said Malik.

It occurred to Eva how ridiculous this was – they were all forced to come up with an opinion that functioned in synthesis with the work of art. The whole field of art was like that. Everyone was striving towards an ideal of consensus. But what existed beyond that? Or was this merely a way to role-play, an approach to art that they had learned? The same way that young people who were politic- ally active spoke of politics the way they imagined that politics should sound.

Finally, Eva decided to speak. She thought she might as well contribute to the discussion.

'At first I didn't really get it. I mean, it's the same thing that you've done the last few times, Ben. Now you've just come up with a whole new title instead of the usual ones that have to do with sex. But then I started thinking, maybe it's an allegory. Maybe you see Afghanistan as an image for your love life.'

Ben started fidgeting. His painting, which was a metre and a half square, was displayed on an easel at the front of the room. He made no attempt to explain anything. Silence descended over the class once again. A few people were drinking wine. Finally, Malik clapped his hands.

'Okay, it doesn't look as if we're going to get any further today. We'll continue on Monday. But that was an interesting theory, Eva,' he said as he went to the back of the room and opened the door. Everyone stood up, a few patted Ben on the shoulder, and the room emptied.

Half an hour later, Eva was waiting for Malik outside the university district, at a café where they often met.

She was thinking about how she longed for clear, sharp insights – the kind that you couldn't make up, the kind that you discovered, as if they had always been there, just waiting for you to find them.

When they were in the car, heading towards town, Malik began talking about the work of the other students as he lit a cigarette.

'The problem with Ben is that he's so emotionally blocked that all he can do is sit in front of a computer and calculate formulas, telling himself that it's art. And then – as if to give the whole thing some sort of framework – he goes and calls the work "Afghanistan" so that he'll seem deeper than he really is. Where's the fucking risk-taking?'

Eva nodded. Malik went on, flicking the ash from his cigarette out of the car window. 'To be perfectly

71

honest, sometimes I just want to shoot myself in the head. Like when the boys start bullshitting about Bourdieu and those damned cultural assets, and they turn to look at the girls' – here, Malik turned towards Eva – 'and their faces are all lit up. And I think to myself what a fucking waste. Boys, there are thousands of other people all around the world right now talking about Bourdieu and thinking that they're the only ones . . .'

When Malik got going like this, nothing could stop him. He loved the sound of his own voice. And Eva refused to admit it, but she actually enjoyed hearing Malik criticise the other students. Whenever he mocked Laurie, he did it with the greatest intensity – and Eva suspected this was because he was pissed off that she treated him with such indifference.

'All her work is extremely narcissistic. Have you ever thought about that? It's like she can only see her own point of view, and she always thinks that she's kicking below the belt, when in reality her work has to do with inflating her own ego. But of course it doesn't matter – she'll do fine. People love that kind of shit. Come here,' said Malik, and Eva leaned towards him.

When they got to Eva's flat, Malik wanted to get high. He claimed to have an inexhaustible supply of Ritalin pills because his doctor had diagnosed him as having ADHD. He'd tried several times to offer some to Eva, but she had a mental block about taking drugs in the middle of the day. She'd tried cocaine at parties, and the first time she'd felt so hyper that she almost chewed her cheeks to shreds. But after a while she started liking the effect it had on her – she felt sharp and smart, and she enjoyed talking to people, without getting into those sorts of embarrassing conversations that often happened if she was drunk.

Malik crushed up a pill and snorted it off the cover of one of Eva's art books, an expensive volume about the Pre-Raphaelites that she'd bought at the National Gallery. Soon afterwards, he wanted to have sex with her. And since he was high, he'd want to spend a long time at it – the drugs seemed to increase his sexual appetite. She didn't mind. Eva thought there was something in the physical act that seemed more comprehensible and pure than the art she'd been trying to create during the past two months. When he entered her from behind, she couldn't help feeling a certain ecstatic pride that she'd made it this far – none of her friends back home in Finland had ever moved further away than to Stockholm.

CHAPTER 6

When Katriina first met Max she was already twenty-two – which seemed terribly grown-up at the time – and he was laying the foundation for his career at the department. In the afternoons, Max used to sit in student cafés, gathering a small audience around him to listen to his ideas and argue. The group included Veronica Pimenoff, Risto Repo, JP Roos, Anssi Sinnemäki, Kari Rydman and Matti Wuori. Katriina thought Max talked too much and was hopelessly self-absorbed, but he was cute, and she thought it might be possible to do something about that annoying side of his personality. Apparently he'd never met a girl who dared to challenge him.

He said as much later on, when they became a couple, and then many times after they were married. 'You're so cruel,' he would say, with pride in his voice. 'I've never met anyone who could put me in my place as expertly as you can. Don't stop.'

It took a long time before she met his parents. They lived in Österbotten, and it was clear to Katriina that Max was nervous about introducing her to his father, in particular. The fact that Max was a Finland–Swede was not something to which she'd given much thought, but for him it was apparently a big deal that her first language was Finnish and not Swedish. Max's father, Vidar, was active in local charity, as well as local politics, and Max didn't think he'd easily accept having a Finnish-speaking daughter-in-law. When Katriina finally did meet them, she realised at once why Max had been so concerned. Ebba and Vidar were a typical post-war couple: he was a domineering alcoholic and she was his stoically submissive wife.

'Can't you see how badly your father treats your mother?' Katriina asked Max after their first visit. She had witnessed how much Vidar drank and how he then verbally terrorised Ebba, accusing her of one thing after another. But Max got upset and refused to discuss the matter. Until the end of his life Vidar never fully accepted Katriina, but he was always kind to his grandchildren. When they visited, he would sit down in his chair to watch TV, hunching his portly body over another seven per cent can of beer, but he sometimes allowed one of his granddaughters to sit on his lap. Katriina always regarded Max's father as possessed of a paradoxical mixture of petty bourgeois Finland–Swedish elitism and a provincially rooted inferiority complex. In his eyes, Katriina was not just a Finn – she was a snobbish Finn from the city.

★   ★   ★

Katriina had spent the whole autumn ploughing disconsolately through an endless series of meetings. Every day she took the bus to work, waiting at the stop on Runebergsgatan at eight o'clock in the raw cold after the rain had frozen overnight, making the roads treacherous.

Weeks had passed, months even, during which Katriina had felt not a scrap of inspiration about her recruitment job at Helsinki health service. It was strange how easy it was to go to work each morning and pretend that everything was just like it used to be. Katriina handled exactly the same duties as she had for the past five years, except that now she did them mechanically, without being fully present, as if she were a robot imitating an energetic mid-level manager at the height of her career.

At first she'd expected someone to notice – maybe one of her colleagues. Heikki, for instance, whose office was right next door. He'd never made it a secret that he coveted Katriina's job. Or maybe Petra, who always required a huge amount of encouragement to carry out even the simplest of tasks. Katriina pictured one of them coming over to her one day and figuratively backing her into a corner.

'Katriina, we've noticed that you haven't been yourself lately. We miss your leadership and inspiration.' 'Katriina, how are you doing? Now be honest.' Something along those lines.

But as it turned out, no one asked her any questions, no one noticed that she was mentally absent.

So Katriina just continued on as before, and strangely enough everything seemed fine, brilliant, in fact, as she pretended to have it all under control. She acted as if she was giving her full attention to her job, even making some innovative changes.

The result of this situation was that she ended up despising her colleagues because they weren't smart enough to realise what a wretched mid-level manager she was. They had basically been duped and blinded by the image of who she used to be, an image that at one time, long ago, might have had some truth to it. Consequently, she was both unhappy with her job and ashamed that she felt this way. Wasn't it irresponsible of her to give less than a hundred per cent?

With such thoughts on her mind, Katriina went to the Tuesday meeting, which had been set up to discuss establishing increased 'interaction' with the patients, or 'clients', as certain people currently chose to call them. The word 'patient' was apparently thought to place an 'unnecessary focus on disease' and hence carried an 'unnecessary negative charge'. (To quote Wivan.)

Wivan had been Katriina's closest colleague for as long as she could remember. Now approaching sixty, Wivan loved words like 'exciting' and 'challenging'. She was a boss who viewed change as a goal in itself. She had recently experienced a major crisis in her life, which had caused her to plant a garden and attend meetings of the Swedish book club 'Life Energy'. Everyone at work was aware of this because Wivan's office was filled with books bearing titles such as *Losing Weight Mindfully* and *Discover and Protect Yourself Against Energy Thieves*.

At this stage Katriina could have given an entire lecture on so-called energy thieves, since it was a subject that had exerted an enormous impact on Wivan. She talked about this phenomenon with every new person she met. Katriina had noticed that, oddly enough, the term 'energy thief' was never directed at herself. It was always aimed at someone else in the room.

Enhanced interaction with the patients – or clients – was supposed to occur primarily via redesigned websites, which would allow individuals to book doctors' appointments online, and thereby shorten the phone queues. The sites would also make it possible for individuals to ask questions about various symptoms, to provide responses from health professionals and even at certain times make 'chat sessions' available with the family doctor.

During the previous autumn, HNS web strategies, which operated under the name *HNS 2.0*, had been the hot topic of conversation. Since Finland wanted to be a forerunner when it came to IT, there was plenty of seed money available to promote innovations for anyone seeking funding for that purpose. At the moment, the staff were discussing the possibility of setting up a quiz on the hospital home page. 'It's hugely popular right now. Everybody's doing it,' said Heikki who, being a male – although not an IT expert, as far as Katriina knew – had an opinion about everything.

'What do you think, Katriina?' asked Paula, who actually represented the doctors' group, but also participated in the planning group that discussed web strategies.

'Sure, I think it sounds fine,' replied Katriina.

Everyone nodded, glancing at one another. Someone made a note of the idea. It was afternoon, and Katriina's energy level had sunk to somewhere between that of a coma patient and a dead fish.

'Or what about a "Question of the Day"?' Heikki suggested.

'What's all of this going to cost?' asked Katriina. She turned to look at one of the people who worked in the IT department. She could never remember the man's name – was it Markku something? – but he seemed to take a disproportionate amount of pride in his work, as if he thought computer engineers belonged to a superhuman race. He'd been on the job for little more than two months, but he was already highly regarded by the whole staff, since he was the only one who knew how to work the projector in the meeting room.

'Well, it shouldn't be a major problem. But we

need a new cms, because the one we have now can't handle a quiz.'

Katriina looked at her colleagues. She had no intention of giving Markku the satisfaction of telling everyone what 'cms' meant, but Paula didn't hesitate to ask. And that prompted him to clasp his hands as he looked around the room and proceeded to speak to them as if they were all children. He had a slightly Asperger's style of explaining things, as if he were forced to translate his own mental processes into a language that normal people could understand.

'If you want the simple definition, you could call it a web publishing tool. And we need to update the one we have.'

'Is that difficult?' asked Katriina.

'Depends on how you look at it. We have to migrate the old home page to the new platform. That can take a while. But if we're talking about redoing the entire website – which is what I'm hearing – then it's going to be a slightly bigger operation.'

'I see,' she said. 'Is this something that requires a call for bids from contractors?'

'That's up to you. There are free versions available. So that's one possibility we could look into. But I can't guarantee we'd get the tech support we need. If anything goes haywire, it could be hard to fix.'

'That doesn't sound good,' said Katriina.

Heikki raised his hand.

'This is just a quiz we're talking about here. It's not rocket science. Do we really have to revamp the whole system?'

Everyone looked at Markku.

'I'm afraid so,' he said, looking almost elated.

Katriina could tell that this meeting was going to go on for ever if she didn't do something. She could already feel the strength seeping out of her body. Dark clouds were piling up in the front of her brain, dousing any spark of life until the only thing remaining was a bottomless black pit marked with the sign WEB STRATEGY. She glanced at her watch and saw that it was almost three.

'Okay, here's what we're going to do,' she said, turning to Markku with a nod. 'I'd like you to draw up a rough estimate of the required man-hours and how much it's going to cost. I'll need to have your report before our next meeting, and then we'll take it from there. How's that?'

She looked at the others, who all nodded. She glanced again at her watch and concluded that the meeting was officially over. Chairs scraped the floor as everyone gathered up their papers. Markku switched off the projector and then everybody left.

Katriina smoked her first cigarette of the day on her way home from work. Normally she allowed herself three, but lately the daily number had risen to as many as eight. She was thinking that the only way to avoid completely falling apart was by plodding onward, as if nothing was wrong, by moving forward and focussing on the next goal. The fact that it was already pitch dark by four in the afternoon didn't help matters.

When she got home she phoned Helen.

'Hi, Mum.'

Katriina could hear the grandkids in the background.

'I'm just calling to chat. Actually, it's about the party for your father's sixtieth birthday. He says he doesn't want to celebrate the occasion, but I was thinking that . . . I mean, we need to come up with something. Not a big party, but maybe a few of his colleagues . . .'

Katriina always liked the idea of a really big celebration. The people, the sounds, all the commotion.

If there was one thing she was good at, it was making other people feel at ease, preferably against a backdrop of the sort of polished bourgeois conviviality that, to her great joy, she realised she had thoroughly mastered. It was a role for which she had subconsciously prepared all her life. Memorising all the lines.

Actually, she had often thought that she would have made an excellent set designer for the theatre. Life was about giving people the right props and the right setting in which to act.

Katriina could hear her daughter speaking to one of the kids – it must be Lukas – and in her mind she pictured how her daughters, and maybe even the grandchildren, would behave at Max's party.

'You know what would be fun?' she now said.
'What?'

'What if you and Eva – you can say no if this doesn't appeal to you – but what if the two of you sang something?'

Helen didn't reply, but Katriina knew that she'd come through. She always did.

'Or maybe Amanda would like to play something?'

'I'm sure she would. We'll see. But Mum, if Dad says that he doesn't want to celebrate his birthday, we can't really force him to have a party.'

A slight reproach was evident in her voice, an insinuating but unspoken rebuke: 'Why do you always have to make things so complicated?' It was an accusation that the whole family often directed at her. But Katriina was the only one who understood why she wanted to do this. It had to do with her special expertise; this party was one of the instances when she knew she'd be able to shine. She could just picture how she'd make the party a little bigger, a little more lavish – and above all more festive – than the ones that Tuula had hosted lately.

'Oh, that's what everyone says about birthdays. They pretend they don't want anyone to go to any trouble, but in reality they'd be disappointed if nothing was arranged,' said Katriina.

She knew this was true about most people but maybe not about Max. His need to socialise had diminished more and more the older he got, and she suspected that he was feeling a bit anxious about turning sixty. Max would never admit it, but the fact was that he admired youth tremendously, and in an entirely different way to Katriina. If anything, his Peter Pan complex seemed to get stronger as the years passed.

'Have you heard anything from Eva?' asked Helen.

'I haven't had a chance to talk to her about the party yet, but I suppose I'll have to offer to pay for her trip home.'

'Is Grandma coming?'

Katriina hadn't given any thought to inviting Max's mother. She assumed it would be too hard for Max's sister to drive her over alone. But she also knew that it was their turn to pick up her mother-in-law in Kristinestad and bring her home for a visit. Ebba hadn't been to Helsinki in two years. Instead, Max had gone to Österbotten whenever he had time.

'We'll see. If she comes, I'd be the one doing the driving.'

'I can help out.'

'So how's it going with your job?' asked Katriina.

'Same as usual. We're getting a new teacher after Christmas. A history teacher. It's kind of a sad story. His wife died in a car accident, so then he and his daughter moved to Helsinki.'

'Oh, that's terrible!'

Helen didn't seem to think it was anything to get upset about. She continued talking in the same tone of voice as before.

'You know our principal? Gunvor? Well, apparently she's hoping he'll be some sort of genius. She's been running around talking about how we need to update our teaching methods, step into the digital age, and things like that. But I don't know . . .'

'To change the subject,' said Katriina, 'I think it's important right now for Eva to work out what she's going to do with her life. She seems keen on this whole artist thing, so I assume that London is a good place for her to get into the right circles and learn something . . .'

'Or else she'll find a husband and have kids. Then at least she'll have something to do.'

'Hmm,' said Katriina, nodding.

She leaned back in the armchair. She loved her Artek chair, not just because it reminded her of her youth, but because it had been such a sensible purchase, one of those things in life that she never needed to regret.

'I think I'd better go now, Mum.'

'Okay, give those little darlings a hug from me.'

'I will.'

After putting down the phone, Katriina went out on to the balcony to have a smoke. It had started snowing, big wet flakes that settled damply on her cigarette. She couldn't see anything except the inner courtyard below. Someone walked across and tossed some rubbish into the bin with a faint splash. She happened to think about flowers: the fact that she needed a lot of flowers for Max's party. Not just a few bouquets here and there, but completely filling the flat. Tuula almost never invested extra energy in flower displays.

She pulled the pack of cigarettes out of her pocket and saw that only one was left.

CHAPTER 7

Max had forgotten all about the interview idea for *Helsingin Sanomat* when Laura Lampela suddenly rang him up one day after he'd given a lecture for his first-year students. He was sitting in his office, just about to leave for home. He agreed to Laura's suggestion that they meet for lunch at the Kosmos on Friday. Max met a lot of young women at the department, but he'd always kept a certain distance, feeling more than anything like an uncle to them. And most of the women preferred to consult his female colleagues when it came to term papers and the like. He hadn't enjoyed this much attention in quite a while. In 1993, the publication *City* had named him one of the 'young intellectuals of the year'. At the time he considered himself too old for such a label, but now he realised how young he actually was back then. He knew that certain factions within the department thought he was a dinosaur, that his views on evolutionary psychology were ludicrous and that he was becoming increasingly isolated professionally. Today's sociologist was supposed to focus on gender studies, environmental issues, or new research in the wake of the influential theories propounded by Pierre Bourdieu.

Max mentioned the lunch interview to Katriina.

'So I guess you'll be home at the usual time on Friday, right?'

'What do you mean?'

'Because you're just having lunch.'

'Oh, right. I assume so,' he said. 'Although I have a tennis game booked for that evening.'

He realised that this whole interview was a foolishly minor event, but if there was anything he needed right now, it was a foolishly minor event to take his thoughts off the book he was writing. His editor, Matti, had phoned to ask him how it was going. The conversation had set his nerves on edge.

In many ways Edvard Westermarck was a mystery, and the biography was a much bigger project than Max had initially thought. How did it happen that in 1888 an unmarried twenty-six-year-old Finn – with very little research experience – had managed to write a book about the history of marriage? And, even more surprisingly, write it in English?

Max had often pictured Westermarck sitting under the great dome of the British Library in London and writing most of the work that would make him a celebrated scholar of international renown. One of the first from Finland.

Westermarck was a man who seemed to possess the huge amount of patience required to gather all the facts, constantly retest hypotheses, latch on to the very latest research and also embark on lengthy travels to parts of the globe where the most primitive conditions prevailed. He was a Finland–Swedish aristocrat from a sheltered world who chose a life that could only be described as cosmopolitan.

The fact that no one remembered Westermarck today was just one more reason to dust him off and restore him to the public spotlight.

When he started on the project, Max had harboured an ambition to travel to at least some of the areas where Westermarck had lived, such as Sicily, Morocco and England. But he never seemed to find time for more than a brief trip to London, and his attempts via phone calls to track down Westermarck's old villa in Tangier had proved fruitless. He'd started his research in Åbo, reading Westermarck's letters, but now it was a matter of actually buckling down to write the biography.

'I'm assuming it's great,' Matti had said on the phone. Max had made several visits to see Matti in his office at the publishing house, each time proclaiming how amazing the book was going to be. He'd told Matti that the work would present a survey of the entire intellectual climate in the early twentieth century – highlighting Darwin, Freud, and the French sociologist Émile Durkheim. And it would show how groundbreaking Westermarck's work had been. Max had enthusiastically recounted the many elements that would add dramatic flair to the text: Westermarck's suppressed homosexuality, his travels to Morocco, his sister who joined the suffragettes, and much more.

By now Max had been working on the biography so long that he'd begun to dream about it. In his dreams he would find himself in a Bedouin tent up in the mountains somewhere near Marrakesh, among bandits and camels, in the nineteenth-century settings that Westermarck described in his memoirs. Max had the same dream night after night: he was sitting on a hill, looking at the lovely women, men and children making their way up dusty trails in the dawn. When he awoke, he was always thirsty.

Matti had sounded less impressed during their last phone conversation.

'Good Lord, Max, we only need fifty to a hundred pages to write up the catalogue copy and the hype for the back cover.'

Max promised to send him something ASAP, but several days had now passed, and today he had no intention of even thinking about the book.

Instead, he devoted the whole morning to choosing the right shirt to wear. He'd also put on aftershave – something he almost never did. He found the tube of Boss cologne, in cream form, which had been in the medicine cabinet for as long as he could remember. He thought it still smelled okay. There didn't seem to be any noticeable difference in the scent from when it was first opened. Helen had given it to him as a Christmas present the year she got her first job.

As far as Max's own profession was concerned, he'd fallen into it more or less by accident. When he was in secondary school, he read the course descriptions in a brochure and thought that sociology sounded the easiest. So he got a copy of *Introduction to Sociology* by Erik Allardt and Yrjö Littunen, the primary text used during nearly all of the 1970s. To his surprise, Max passed the exam with high marks, and when he entered the university, he realised that he had a talent for the type of research still prevalent in the field of sociology at the time: Marxist tinged and yet solidly anchored in positivism and the idea of correlations – i.e., that c follows a and b, and so on. Max's father knew nothing about university studies, but both parents had gone to secondary school. So Max was expected to make the move to Helsinki to continue his studies, no matter how suspicious Vidar might be about his son's chosen field.

'Aren't they all just a bunch of communists?' he'd asked. Max had staunchly denied this claim, even though sociology was crawling with communists.

He felt the same need to defend himself now, in the Kosmos, as Laura sat in front of him with a notebook and asked him whether sociology wasn't merely a 'typical 1970s discipline'.

'No, on the contrary. The whole nineties period

was incredibly exciting for us, because of what happened with the economy. Plus there was our study of Finnish sexual practices. And now all the focus is on the Nordic welfare model – and how it's being dismantled. There's a lot going on. Although these days I have a more social-psychological perspective . . .'

Laura nodded and took notes. Before they'd started the interview, Max had been subjected to a tedious photo session lasting a good fifteen minutes. When he arrived at the restaurant, Laura and the photographer had been waiting for him outside. The photographer was a young guy, barely twenty, with a bizarre haircut, and it was obvious that he didn't know who Max was. Nor did he have the slightest interest in finding out. He wanted to take the photos outside because it was snowing. He asked Max to put on a 'pensive' expression and look up at the sky. Max felt like a real idiot but did as he was asked.

When he was finally able to sit down with Laura – and at first he'd worried that the photographer would accompany them inside, but fortunately the guy went back to the newspaper office – they started off with some polite chit-chat. Max asked Laura about her job, and she gave him the short version of her life story. After studying sociology, then journalism, she'd taken a year off (Max thought to himself: how typical, these kids and their gap years). During that period she travelled to Australia and New Zealand, and then spent some time in

Shanghai, where she wrote freelance articles for the Finnish media, mostly about the Chinese economy. When she returned home, she became a freelance reporter. She shared an office with some friends in Berghäll.

No boyfriend? Max wondered, but he decided to save that question for a later time.

'But it's cultural issues that I want to write about,' Laura told him as the waitress brought their first course. They had both ordered borscht, which seemed appropriate for this sort of winter day with heavy snowfall that was making Helsinki look like a city in an old Russian postcard from the nineteenth century.

They were sitting at a corner table next to the window. Max had insisted on ordering wine with their lunch. ('Is that okay? I don't have any lectures this afternoon.') Now he filled Laura's glass for the second time.

'Since the newspaper is paying, I'd love some wine,' she replied.

For Max, the Kosmos restaurant was a familiar stomping ground, even though lately he came here mostly for nostalgic reasons. The customer base had changed, with the journalists and artsy bohemians now replaced by business people and tourists.

The only thing that bothered him a bit was that a history professor from Tampere whom he happened to know slightly, a man by the name of Pekka Kantokorpi, was sitting at a table not too far away. Pekka was with a woman that Max didn't recognise.

He found the professor's presence annoying, since this was an opportunity that wouldn't come along again. He could feel himself sweating under his jacket as he tried to make Laura think he was perfectly relaxed.

She set down her wine glass and picked up her notebook. 'I think we should start with one of those "fact boxes". Do you mind if I ask you some questions they always print in women's magazines? You know: age, marital status, and so on?'

'Sure, go ahead.'

'Okay. I know that you're about to turn sixty. Are you married?'

'Yes, my wife's name is Katriina.'

'Okay. And what kind of work does she do?'

'She handles human resources and staffing issues for the hospital districts of Helsinki and Nyland.'

'Is she a doctor?'

'No, she has a degree in political science.'

'Any children?'

'Helen and Eva. Helen is . . . let me see . . . She's thirty-two. And Eva is three years younger, so she's twenty-nine.'

'No other children?'

'No.'

'What do your children do?'

'Helen is a teacher. Eva is studying art in London. From what I understand, it's supposed to be an exceptionally fine university.'

'Art? Do you mean art history or something like that?'

'No. As far as I know, they paint and work in other media.'

'Sounds exciting.'

'Uh-huh. I suppose so. But Eva has always wanted to go her own way; that's a big deal for her. Maybe because she's the little sister. To be honest, I don't know how she's managing to make ends meet in London. What we send her isn't much, at any rate. Although . . . You're not going to write about any of this, are you?'

'No, the article's not about your children.'

The waitress served their food. Max had chosen filet de bœuf with sauce rouennaise and racines alimentaires rôtis. Laura had selected one of the restaurant's classic dishes: Sylvester sandwich au gratin, which consisted of toasted black rye with a rum and morel sauce. They drank a toast and then started eating.

'So how do things look for the field of sociology nowadays? When I was a student, there was a lot of talk about population statistics.'

'Right. And there always is,' said Max. 'Although lately there's also a great deal of focus on feminism and gender studies. Lots of attention paid to post-modernism and post-everything.'

'Are you a feminist?' asked Laura.

It had been a long time since Max had thought about that question. Of course he was a feminist, or at least he'd convinced himself that he was during the seventies and eighties.

'You know, I'm so old that I can remember when we organised groups for men out in the archipelago so we could talk about feelings and explore our feminine side. With exercises where we would hug each other and walk around naked, and things like that.'

'And that made you become a feminist?'

'Yes. In reality, some of the Stalinists thought that the women's movement was nothing but bourgeois bullshit. In a socialist society the differences between the sexes were supposed to be automatically erased.'

'But you don't agree?'

'I think that feminism is necessary. But . . . maybe I shouldn't say this, but I think it's a shame that it has taken centre stage in such a dominant way. It scares off quite a few students, in my opinion.'

'What do you mean?'

Max paused to think. He wasn't entirely sure that he wanted to have this discussion at the moment.

'Well, why do all relationships between people have to be interpreted from a feminist perspective, so that nothing is ever left to chance any more? All behaviour is explained by the so-called balance of power between the two sexes. I understand the theoretical significance, and I understand why it's important for us to take a critical view of norms, but I don't understand why everything that happens to people, everything that people experience, all the sorrow and longing and clumsiness, has to be explained by feminism. Sometimes men act like real bastards – that's true – but it's not always because of the sexual power hierarchy. Some men are just bastards, plain and simple. And sometimes there's an even bigger overriding structure involved, like capitalism. I think we need more complex models for explaining things.'

Laura took notes, nodding as she wrote.

'So you're talking about intersectionality?'

This was a term often heard at the department, as well. Every time Max discussed this particular topic, he involuntarily landed in some sort of culturally conservative trench. And the more he talked about feminism, the more he yearned to read about Edvard Westermarck and his Bedouins and Berbers.

'You're right. I suppose that's what it's called. But what I mean is that in a world where everything is defined from a structuralist perspective, there's no room for mystery or excitement. Who wants to live in a society in which everything is organised according to the concept that no one ever acts inappropriately or feels bewildered; nobody goes too far or follows his emotions or does anything in direct contradiction of all the rules? It feels like there's something normative built into any criticism of societal norms, a desire for everyone to be the same, so that they will all fit into the advocated world-view.'

This was not what he'd intended to talk about. He was just trying to impress Laura.

'What's the angle you're going to take for this article?' he now asked.

'What do you mean?'

'I mean, are you going to slant it to portray an old guy who's complaining about the feminists? Or will you slant it to show a researcher who's at the height of his career? Sorry. I don't mean to push you one way or the other. It's just that I feel . . . well, I don't want it to sound like some sort of defensive speech.'

Laura nodded. Max studied her as she tilted her head to one side. As she talked, he thought to himself that she ought to pin up her hair. He'd like to see all of her neck.

'Okay. I understand. But I think we can try to cover a lot of ground in this article. Let's take a look at the nineties. It feels like intellectuals in Finland started getting much more attention in the media. There were plenty of intellectuals writing for *City* and other publications. You were one of them, Esa Saarinen was another. And you talked a lot about sex. Am I right?'

Max proceeded to answer as best he could. He cast a few glances at Pekka Kantokorpi and his female companion sitting at the nearby table, but they didn't seem to have noticed Max.

'Yes. There was a time when Helsinki University, and especially the humanities departments, had a reputation for being very . . . sexy. Today it's journalism and the various media that are hot. Seems as though everybody wants to be a TV news presenter. But you need to remember that Finland is a young nation. The seventies were highly political, and then in the late eighties everything was totally apolitical. After that, a middle ground was reached – a combination of what was new and superficial with what was old and intellectual. Including a place for philosophy. Maybe it was partially due to the growth of the middle class. People gathered in front of the TV to watch programmes about philosophical topics because they had the educational background to understand what was being discussed.'

Laura continued to take notes.

'Interesting,' she said. 'But you don't think this is true any more? Is the field of sociology no longer sexy?'

Max hoped it still was. Above all, he hoped that he was still sexy.

'In a matter of only a few years people have adopted a different attitude towards a university education. Partly because there's no longer the same guarantee that a degree will lead to a job. Other qualifications are required these days, like work experience. The other reason is that the whole university system has been restructured. Nowadays, the goal is to churn out graduates faster and faster.'

Out of the corner of his eye Max saw Kantokorpi get up and head for the loo. He decided to follow. He needed to take a break.

'Excuse me, but would you mind waiting a bit? I just need to . . .'

'Of course.'

He walked past the maître d' and went into the small men's room beyond the cloakroom. Kantokorpi was standing at the urinal and Max went over to stand next to him. As he washed his hands, Max pretended suddenly to recognise the professor.

'Hey, I can't believe it! What are you doing here?'

'Max! Long time, no see!'

They shook each other's hands, which were both still a bit damp. The Kosmos was an old restaurant, and there was something very fitting about two middle-aged men running into each other in the men's room. Max had a feeling that he needed to explain his presence, even though Kantokorpi hadn't even noticed that he was sitting at a table with Laura.

'So . . . What are you doing in Helsinki?' asked Max.

Pekka shrugged.

'Oh, nothing special. I'm just in town for a few days. Having lunch with an old colleague of mine. Maybe you know her . . . What about you?'

'No, you know, nothing much. I'm just here doing an interview for *Helsingin Sanomat*. I'm about to turn sixty, you know. Yeah, it's awful, isn't it? But what can you do? Everybody gets old, right?'

'Uh-huh. No way to get around it. But let me at least wish you happy birthday. Shall we?'

The professor opened the door for Max, and they said goodbye before going back to their respective tables. As Max sat down, he noticed that Kantokorpi glanced in his direction and then at Laura. Then he signalled a 'thumbs up', which made Max instantly lower his gaze.

'So. Where were we?'

They talked for an hour, and Max finally managed to get the ball rolling. Laura took few notes, focussing instead on running her fingertip along the rim of her wine glass – in a devastatingly sexy way – and laughing whenever Max said something amusing.

Speaking about his career in grand narrative arcs always came easily to Max. He made use of anecdotes that he'd told many times before to considerably larger audiences. At the same time, he couldn't help thinking how easy this was, perhaps a little too easy. As if a person's life could be defined by these big, vital themes. As if an individual reached certain points in his life when everything seemed to culminate, when decisive events occurred. But really, Max had always thought that such constructs were formulated by people after the fact. In reality, life consisted of a series of disparate embarrassments and episodic intervals that didn't necessarily add up to a coherent whole. The moments that had the greatest impact on our lives were often those that we never talked about because they had to do with personal failures: divorces, children with whom we'd lost

101

contact, painful misunderstandings. There was less controlled rationality in people's lives than they outwardly projected.

Yet Max did understand the merits of a good story. One important criterion for all research was that it had to be possible to explain the basic ideas in a simple manner. A good doctoral dissertation could be comprehensively summarised over lunch. Taking this to extremes: a good researcher should, in principle, be able to speak with such enthusiasm that his words could function as a series of pick-up lines.

Right now, Max was discussing the atmosphere at the university during the seventies.

'The most rabid Marxists were always citing Hegel, even though they really had no idea what he stood for. There was a lot of hype about Marxist literature, which meant that all other forms of sociology research were shoved to the background – and no one could write an article without first quoting a few fundamental state-ments from *Das Kapital*. Anyone who didn't follow Marxist dictates was branded a bourgeois sociologist,' he explained.

Laura then asked him to say more about the intellectual landscape within the field of sociology during those heavily politicised decades. Max thought she seemed like a student trying to get extra credit by delving into things at such a detailed level, but maybe she was actually inter-ested in what he had to say. When the waiter came over to their table to ask if they'd like more wine, Laura offered no objections.

'What happened after that?' she asked.

She was looking at him with a different sort of curiosity in her eyes. Maybe it was the alcohol, but Max thought there was something informal and even intimate in her expression.

He went on: 'When the Marxist boom gradually subsided in the early eighties – and then the Berlin wall came down – we found ourselves at a cross-roads. A number of sociologists turned their attention to manners and customs, or etiquette. In other words: how we use a knife and fork. Those who were younger, who had entered the university in the eighties, started reading Bourdieu and writing papers on "the sociology of fashion", and things like that.'

'What about you?'

'I suppose I found myself somewhere in between. I got interested in evolutionary psychology, and, well, of course I have nothing against reading Bourdieu. And that's where we are today. I offer introductory courses in the history of sociology while I try to write my little book about Westermarck.'

It had been a long time since he'd had the pleasure of talking so much about what interested him.

'Fascinating,' said Laura. Her eyes narrowed, and then she turned to survey the room. For a moment she seemed puzzled, as if she didn't really know where she was. But then she closed up her notebook and slipped it into her handbag. She got up to go to the ladies' room.

'Clearly I'm a bit tipsy,' she said. 'I'll be right back.'

She spent a long time in the loo. When she returned, Max could see that she'd touched up her lipstick. He took that as a compliment.

'So, are we done here?' he asked.

'I assume so.'

'And you're positive that the newspaper will reimburse you for the lunch?' said Max.

'Absolutely.'

They stood outside in the snow, putting off saying goodbye. Laura didn't seem to be in any more of a hurry than Max. She wore the same chic black coat she'd had on when he saw her for the first time in the café, and a purple scarf. They watched the people walking past on the street, and Max lit a cigar.

'So where are you headed now?' he asked.

'I suppose I should be getting back home. I have to write up this interview for Monday. It'll be published next week. Could you read through it for me?'

'Sure, I'd be happy to. Unless there's someone else who could do that.'

'Someone else?'

'A boyfriend, maybe?'

Laura laughed. 'Nope. No boyfriend. And even if I did have one, I think I can write my own articles without any help. I meant that you might want to read it to make sure all the facts are correct.'

'Oh, of course. I can do that.'

She smiled at him. Max took her smile to mean that she didn't think he was a total idiot. He earnestly wanted to stay right where he was.

'Actually, my wife is organising some kind of party for me, it'll probably be awfully boring, but apparently I can't get out of celebrating my birthday. You could come, if you like. I told her that I didn't want any big production, but if I know my wife, she's going to invite half the city. So it won't matter if you don't know anyone.'

'Maybe. But thanks for inviting me.'

'It would be really nice if you came. Something for me to look forward to. To be perfectly honest, I hate these kinds of social functions. You could offer me some moral support.'

'It's nice of you to have such faith in me.'

She gave him another smile. She had beautiful teeth. It was something he'd thought about all during lunch. If they hadn't been standing outside on the street, he would have leaned down and kissed her.

'Strangely enough, that's exactly how it feels. Like I have faith in you, I mean.'

She shrugged. 'That's sweet of you. But now I'd really better get going.'

She held out her hand, and Max took it, at the same time leaning down, as if to kiss her on the cheek.

'All right, see you!' she said, stepping out of reach. He managed to catch the scent of her perfume.

Then she was gone. For a moment Max didn't move, hardly aware of the snow falling all around him. Suddenly Pekka Kantokorpi appeared half a metre away, along with the woman who was his lunch companion. Max greeted them with some reluctance.

'So, that was the journalist from *Helsingin Sanomat*?' queried Kantokorpi. 'Nice-looking girl.'

CHAPTER 8

Eva could have stayed in London, saying that she couldn't afford the expense or take the time to fly home until Christmas (which was true), but then her parents would have started worrying about her finances, and she didn't want that. So when her mother phoned – Eva could hear Helen's kids in the background – she promised to book a ticket on Norwegian Air so she could be home for her father's birthday.

'Only two days? Can't you stay a little longer?' said her mother.

'I don't know, Mum. I've got a lot of work to do.'

'Just tell me that you're happy over there.'

'Yes, I'm happy.'

'Okay, okay. It's your life. By the way, to change the subject . . . Don't worry about getting a present. We're going to buy him something from all of us. I was thinking of having a party here at home, nothing big, just a few colleagues and you girls, and maybe some of our friends.'

When Katriina started talking like this, Eva would sometimes put the phone down on the table and pick it up again only when she could hear that the flood of words had stopped. She pictured Katriina lying on the sofa, wearing her reading glasses and paging through some women's magazine as she talked, with her thoughts leaping from one topic to another. There were seldom any awkward silences in conversations with Katriina, since she just didn't react to those sorts of signals. It was as if the synapses in her brain were so active that she never registered the more subtle emotional moods.

Eva pressed the phone to her ear and said that she still might want to buy her father a present.

'Your sister is here, by the way. Do you want to talk to her? Wait a minute and I'll give her the phone.'

Before Eva could say a word, Katriina handed the phone to Helen. 'Hi, Eva.'

'Hi, Helen. How are things?'

'Well, as you can hear, Mum is planning a birthday party for Dad. She thinks that you and I should sing something.'

'God, no.'

'I know what you mean. I told her that we haven't done that since we were teenagers.'

When they were younger, the two sisters had always sung at the parties given by their parents. It had been Katriina's idea, since people were always telling Eva what a great voice she had. Now that they were adults, Eva wasn't entirely sure that her voice had ever been that great. At least, no one had complimented her singing in a very long time.

'How's it going in London?' Helen asked now. 'Is it exciting to be part of the art world?'

'Uh-huh. And I'm actually really busy. It's going to take a while for me to get fully acclimatised. What about you guys?'

'Apart from the fact that I've been ill all autumn, everything's fine. Except we had lice. Did you know people still get lice? We never had lice when you and I were kids, did we?'

'Not that I remember.'

'Or maybe we did, but Mum and Dad never had time to check. I had to go through three rounds of treatment to get rid of them. But Lukas was lucky. Apparently they didn't like his hair – too grubby, I guess. It's impossible to get him to wash his hair.'

Eva could hear her mother trying to say something in the background.

'Helen, I have to run. I'm on my way to meet a friend. Give Amanda and Lukas a kiss for me. Do you think they'd like me to bring them something from London?'

'I'm sure they would. Do you want to talk to Mum again?'

'I'd rather not. Tell her goodbye, okay?'

It took a moment for Eva to refocus and remember where she was going. She was standing at a large crossroads near Liverpool Street. It was Saturday, and it was raining. A depressing, grey sky had hovered over London all week. Eva paused at the stairs leading to the Tube as she waited for a large black woman to carry her pram down to the platform. The sweet scent of her perfume blended with the smells of the big city: urine and greasy takeaway.

A man wearing a suit and carrying a briefcase raced past, nearly knocking over the woman with the pram. When she angrily shouted after him, he just kept on going, down into the tunnel that led to the Tube. Eva and the woman exchanged glances, as if to confirm that the man was a dickhead, and then Eva continued down the stairs.

It was lunchtime, and the whole city was crowded with Saturday shoppers. London was chaotic and enormous, with both wide and narrow streets criss-crossing each other, new and old buildings jumbled together, business districts and tourist areas and hipster neighbourhoods all mixed up with no rhyme or reason to their location. In a city like Paris, you always knew where every district was situated, since the whole place had been mapped out all at once. London lacked any similar sort of urban planning, and had been allowed to develop organically. Its layout was said to be so complicated that out of necessity cab drivers had developed larger brains.

The city was filled with galleries. In the beginning, Eva had tried to visit as many as possible, although most of the art she saw was dull and boring. But she liked the architecture of the big museums, especially the Tate Modern, which was huge, as big as an aeroplane hangar.

During the past few weeks the hot topic of conversation had been the Occupiers living in tents near St Paul's Cathedral. The anti-capitalism movement had spread to London, and now the area surrounding the cathedral was besieged by tents that had been set up on pallets. Eva sometimes walked past late at night, wondering whether anyone was really asleep inside those tents, or whether the Occupiers just came over in the daytime. Apparently some people did spend the night there, because if she walked very quietly, she could hear movement coming from inside the tents and someone's radio playing. Or she might see a faint light shining under one of the tarps. In the daytime the area was an odd mixture of grassroots activists and tourists. Foreigners seemed just as delighted by the demonstrators as they were by the old cathedral.

Eva was on her way to a chemist's. She had decided that she could no longer put off taking a pregnancy test. The whole thing was an inconvenience that she would have preferred to avoid, but this was the situation she found herself in and she would have to deal with it.

She hadn't told anyone about it, not her sister, not Natalia. Aside from Malik and Natalia, she was friends with only one other person in London, and that was her classmate Russ. One day when they were working in the studio he'd come over to talk to her. It was hard for her to know what he really wanted to say, since he kept mumbling into his moustache, saying something that sounded like he thought the opinions that she offered during one of the seminars had been 'valuable'.

Russ was extremely private about the paintings he did. If she came near his easel, he would always act embarrassed. He spoke quietly, keeping his voice low, but he had a vulnerable and self-deprecating – on the verge of self-annihilating – sense of humour that merely served to underscore his almost slapstick appearance. His moustache, which he kept carefully waxed, was the comical type that you saw in old photographs of workmen, butchers and shoemakers from the late nineteenth century. The only difference was that Russ was dark, with a complexion that revealed his Near Eastern heritage. (Eva soon learned that his family had roots in Algeria.)

She didn't tell him anything about Malik. Russ seemed so timid and prudish, and he probably would have been shocked to hear that she was sleeping with their professor. But it didn't really feel like she was doing anything that was strictly forbidden. When it came down to it, Malik was no more than twelve years older, and she was an adult, after all. Malik was discreet when they were at college. He claimed that he'd get kicked out if their affair became public, and Eva didn't doubt it – and that gave her a thrilling feeling of power over the whole situation.

Now she was standing at a crossing in Covent Garden. She tried not to think about it, but if she turned out to be pregnant, she had already decided to have an abortion in Finland. There was no other option.

The chemist shops in London were big and air-conditioned and brightly lit, following the American example. She asked one of the shop assistants where she could find a pregnancy test and then took from the shelf one in the middle price range. The box was small and yellow and cost two pounds. She had told herself to handle the whole situation with all the composure she could muster. But the package burned in her hand as she went over to the cashier to pay for her purchase.

When Eva arrived at the flat, Natalia was in the kitchen. She looked at Eva and then pointed towards her room. Eva went in and found Malik lying on her bed.

'Hey, babe. Your friend let me in,' he said. He was paging through her sketchbook.

'You know what? These aren't half-bad. I mean, you're no fucking Turner, but they're . . . pretty good. What's in the carrier bag?'

CHAPTER 9

'You fucking cunt,' said Malik. 'You tricked me.'

He was restlessly pacing Eva's small room. This was how Malik always talked whenever he was angry, so she didn't take his words seriously. She'd heard him call one of his best friends a 'fucking cocksucker' right to his face.

Eva had taken out the pregnancy test she'd bought at the chemist's shop and shown it to him. He peered at her with a blank expression and then slammed his fist into the wall, really hard. Eva thought it must have hurt terribly. Why did men do things like that? She wondered if it was something that Malik had learned from watching films. It seemed like the craziest thing to do, and Eva couldn't help laughing.

But Malik was furious. 'What the fuck? What's so damned funny?'

Natalia came in, wanting to find out what was going on. Her usual cheery expression showed a touch of concern.

'It's okay,' said Eva, not sure whether that was true or not. It felt as though she always ended up in these kinds of situations with men. She managed somehow to bring out their inner despair. 'My period is late, so I went out to buy this . . .'

'If it turns out you're pregnant, are you thinking of having an abortion? End of story?'

Eva nodded. 'I assume I will.'

'You assume you will?'

'I mean, yes, I will.'

Malik calmed down. His whole body had looked as tense as his fist, but now he relaxed.

'Okay. Go and do it. Let's find out.'

So Eva went into the bathroom, took the device out of the package and read the instructions. She'd taken a pregnancy test twice before, and both times it had been a false alarm. She stood there in the bathroom, listening to Malik shuffle around her room. After ten minutes she opened the door and joined him.

'I'm not pregnant.'

'Okay,' said Malik. He came over to give her a hug. 'I'm sorry, babe. I shouldn't have lost my temper like that. But you know that I wasn't plan-ning on . . . on our relationship being anything more than some innocent fun. I'm just not prepared to be a dad.'

'Yeah, I know that,' she said, and sat down on her bed.

Innocent fun was exactly what it had been. From the very beginning the only reason she had slept with Malik was because she was lonely in London, and it was something to do – someone to talk to.

One day after class he had shamelessly made a move on her. ('Eva, could you wait a minute? I'd like to talk to you.') It had started with a drink, and after the second drink, he'd thrown himself at her. She liked his aggressive ardour – it was both embarrassing and exciting at the same time, like a love story in a novel; not very cool but slightly irresistible.

Later, she began treasuring their time together after making love as much as the sex itself. Malik enjoyed telling her – although boasting was probably a better word for it – about the art boom in the eighties, and all the parties and exhibitions, about 'fucking Saatchi', 'fucking Venice', 'fucking Basel', and so on. Eva soon realised that Malik's self-described underdog status was just a pose. He actually came from a well-to-do family who owned a grand house on 'embassy row' in Belgravia. He'd gone to all the best schools and spent his holidays at French ski resorts. She'd even seen a picture of him as a fourteen-year-old schoolboy wearing a Lacoste pullover. But he chose, of course, to view himself as the black sheep of the family.

The fact that he'd become a teacher was the result of a huge concession on his part. His father had demanded that Malik, after he turned thirty, should find a way to become self-supporting. But Malik also claimed that by then he'd lost all interest in making art in the twenty-first century because the whole climate had become so individualistic.

'Artists need to find like-minded peers so they can toss their ideas around. If you look at the history of art, it's filled with movements. The Impressionists all knew each other, hung out together, drank together, fucked each other's wives, married each other's cousins.'

Malik wanted to divorce Sarah, but since he was part-owner in her gallery, they hadn't yet signed the papers. They had no children, and Malik claimed that he never wanted to have any. ('This world is too fucked up to have kids.')

It struck Eva that Malik might have interpreted the whole pregnancy scare as some form of black-mail, a way of getting at his family's money.

'I'm sorry. I shouldn't have said anything about it, since I wasn't sure,' Eva now told him.

'No, no, I'm glad you did. It's not just your . . . problem.'

Later in the evening, after Malik went home, Eva lay in bed and found herself thinking about Alexander. He'd been the boyfriend with whom she'd had the longest relationship. After four years they got engaged, moved in together, and then split up two months later. They'd talked seriously about having children, but put off the decision several times, since Alexander first wanted to finish his studies and get a job. According to him, they would then move into a terraced house in Esbo or Vik and have three kids (a girl and two boys, if Alexander had his way).

But one day Eva developed an inexplicable sense of anxiety about everything, about all his plans and the fact that their life together seemed so constrained. She felt as though she couldn't tell what was left of their actual relationship behind all the ideas about their relationship. She discovered that she felt happiest when she was home alone and forgot about Alexander, forgot about his very existence, and this led to the realisation that she didn't want to be with him. For her, a life in Esbo seemed to hold no promises for the future.

Katriina was furious when Eva called it quits, since she'd become very attached to Alexander, and for several months she'd held out hope that they'd get back together.

When the wedding invitation arrived a year later, everyone finally realised that it was over. Eva decided to go to the wedding, mostly because so many of her friends would be there.

That was a mistake.

Alexander and Marika got married on a large estate just outside of Borgå. It wasn't a bad ceremony. Marika's nieces were the bridesmaids, and Alexander's best man organised a spontaneous sort of flash mob inside the church. Lots of the guests stood up and started singing as the newly married couple walked back down the aisle. It was the type of meticulously planned spontaneity that Eva realised someone of her generation ought to perceive as the height of romance.

Immediately after the wedding cake was presented but before the disco dancing started up – and before the wedding ultimately degenerated into an inferno of sickly sweet self-promotion and kisses on the cheek – Eva decided she couldn't take it any more. Two guys who she remembered had studied economics at university had rented a DJ console, and they began playing horrible Swedish music from the eighties while, with their naked torsos glittering, they pumped their arms in the air. She went over to a table where she found an open bottle of white wine, so she sat down and poured herself a glass.

Pulp's 'Common People' began blaring from the loudspeakers. Eva got up and walked past Alexander's parents, straight across the dance floor and out into the summer night.

Several people were standing on the stairs, smoking. She asked a guy she didn't know – presumably one of Marika's relatives – if she could blag a cigarette from him. He was a few years younger and close to six foot six, with a nose that was both crooked and flattened, as if someone had punched him in the face a number of times, and it had never regained its former shape. He dug around in his jacket pocket and pulled out a cigarette.

Eva took it from him, murmuring her thanks. He offered her a light, holding the lighter in a big pale hand with long bony fingers.

'Eva,' she said, holding out her hand.

'Johan,' he told her, shaking her hand.

'How do you know . . .?' she asked.

'Marika. And you?'

'Alexander. We used to be an item.'

She glanced inside at the party. They were now the only ones left outside on the stairs.

'They seem happy,' she said.

'Uh-huh. They seem to be. Are you here with someone?' he asked.

'No. Solo.'

'Are you having fun?'

'I wouldn't say that.'

Eva was rocking back and forth on one of the steps of the small stone staircase, as if preparing to suddenly take off and flee. She exhaled a cloud of smoke and looked at his face. He was nice, even though he was younger than she was. Eva considered asking him to dance, but suddenly she heard the opening bars of a tune that she instantly recognised. She couldn't believe her ears.

Johan must have noticed, because he asked cautiously, 'Is everything okay?'

Eva felt confused.

'It's just . . . That song they're playing. It was our song. Alexander's and mine.'

Johan took a drag on his cigarette and then blew out the smoke.

'Hanlon's razor,' he said.

She didn't understand what he said.

He repeated it. 'Hanlon's razor. It's an adage or a law, sort of like Occam's razor, you know. "Never attribute to malice that which is adequately explained by stupidity.'"

Eva started laughing. It was the first time all evening that she'd found anything amusing.

'Where'd you hear that?'

'I don't know. I guess I'm just a nerd.'

'You don't look like a nerd.'

'Believe me, I am.'

She studied him for a moment. 'You know what? Nerd or not, I think the only way for us to survive this event is to go inside and dance and pretend we're having fun. What do you say? I think the bar is open.'

He nodded, so she took him by the hand and they rejoined the party. They went over to the makeshift bar and poured themselves a couple of strong vodkas. The dance floor was an explosion of skin and glitter, blisters, sweat and euphoria.

When Eva awoke the next morning with a stale taste in her mouth and a pounding headache, she first had to figure out where she was. It took a moment for the penny to drop. She looked around at the shiny tent wall with light seeping through the cracks, heard people laughing outside, breathed in the stifling air, and then, when she turned over, she saw him. The tall dark man lying there, his cheek pressed against the green ground cloth. The texture of the material had left an impression on his skin so it looked as if his face had been flattened in a waffle iron. When she saw his crooked nose, it all came back to her. She was still in Borgå. It was day two of the wedding celebration. They were supposed to get up, have breakfast, drink some coffee, and look alert.

She lay there in the tent without making a sound and tried to go back to sleep, but she was both too wide awake and too tired to sleep any more. And besides, it was much too hot. She'd slept with her sweater on after waking up and freezing in the night. Now the sun was right above the tent, and she was sweating. As Eva began moving about in her sleeping bag, he turned over and pressed his face against the tent wall. She tapped him lightly on the shoulder.

'Are you awake?'

He mumbled something, as if speaking from a deep slumber, from some distant place.

'What time is it?'

'I don't know.'

Eva reached her hand towards her feet to see if she could find something to drink, maybe a bottle of water. Nothing.

She wriggled out of her sleeping bag and unzipped the front flap of the tent. Sunlight came streaming in, and she could see the clear blue sky overhead. She heard him stirring in his sleeping bag.

'I promised to drive my sister and Alexander to the airport today. I hope it's not past eleven,' he mumbled.

Eva stared at him.

'Your sister? Marika is your sister?'

He looked at her with bleary eyes as he scratched his head.

'I thought you knew that.'

That morning she rang her mother and asked her to come and get her. She would have preferred to ask Max, but he didn't have a driving licence. When Katriina turned up, Eva was waiting on a gravel road outside the building where the party had been held. She wore a dress that looked as if she'd slept in it, which she had. She tried to look alert and cheerful as she hugged her mother, but she knew it was hopeless.

'So, late night, huh?'

Eva smiled, but avoided looking at her mother. 'Yeah. It was.'

'Was it a nice wedding?'

'Well, er . . . sure, it was fine,' she replied, staring straight ahead.

'You didn't have to go, you know.'

Eva didn't say anything. All of a sudden she started crying, just a little, but loud enough for Katriina to notice. She kept her gaze on the road as she drove.

'Eva, these sorts of things take time. It's okay if you still have feelings for Alexander.'

Eva couldn't believe her ears. She leaned against the car window, not saying a word. The sun was shining through the glass, but she was filled with anxiety.

'What's the name of his new girlfriend? I mean, his wife?'

'Marika.'

'Do you know her?'

'She's part of the same bunch of friends.'

Katriina turned to look at her daughter. 'You'll find someone else.'

Eva sat up straight. 'But that's not what this is about! Don't you understand?'

'Okay, okay. I know. Sorry.'

It was partly because of Alexander's wedding that Eva decided to move away. When the acceptance letter arrived from the art school in London, she didn't hesitate for a moment. It couldn't have come at a more opportune time. Now she could simply leave the whole insular Finland–Swedish social circles of Helsinki behind and start a new life.

CHAPTER 10

Katriina had taken a cab home from the florist's shop and then called Max as she stood on the slushy sidewalk, and together they'd carried all the flowers up to the flat.

Now she was standing in the living room, unwrapping the bouquets so she could place the tulips, narcissi and amaryllis in vases. Amanda was helping her.

'What time does Eva's plane get here?' asked Max, going over to the table with the liquor bottles. He poured himself a whisky.

He was looking forward to having all the children and grandchildren gathered in one place. But he had no interest in any other part of the festivities. At the department they'd put together a Festschrift for him, which Max had accepted with much embarrassment, and he still hadn't dared read it. He knew it would be like reading his own obituary.

And now Katriina had organised a big party, and he was the guest of honour. He would have liked nothing more than to escape, but there was one thing keeping him here – the thought that he'd get to see Laura. Max had phoned to thank her for the interview, and that was when she'd told him that she'd decided to come to the party.

'The plane's supposed to land at five o'clock, so she'll probably turn up in a couple of hours. By the way, I think you should wear your grey blazer tonight. And that dark-blue cotton shirt. I washed it on Monday, and I've already ironed it. Could you help me with this?'

Max put down his glass and went over to his wife.

Katriina had painted her nails red, and she was arranging the flowers and greenery in even piles. It was hard for him to tell whether the strong fragrance was her perfume or the scent from the flowers. He put his arms around her, leaned his face against the back of her neck and put one hand on her breast. The physical sensation of Katriina's sweater and her soft roundness underneath washed over him and made him feel almost serene. In a perfect world he'd be able to love both Laura and Katriina. Wouldn't he? What sort of idiotic rule made that impossible? It was so easy to love. The easiest thing in the world.

'Okay . . . Cut it out, Max. Come on, go to the kitchen and get the big vase that's on the window-sill. I'm thinking of putting it on the table as a centrepiece. Fill it halfway up with water. Helen, could you help me trim these tulips a bit? And then I'd like you to do something pretty with these amaryllis that are left over.'

Helen, Christian and the kids had come over in the morning. Max's sister had also arrived, and he knew that Elisabeth thought he should have worked something out so that their mother could have come to the party too. But what could he have done? It was impossible to imagine his mother travelling by train. If anything, Elisabeth should have brought her in the car. They'd argued about it on the phone.

'But what if Mamma falls? Or if she needs to use the bathroom during the trip? I can't lift her out of the car.'

Max's mother had phoned that morning, sounding left out. She wanted to take a cab all the way to Helsinki, but he promised that instead they'd organise a family get-together in the spring, and hold it in a place where everyone would be able to attend.

On his way to the kitchen Max stopped in the hall. The entire wall was covered with photographs of family members. One of his favourite pictures was of Katriina at the San Francisco Zoo. In the photo she was kissing a chimpanzee. She had a deep tan, and she looked happy, as if for a moment she'd totally forgotten about the camera. Katriina was fearless in that regard – she would never have hesitated to kiss any kind of animal.

The rest of the photos were mostly of the girls. Pictures of Eva as a tiny newborn next to Katriina; pictures from the day-care centre and school; pictures of Helen and Eva on horseback;

and lots of photos of Katriina, Eva and Helen in Berkeley. There was also a certificate that Max had received from the Finnish Academy and a framed copy of his parents' wedding photo.

There were no pictures of him.

'Is my shirt in the bedroom?' Max yelled.

'Yes, it's hanging in the wardrobe,' replied Katriina.

He went to the kitchen and got out the vases. On the table he saw a copy of *Helsingin Sanomat* lying open at the cultural section, to show the feature article about him. He thought he'd allowed his rambling to go a bit too far this time. He knew that some of his academic friends sneered at his sociological one-liners.

The headline was a quote from him: 'Total freedom is not an ideal state.' Max had talked about that subject the way he always did, saying that the sheer number of choices available to us make us depressed. In the photograph – which was at least seven columns wide and covered the full length of the page – he wore an anxious expression, as if the photo was taken just as someone reminded him of something sad. In reality, he'd had a hard time understanding what the photographer wanted from him. He looked at the picture again and wrinkled his nose. He suddenly thought he recognised something of his mother in that troubled expression. Didn't all of her relatives look as if they might burst into tears at any second?

Katriina had placed the newspaper on the table so that their guests would see it. He considered folding it up and tossing it in the recycling bin. But the article wasn't bad. He'd read it before it was printed and emailed Laura some suggested changes and clarifications. Earlier in the day he'd looked up the paper's website and read the discussion threads under the interview. The tone of the comments had surprised Max – apparently there were still people who thought he had something sensible to say.

By six o'clock the flat was filled with people: Helen and her family; Max's sister Elisabeth; his colleague Antti, who'd come early; as well as a younger colleague from the department, an incredibly ambitious doctoral student named Sara. Max hadn't wanted to invite his editor, Matti, since he had no desire to talk about the Westermarck book, but Katriina was in charge of the guest list, and of course she had refused to leave anyone off.

The noise level had risen to a pleasant hum, and Edvard was running around, wagging his tail as he greeted and sniffed at everyone. Max was doing his share of conversing as he showed the guests his study and the desk where he usually sat, but the whole time he was on the lookout for Laura. Each time he heard the door open, he was hoping it would be her.

By seven, most of the guests had arrived. Katriina had stood at the door with Max to welcome everyone, although he occasionally slipped out to the balcony to smoke a cigar.

Now he was moving through the crowd, making an effort to smile at everyone. He didn't always know who he was talking to, but afterwards it was the details he remembered: Katriina's earrings, the décolletage of the wife of a colleague, a red hand-kerchief, a pair of white trainers. At eight o'clock Laura finally appeared, wearing a short purple dress, her black hair glossy, and with a cautious but endearing smile that she directed with complete self-control at Katriina under the muted lighting in the front hall. Max stood back, trying to main-tain as neutral a demeanour as possible, which was difficult since he'd already had a few drinks, though he wasn't sure exactly how many. He felt a smile tugging at the corners of his mouth, and he hoped no one noticed. He waited as Laura went into the flat with Katriina to say hello to the other guests. He stood there, watching them from a distance, those two women. Then he waited until Laura was alone, at most five minutes, although it seemed like an eternity, before he approached her.

She didn't seem to know anyone else, which was a relief to Max. It meant that he had an obligation to entertain her.

'Hi. You came.'

'Yes.'

'I have to say that the article turned out great.'

'You think so?'

'Yes, I do. You really understood what I was trying to say. And that doesn't happen very often. I've heard lots of positive comments about it.'

'It wasn't that special, but thanks.'

'You should definitely get into reporting on cultural issues full-time,' he said.

Laura merely nodded, so he went on talking, since that was the only thing he could think to do. He was aware that he could look right down at her cleavage, and it took a real effort not to do so. He looked at the other guests and noticed that Matti was on his way over. He was still at the other end of the room, but his eyes were fixed on Laura. Max quickly tried to think up some way to out-manoeuvre him. He'd been trying to avoid Matti all evening, since he knew his editor would inevitably ask about the book, and maybe even demand to have a look at it.

'Maybe I should introduce you to everybody.'

'No, you don't have to do that.'

She seemed a bit shy as she looked at the other guests. By now Matti had almost reached them.

'But I really should,' said Max.

He raised his glass and began tapping on it with his cigarette lighter, but it made no sound. None of the guests turned around, so he went over to the table, where the coffee service had just been set out. He picked up a knife and struck his glass harder. The sound sliced right through the noise of the party, and the wine in his glass sloshed over the rim and on to the floor. Now he had everyone's attention.

'Er, hello, I just want to say one thing. As you all probably know by this time – thanks to my

131

wife, who never lets this sort of thing go unnoticed – in today's issue of *Helsingin Sanomat* there's an article about me, in honour of the occasion. You know that I usually detest journalists . . .'

Scattered laughter in the room. Max was good at playing to the crowd.

'. . . but in this case I made an exception because the journalist in question is a former student of mine, one of the most talented, and she's actually here with us today. Laura, where are you?'

He pretended to search for her. Laura was still standing in the corner, and she gave everyone a little wave.

'There you are! Not only is Laura an amazing cultural journalist, she's also an expert on financial matters, reporting on Asia, in particular.'

Laura was clearly embarrassed. The guests looked at their host, then at her, not sure where to direct their attention.

'Well, that's really all I wanted to say. I hope everybody got enough to eat, because now it's time for coffee and cake.'

Everyone raised their glasses in a toast. For a moment Max felt very pleased with himself. But then he saw that Matti had reached Laura and was shaking her hand. Now he was motioning for Max to join them, and he had no choice but to comply.

Matti had a slightly macho way about him that Max found annoying, but he realised that certain women fell for that sort of thing. His editor was in his fifties, good-looking and cocky, but also well read and a thoroughly hardnosed businessman. Max had a feeling that he was about to lose out to him. Matti had already placed his hand on Laura's bare shoulder.

'I was just telling Laura here what a damned good article she wrote. It's rare to read anything that good in the paper these days.'

Max nodded. Laura seemed pleased with the attention.

'You know, Max, since this is your birthday, I wasn't thinking of bothering you with any questions about your damn book. But I thought I'd make a suggestion, and it's lucky that the two of you are here right now, since this has to do with both of you. Today when I was reading the paper, I came up with an idea, and I think it's a damned good one. How would it be if Laura helped you out? She seems to understand what you're talking about. Why don't you let her have a look at the text? Then I won't have to do it.'

Max glanced at Laura in surprise. Yesterday he'd actually fantasised about taking his manuscript over to Långa Bridge and tossing it over the side.

'I don't know . . . I'm actually almost finished . . .'

Matti gave him an amused look. 'Damn it, Max. Let's be honest now. Tell me how it's really going with your book. So far I haven't seen a single sentence of the bloody thing.'

Now Matti turned to Laura. 'I have no doubt

that Max has written something, but as long as he won't show it to me, I can't be sure, can I?'

Max knew he had to defend himself. He was pissed off by the situation, with Matti embarrassing him in front of Laura and making him talk about this topic.

'If you like, you can have a look right now. I've got it in my study.'

'Okay, okay,' said Matti. 'Maybe it's a dumb idea. I'm just thinking that it might be good for someone to wrest it out of your hands. There's no harm in that, is there?'

It occurred to Max that so far Laura hadn't said a word. The noise level had risen, and Max had to lean towards her to hear what she said.

'Of course I'll have a look. If that's what you want, Max.'

He looked her in the eye and felt something that resembled tenderness – she had no idea how much it meant to him to have received a little media attention again. He was ashamed that he was such easy prey to flattery.

He was just about to reply when the doorbell rang.

Helen shouted, 'I'll get it!'

Max thought it might be Eva, but when the door opened, he heard an unfamiliar man's voice out in the hall. Max excused himself and left Laura and Matti to go and see who had arrived. He realised that the man was a stranger to him. He was unshaven, with dark hair and a foreign look about him. Maybe from India? Max couldn't hear what he and Helen were saying because of the noise from the party.

'Can I help you?' asked Max.

Now Katriina came into the hall.

'Are you Max Paul?' asked the man in English. His clothing was odd – he looked like a combination of an old-fashioned vagabond and someone who had put on a costume. A silk handkerchief stuck out of the breast pocket of his worn jacket.

'Yes, that's right. Are we making too much noise? I can ask our guests to keep it down a bit. It's my sixtieth birthday, you see.'

'No, that's not it. But I'm looking for your daughter, Eva. I understood that she would be here tonight.'

'And you are?'

'I'm her . . . friend. Russ.'

CHAPTER 11

Malik's attraction to Eva began to cool after that evening when she frightened him with the pregnancy test. He demonstrated his waning interest over the following days by standing behind Laurie and leaning close as he showed a new-found eagerness to discuss the technical aspects of her paintings. Eva could see how his arm kept searching for a new position – looking as if it were getting close to the fastener on Laurie's very visible bra. Suddenly, the only reminder of Malik's presence in Eva's life were the white streaks of Ritalin inside her art books. During class he would lapse into harsh criticism, and nothing the students did seemed good enough. Ben, in particular, repeatedly heard that he was an incompetent bungler who 'couldn't tell art from his fucking elbow'.

Eva had quickly made up her mind as she sat hunched on the toilet in her flat, with Malik right outside the door. She had no intention of telling him that the test was positive. The truth was, she was a little afraid of him.

She considered reporting him to the dean of the

college for assault, but she realised that that would be a lie. She had been a willing participant in their affair. She had enjoyed it, enjoyed how it made her feel.

Instead, she began taking walks every day after college, until one day she found herself standing outside the gallery that belonged to Malik's wife. She had no idea how she'd ended up there. This was on a Thursday evening. It was already past seven, but the gallery seemed to be open, judging by the sign placed outside on the pavement.

The premises looked like an abandoned shop that someone had transformed into a venue for art. It was nothing like the spacious and minimalist galleries so prevalent in the East End.

Eva had always pictured Sarah and Malik's gallery as elitist and expensive. A place that was exclusive, in white and black, and intimidating. Not this Berlin-style do-it-yourself place in an abandoned building.

The wall facing the street was covered with graffiti, and the window was so dingy that it was hard to see inside.

A dark-haired, broad-shouldered woman in her forties was sitting on a stool behind a counter that looked as if it belonged in a hotel lobby. Her arms were covered with tattoos, which merely served to enhance the ordinariness of her features.

She nodded a greeting as Eva came in. 'Just tell me if you have any questions. My name's Sarah, by the way.'

Eva gave her a wary smile and turned to walk around the room. Grey clouds had hovered over London all week, and the damp light seemed to seep through the window, filling the gallery space. It was not painted white, like most other galleries. Instead, it had the feel of a renovated warehouse, with a grey cement floor and patches of exposed brick on the walls.

From somewhere at the far end of the room Eva could hear a whining noise that seemed to be emanating from a work of art. Sarah had gone back to reading her book.

Was this really Malik's wife? Eva had imagined someone completely different – a chic Londoner with a strong presence and cold eyes, an excessively thin woman who knew all the right people and who could crush any opponent with her little finger. Considering how Malik had talked about Sarah, Eva had the impression that she was a terrifying person who wouldn't stand for any bullshit. But this woman was downright . . . motherly. And she didn't look the least bit chic. She was more like an ageing Goth, with her black-painted nails bitten to the quick and matted black hair.

Eva wandered around the gallery, looking at the artwork.

The overall theme seemed to be gender issues. The first piece, closest to the entrance, was some sort of insipid Pop Art painting in garish colours – there were allusions to Warhol, but the figures lacked impact. As a concept, it wasn't especially exciting, but from a technical viewpoint, it was well done. Eva saw from a sign on the wall that the paintings were the work of a local woman artist.

'The art on that wall changes every week. On Monday there'll be a new exhibit. You should come back then. It's going to be great,' said Sarah, who had noticed that she was looking at the paintings.

Eva nodded.

'We want part of the gallery to have a low threshold so that young artists who might not have much experience get a chance to show their work.'

The main exhibit was devoted to an artist by the name of Claire Kelly. There was a photo of her in the catalogue that was lying on a table. She was a Londoner, born in 1972, who had 'studied art in Bergen and Istanbul', and now lived 'with her cat and her husband in Paris'.

The exhibit consisted of small sculptures, with rose-pink as the dominant colour. Eva thought it was a kitschy, nightmarish version of the sorts of things found in girls' bedrooms in the eighties: ponies and dolls, little animals made of plastic with wisps of hair sticking out. Kelly had placed the sculptures inside cloth-lined boxes with dim, porno-type lighting – grubby and stained, as if they represented a dark back room, an alleyway, or simply an image of poverty. They were like a miniature world in which everything that was nice had been mangled by a social-realist filter, like crime scenes in a girl's bedroom.

There was something inexpressibly sad about this monument to lost innocence, and yet the work had humour. A little girl's dreams that had been confronted by a filthy reality, but that somehow also radiated a certain playfulness. Eva was reminded of something from her own childhood: those endless games that she'd played with Helen, how they'd sewn clothes for their Barbie dolls, how they'd sometimes visited friends and exchanged dolls with them. That unfamiliar smell of her friends' toys. The feel of the Barbie doll's hard sheen.

Another piece was a video installation in which Claire Kelly wore a full-body suit made of flesh-coloured rubber. It made her look like an air-filled, pregnant sex toy. This was where the whining sound was coming from.

About halfway through the forty-minute film the artist pulled out a rubber penis from between her legs, which she then proceeded to inflate with a pump she was holding in one hand, all the while grinding her hips towards the audience standing in front of her.

In another video, the artist wore a bridal gown over a bulging stomach, as if she were pregnant. She was standing next to a motorway, trying to thumb a ride.

It made Eva think about the last scene in Mike Nichols's film *The Graduate*, when the young couple runs out of the church. Except that here, it was a lone woman who was running away, with her little baby inside her womb.

At the end of the video Claire Kelly was sitting in the back of a bus, speaking directly into the camera, talking about men that she'd met and their personal stories. She counted them off, one by one: old boyfriends and several one-night stands, although she never mentioned their names, just rattling them off like letters of the alphabet; sometimes telling a lengthy story, sometimes keeping it brief. One man she'd been with was from the suburbs, and he'd told her about his childhood. When he was a teenager, he'd killed his older brother, and that transformed the story into something biblical. For a while Eva actually forgot where she was as she watched and listened; there was something hypnotic about the whole installation. At the same time, it felt very radical because it was a woman telling the stories, like a prison guard talking about her prisoners.

Eva remembered the glass of water they'd seen in their first class. Now she understood why it hadn't really appealed to her. There was no story. Nothing to latch on to, no narrative. In order for anyone to believe in an artist's illusory trick, the artist first had to establish a level of trust.

As she was leaving, Sarah glanced up from her book to give her a smile. 'I hoped you liked it.'

'Definitely,' said Eva, thinking what a strange comment that was. Malik had been telling them

141

all autumn that the point was not to make art that people liked.

When she got home, Eva thought it would be best to start packing. Her plane left the following morning, with a layover in Frankfurt. Natalia was sitting in front of her computer in the kitchen, and she pointed towards Eva's room.

'You've got a visitor. He seemed a bit scared of me, so I let him wait in your room.'

Natalia smiled. Eva gave her a surprised look. She had no desire to talk to Malik right now.

But it wasn't Malik. It was Russ. He was sitting on her bed, deeply immersed in a book about Dutch paintings, and he began talking without looking up.

'I've never understood how they did it,' he said. 'I mean, check this out.'

He held up the book to show Eva. She recognised it at once – a painting by Vermeer.

'It's like the only instance in human history when evolution unquestionably moved backwards. Do you think Julian Schnabel could paint something like this? Do you think anyone could do it today?'

Eva was still standing in the doorway.

'Hi,' she said.

Russ put the book down. The first and only time they had spent any time together outside of class, he had taken her to a dreary pub near Liverpool Street Station. The place was dark even in the middle of the day, and it seemed to suffer from a lack of oxygen.

Eva liked Russ. He appeared to have a real sense of integrity, and he didn't care for Malik. But she found his negative attitude hard to take. During that first pub visit, the only thing he'd talked about was how the London art world was a vicious circle in which nobody cared about anything except status and money. He'd asked her hardly anything about her life.

Now he was sitting cross-legged on her bed, and Eva noticed that he hadn't taken off his shoes.

'Do you want something to drink?' she asked.

'Sure. Thanks. Do you have any beer?'

'I'll see what I can find.'

Eva went back to the kitchen, where Natalia was still working at her computer.

'Weird guy. Is he a friend of yours?'

'I guess you could say that. But I don't know him very well.'

'He seems nicer than Malik. He doesn't look like the type who would hog the shower for two hours every morning.'

Natalia had been extremely critical of Malik. She claimed that he'd pawed through her things in the bathroom and that he sometimes left his dirty underwear on the floor next to the shower.

Eva went over to the fridge and took out a beer. She went back to her room and handed it to Russ.

'Thanks,' he said.

'So,' she said. 'What brings you here?'

'Nothing special. I just happened to be in the neighbourhood.'

His moustache somehow made him look even more like a schoolboy.

'And you decided to drop by?'

'Exactly.'

After that, neither of them seemed to have anything more to say, and Eva thought that might actually be good, maybe even pleasant. She had no idea why Russ had turned up at her flat, but since he had, there wasn't much she could do about it.

'What do you think about our course?' she finally said.

Russ was silent for a moment. He seemed to be pondering the question. Then he said, 'All that stuff about sitting around and discussing each other's work . . . I don't believe in it. That whole "crit" approach. I don't think it means anything. You know? We should be working, instead of talking. Like those Occupy people. At least they're doing something that makes sense, something that has an impact in the world. Not making some stupid piece of art that gets displayed in a gallery and then hung on a wall in the home of some pampered upper-middle-class family.'

Eva sat down next to him on the bed. 'I'm sure my father loves the Occupy movement. He's always complaining that young people today no longer believe in change.'

'But that's the thing – maybe we don't. I don't

know who those people are, but they do seem to believe in something.'

'At least they believe in the possibility of not paying any rent.'

Eva immediately regretted this last remark. She regretted sounding so caustic, resorting to the sarcasm that was typical of her whole generation – except Russ, for some reason.

'I'm sick of everybody thinking only of themselves. I want to have a sense of belonging. The art world is so oriented towards the individual. But it hasn't always been that way.'

'Now you sound like Malik,' said Eva, and then regretted that remark too.

'Are you kidding? He's the biggest idiot of them all! There's nobody in England who cares more about himself. His ego is so huge that you could orbit around it. And the sickest part of all – what's so ironic – is that he hasn't had a show of his own work in fifteen years.'

Eva realised that Russ was right, but she didn't let on that she agreed. Instead, she tried to say something nice.

'Well, at least you have a clear idea of what you want to paint. I still don't know what I'm going to show when the six weeks are up.'

Eva looked at him with an expression that might have revealed an unintended tenderness, because Russ leaned forward to kiss her. She felt his moustache brush her lips, and it tickled so much that she pulled away, and without thinking she put out her hands to push him against the wall. She heard a loud thud as his head struck the cement wall, at the very spot where Malik had slammed his fist a week ago.

'Sorry! I didn't mean to do that. I was just so surprised.'

Russ put his hand on the back of his head, and his face flushed bright red.

'Does it hurt?'

He didn't answer, just gave her a miserable look.

Eva was just about to say something else – explain her behaviour, anything – when he got up from her bed and picked up his bag.

'So, are you coming to college tomorrow?' he asked.

She looked up at him. He was still holding his head.

'I'm afraid not. I'll be away for a few days. I'm going to Finland. It's my dad's birthday.'

CHAPTER 12

Nothing gave Katriina such a sense of peace as the intense buzzing of a successful party – the knowledge that she was the one who had gathered all these people in one place, that she was the one who had created the atmosphere upon which the festivities depended. But before the guests arrived Max hadn't once taken the time to thank her for everything she'd done. Instead, all day he had whined like a child about not wanting any sort of celebration, and he'd started drinking well before noon. The speech that he'd given for Laura was both peculiar and embarrassing. Everybody could see that he was openly flirting with her.

And now a complete stranger had turned up. No one had any idea who he was.

Katriina rushed back and forth from the kitchen to the living room, making sure that there were enough coffee cups and glasses, and that all the guests were having a good time. She had on high heels and a print dress that was black and neon-pink, which she'd bought in a hurry at Stockmann's department store the day before.

Elisabeth had arrived by train to help Katriina with all the preparations. Max's older sister was married, had three children, and lived in Närpes. She made her living by selling some sort of natural supplement, and she talked about her cats as if they were people. But she'd raised three sons. One was a doctor in Uppsala, Sweden, and the other two had respectable jobs up north in Österbotten. And she had a good sense of humour. Each time she visited, Elisabeth would stand in the middle of the living room, look around, and say that she'd never seen 'rich folks living such a shabby existence'. It was a joke, of course, because the flat where Katriina and Max lived was 1,500 square feet. But according to Elisabeth, what mattered was that they had no yard, and the fact that they both worked in professions that were abstract and, frankly, ridiculous. She always teased Max whenever he received media attention. Back in the nineties, after he'd published his sex study, she claimed that their father would turn in his grave if he knew about it. ('Who knew that somebody could get famous from talking about the ten ways that complete strangers fuck?')

Katriina quickly surveyed the room. The unexpected guest was sitting on the sofa, waiting for Eva. His bony fingers were resting in a rather affected manner on his knees as he looked around. His gaze stopped on a large painting by Heikki Marila that Katriina had acquired at an exhibition at Korjaamo. She had never before bought anything so expensive just because she liked it, but in this case she knew she wouldn't regret the purchase.

Katriina had tried phoning Eva, but her mobile was turned off. Helen had checked the Internet and found out that the flight from Frankfurt would be two hours late.

When Katriina tried to ring again, she suddenly got through.

'Hi, Mum. I'll be home soon. I'm on the bus at the moment.'

'Good, good. You need to hurry, because there's someone here to see you.'

'There is?'

'Yes. A young gentleman. He says that he knows you. I think his name is Russ. Dad is talking to him in the living room right now.'

For a moment there was only silence on the line.

'Russ? Are you talking about a short, dark-haired guy with a moustache?'

'Right. That's him.'

'But what's he doing there? How'd he get there?'

'How would I know? Is he your boyfriend?'

'No, he's not my boyfriend.'

'Then who is he?'

'He's somebody who definitely shouldn't have flown to Finland without telling me.'

'Well, he says he tried to ring you all week, and you never answered.'

'But I talked to him yesterday! He told you that he'd tried to phone me?'

'That's what he says. The two of you will just

149

have to work this out. Although I can't say I care for that moustache.'

Katriina ended the call and left Max to take care of Eva's guest. Max sent her a look that said he had better things to do, but she pretended not to notice.

She went into the kitchen, where she found Helen with her husband, Christian.

'I finally got hold of Eva. She's on her way.'

'Did she tell you anything about that guy?' asked Helen.

'She said they're friends. But he's not her boyfriend.'

'He looks kind of odd.'

'I suppose so.'

He did look a bit odd, compared to Katriina's son-in-law. Christian was tall and solidly built. He had the physique of a skilled workman, with sinewy arms but also a certain weight and strength about him. A real man. There was nothing that Christian couldn't do. When he quit the architecture firm to become a carpenter and furniture upholsterer, they all thought at first that he was crazy. But after five years he had his own company and was a professional consultant for the Museum Department. He now earned more money than he ever had as an architect, and he'd also renovated a beautiful house for his family near Kyrkslätt, right where Esbo turns into countryside.

Katriina leaned against the worktop. Water was splattered around the sink, and she started wiping

150

it up, but it just kept spilling over the edge. She gave up and tossed the dishrag in the sink.

'Helen, take a look at this,' she said.

She yanked out the drawer that never opened smoothly.

'Yes, I know. We've seen it, Mum. You've showed it to us before.'

'Do you think we'll ever get a new kitchen?'

'Well, just talking about it won't make it happen.'

'But Dad refuses to even consider it. Plus, there's no time. After Christmas I'm going to the Philippines. Wivan is sending me on a mission to recruit nurses.'

Katriina slammed shut the drawer.

'Christian, what's your opinion?'

'About what?'

Christian looked as if he'd been startled awake from a deep sleep. He was the most diplomatic person Katriina had ever met – and there was something rather undiplomatic about that very fact, because it was impossible to be on everyone's side at all times. Mostly he tried to stay out of the domestic matters of the Paul family.

'What do you think about this kitchen? Shouldn't we have it completely redone?'

'It is looking a bit worn out.'

'So do you think it's fixable? Max says that we could just repair whatever's falling apart.'

'Maybe. But it's often cheaper to start from scratch, unfortunately. That's how it is these days. The cost of hiring workmen has gone sky-high. I think you could have some of these cupboards refinished. But if you need new shelves . . . The question is: what would be less expensive?'

Max came into the kitchen with the young man who was Eva's friend. 'So, have we heard anything from Eva yet?'

He spoke English, so that Russ would be able to understand. Katriina also replied in English.

'Yes. I just spoke to her. She should be home any minute.'

'You have a lovely home,' said Russ. Katriina wondered what he really meant by that. Was it sheer flattery on his part, or was he genuinely impressed? It was impossible to tell whether he came from a family with little money, or whether he simply chose to dress in such shabby clothes.

'Thank you,' said Katriina. 'But our kitchen is terribly outmoded. Don't you think we ought to have it refurbished?'

Max raised one eyebrow and looked at Helen, as if to get her to cooperate in some tactic against her mother, but Katriina saw that Helen refused to acknowledge her father's unspoken request.

'How about if we had it painted?' said Max.

'Your dad is so romantic,' replied Katriina, with what she hoped was a casually ironic tone to her voice.

A strand of hair had come loose from her ponytail.

'But I *am* romantic,' Max insisted and then laughed. It was the kind of laugh that Katriina hated, because it was an attempt to erase anything serious from the situation. At this particular moment she was sick and tired of Max.

She couldn't help it, but suddenly all the stress of the day flooded over her, and she almost fainted. She knew she should keep quiet. Instead, her voice rose shrilly.

'Then why the hell don't you ever show it, Max? Why do you show it only to everyone else, in your books, in your articles, to your colleagues, and God knows to how many of the young women you meet? But you never show it to me.'

Silence descended over the kitchen.

'Mum. Dad. I don't know if we . . . Maybe you should talk about this some other time.'

Helen cast an embarrassed glance at Russ. She looked very uncomfortable and wanted to change the subject.

'It seems cold in the flat. Have you noticed? Don't you have the heat on?'

'It's your father who refuses to turn up the thermostat. He thinks we need to save on electricity and just put on warmer clothes,' said Katriina.

'Or we could warm each other up. That's romantic, isn't it?' Max ventured.

Katriina sighed and tucked the loose strand of hair behind her ear. 'I don't feel like arguing with you right now. This is your party, and you should celebrate however you like. But if you're planning on getting drunk, you should at least have sense enough not to give any more speeches.'

153

Helen covered her ears. 'Mum and Dad, I don't want to listen to this. And I don't think our guest does either.'

Now she turned to face Russ. 'I apologise. My mother and father can't stand each other, and they think the rest of the world should know about it.'

Everyone was now looking at Russ, who tried to muster a smile.

Max was set on defending himself. He said to Russ, 'Don't worry, it's not serious. We've been married thirty years. This is just what happens. When you turn sixty, you should be happy just to be able to locate your socks in the morning.'

Max raised his glass, spilling a little of his drink. 'Oh, well. Happy birthday, by the way,' said Russ. 'Thanks.'

HELSINGIN SANOMAT

Complete freedom is not an ideal condition

Professor Max Paul turns sixty today, but he has no intention of stopping working. 'Work is the most direct path to happiness,' he says.
by Laura Lampela

He begins by quoting Tolstoy.

'I think that Tolstoy said it so well. You should "work for those you love and love your job",' says Professor Paul.

We met at the Kosmos restaurant, which

holds a special place in Paul's heart. This was where he went as a student to celebrate passing his exams.

'We also came here on those occasions when we didn't pass. We often couldn't afford to order any food, but they would let us sit here and drink. When my parents came to Helsinki to visit me in the early seventies, we had dinner here after seeing a play at Lilla Teatern,' he explains.

He is easily recognisable from his appearances on TV. He has the same slightly anxious look in his eyes and the same quick wit that made him such a popular guest on talk shows in the nineties. A 1993 article in *City Guide* dubbed him the 'young intellectual of the decade', and that made Max Paul the big star among Finnish intellectuals.

Lately we haven't seen much of you in the media. What happened?

'It's partly because these days I'm better at saying no, and partly because the intellectual climate has changed, in my opinion. Plus, philosophy was a hot topic in the nineties, but not so much today. Unfortunately, this has also been felt at the university. Other subjects are now more fashionable, and those students who have real talent – and especially the men – choose fields that offer better job prospects,' he says.

But Max Paul has not given up his enthusiasm for sociology.

'On the contrary. Sociology is a very generous discipline. It allows a man to have other lovers. It's polygamous by nature. I'm very interested in social psychology and the history of ideas. At the moment I'm working on a biography of the "grand old man" of sociology in Finland, Edvard Westermarck.'

It has been a while since Professor Paul published anything. His break-through book, *Under the Metropolis Star*, was nominated for a Finlandia Prize. It was a cross-discipline examination of the post-war generation in which Paul conducted interviews with war veterans and their families to discuss how the Western concept of happiness became shaped in the modern era. The book put him on the map as one of the foremost interpreters of how the war years affected the soul of the Finnish people.

'I still receive invitations to speak about that book, even though it's been twenty-five years since it came out. In Finland the war marked all of us in such a fundamental way that we still turn to those years for answers to our problems. Sometimes it can be a little absurd. Last year a journalist phoned me to ask whether the war years could somehow explain Nokia's recent decline.'

Paul's answer to that reporter was: 'Of course.'

'Personally, I think the real answer lies in the global market, and in Nokia's case, the company simply needed to reinvent itself. At the same time, I think the fact that Finland is a young nation has affected how Nokia is treated in the media – criticism has been conspicuously lacking. When Nokia was strong, nobody bothered to dig around in what the company was doing, and that says something about what a powerful function Nokia served in terms of the national identity. Maybe there wasn't enough vigilance. Finns have always needed a narrative to cling to, just like all small countries. When we joined the EU, we behaved much like a provincial family in a novel from the late nineteenth century. We agreed to everything just so we could marry into the grand landowner's family. That's okay, except that you also lose some of your integrity and set yourself up for a very big fall,' the professor explains.

In Paul's opinion, the Finnish inferiority complex shows up in a paradoxical way in politics.

'From an economic point of view, we're one of the most financially healthy nations in Europe, and yet for a long time we've suffered from a lack of self-confidence because we consider ourselves poor – maybe not monetarily, but culturally. That's why I was personally overjoyed when the Social Democrats showed some initiative with regard to the Greek question,' he says.

In the nineties Max Paul was frequently in the tabloids, thanks to his study on Finnish sexual practices, which was the hot topic of conversation in the autumn of 1994. Today he merely shrugs when asked about the study.

'It caused a big stir, even though the results of the study weren't exactly revolutionary.'

Yet Max Paul is still preoccupied with the question: what is happiness?

Why are you interested in such a worn-out topic?

'It's not really that strange. Everyone wants to know how to be happy, and I'm no exception. I link the whole issue to the choices that people have, and why we make the choices that we do.'

The professor admits this may sound a bit vague. But he points out that these are issues that even Socrates grappled with in his day.

'I think we still have a lot to learn from Socrates, and Aristotle as well, who viewed happiness as a constantly evolving condition. In other words, you can "be" happy without having to work at it all the time – much like democracy. It's also exciting to look at the new aspects of psychiatry, and especially the neurosciences, which have made enormous breakthroughs even in the last ten years with regard to behaviour patterns.'

According to Paul, those who speak of happiness are often viewed with scepticism – such remarks are better suited to self-help books.

'I think that happiness and consumerism have become very much the same thing, and talking about happiness in any other way than as pure self-fulfilment seems old-fashioned. Unfortunately, we can't get around using it, because it's the only word we have.'

One reason for unhappiness, according to Paul, is that we're constantly confronted with an endless array of choices.

'We think that we'll be happy if only we make the right choices. That's something that permeates every facet of our lives. For instance, at this very moment: what should I have for lunch? But when it comes to the really important questions – those that touch on the future of everyone – we actually have no choice at all. Decisions are made at levels far beyond our control. No one asked us, for example, whether nuclear power should be expanded in Finland.'

You say that work can be a pathway to happiness. Is it possible to be the creator of your own happiness?

'Rousseau said that it's impossible to be consciously happy. You can only recognise your own happiness retroactively, after you've lost it. When you're happy, you don't notice it; if you're aware of it, you can't have it. Hannah Arendt says something similar: to rise up, you have to have been to the bottom. Life is really a continuous cycle of happiness and unhappiness; the one presupposes the other.'

Are you personally happy?

'Fate has been good to me. I'm in good health, and I have healthy children and grandchildren. And I have work that I enjoy doing. Complete freedom is not an ideal condition. And I say this as someone who lived through the 1960s. Freedom was the only thing we wanted. But today I realise that my father's generation, which went through the war, in some ways had a less complicated view of happiness than my generation has. For them, change was a necessary means for achieving stability. For today's young people, change is a goal in itself.'

CHAPTER 13

'And basically, that is why I'm here.'

Russ turned over as he lay on the mattress on the floor. He'd been talking for almost an hour, explaining that after his conversation with Eva, he'd decided to book a plane ticket to Helsinki. He needed to see her again because he hadn't said what he'd intended to say, what he'd gone to her flat to tell her. Then he launched into a long preamble about seeing Eva at the first class session, and how even back then he had decided that he wanted to get to know her better. During his rambling monologue Eva caught words like 'in love' and even 'obsessed', but she had a hard time taking in all the information because Russ spoke in such an incoherent way, almost like a witness to an accident who was still trying to sort out in his mind everything that he'd seen. But now he had finished and was silently waiting for her reaction.

'You have to say something. Anything. I'm going to die if you don't say something soon.'

But Eva had no idea what to say.

It was actually rather sad that it had come to

this. She had hoped that they could be good friends, but apparently that wasn't going to happen. He had practically just declared that she was the love of his life.

What should she do? She felt so confused.

She wished she could have talked to Helen. About everything, actually. But there had been no chance for that all evening, since Russ was here, and she felt responsible for him. Of course she did.

Eva couldn't help feeling a stab of jealousy when she saw her father talking to that young journalist, Laura, later in the evening – he was leaning in close, and she was laughing. Eva wished that she too could have been that happy, but she had felt obliged to sit next to Russ. She was possessed by a dream-like feeling that the world was about to split apart, although no one else could see it.

Katriina had made up beds for them in Eva's old room, which looked as if she was still living there. The walls were painted the same old-fashioned green colour that she'd chosen when she was in secondary school. Next to the window hung a Nick Cave poster, and on the windowsill stood an ugly ceramic sculpture that she'd made in middle school. The bed was the same, and stored inside an old wardrobe standing against the wall – the wardrobe from her paternal grandmother's house in Kristine-stad – were all her old LPs. As a teenager Eva had collected vinyl, buying a lot of records from Black & White in Hagnäs and from

Keltainen Jäänsärkijä on Urho Kekkonensgata. The wardrobe also contained a plaster model of her teeth before she got braces; a box of cassette tapes in which she'd kept marijuana during the summer after her second year in secondary school; several old textbooks; and a shoebox filled with old letters from middle school, mostly from her cousins in Österbotten.

'Thank you,' Eva now said. 'And I really mean that. Thank you for telling me all this. I'm very . . . flattered. What else can I say?'

'You could tell me how you feel. Do you share my feelings at all?'

'Sure. I like you. Definitely. But you're more like a . . .'

Eva had intended to say 'brother', but she caught herself.

'What I mean is, I'm not sure I'm ready for a relationship right now. I'm . . . I have a lot of things I need to work out.'

'I can be very persistent.'

'Obviously. You flew here, after all.'

'Yes, I did.'

'Russ, I'm sorry, but could we talk about something else?'

'Of course. What do you want to talk about?'

'I don't know.'

'Okay. What do you want me to tell you?'

'Tell me anything.'

'Well, I've just told you that the only thing I can think about is you.'

'Something else. Tell me about yourself. I don't know anything about you.'

Eva was actually too tired to talk, but she couldn't fall asleep when there was so much tension in the air because she was expected to respond to what Russ had just revealed. She didn't want to think about anything at all. She'd slept badly for the past few days, and having Russ in the same room was not the most ideal situation, but Eva couldn't bring herself to explain to her mother why she would have preferred to sleep alone. Apparently Katriina hadn't fully understood that Russ was not her boyfriend.

'Eva, I realise this whole thing may be a bit sudden. You don't even know me.'

'That's true. I don't really know you. So talk to me. Do you have any brothers or sisters?' she said, even though she wasn't sure that she was particularly interested. She'd had a few glasses of wine and could feel the soft bed enticing her towards sleep. There had been too many people at the party for her to have a real sense of being back in Finland. The flat looked different when it was filled with guests all dressed up; it was almost like being in a film.

'Yes, one sister. She lives in Brighton and works in a restaurant. Married with three kids, even though she's only twenty-six. She had her first child at the age of nineteen.'

'Have you always been interested in art?' asked Eva. 'I mean, even when you were little?'

'I was a very timid child. I cried when I had to go to nursery. I remember that my mum took me there on the Tube, and I refused to hold her hand because I didn't want to go. One day I tried to run away, so she just left me there on the platform. I panicked and thought I was going to die, but she was standing behind one of the pillars the whole time. "That's what happens when you refuse to hold my hand," she told me. Talk about methods of childrearing.'

'Where'd you grow up?'

'In the East End of London, but it was different back then. Before all this gentrification shit. My mum and dad split up when I was eleven. So I'm one of those children of divorce who creates art to mend the hole in his heart.'

Russ laughed. He lay on his stomach, staring at her. His eyes shone in the dark.

Eva fixed her gaze on him and asked, 'Are you really thinking of quitting the art school?'

'Oh, I don't know.'

'Have you made other plans?'

'To be perfectly honest, my original plan was to become a rock star. I know that sounds ludicrous. I've never even played an instrument, but I wanted to impress the girls. Art isn't really sexy in the same way, but there's less competition. Have you ever been to a gallery opening? These days eighty per cent of the guests are women. That means four women for every man. Even better would be taking up acting. All the theatre audiences are women.

The only men who go to the theatre have been dragged there by their wives, or else they're gay.'

Eva rolled on to her back and stared up at the ceiling. She could hear someone walking about in the flat. Probably her mother, cleaning up. She wondered how long her parents would leave her room untouched before deciding to redo it.

'My mum and dad hate each other,' she said. 'For as long as I can remember, they've slept in separate beds. I wonder why they stay married. I mean, Helen and I have both moved out. And they hardly spend any time with each other. I don't think Dad is home much, and when he is, he holes up in his study, pretending to write. And Mum works herself to death, even though she hates her job. I hope I'm never like the two of them.'

'I think they seem great. Your mother arranged the whole party for him, and you don't do things like that for people you hate. It would make me really happy. And your dad is cool. He showed me his library and all the books he's written.'

'Tonight?'

'Uh-huh. While you were doing something else.'

'That's so typical of him. As soon as somebody new turns up, he drags out all his old stories. Don't listen to what he says; just ignore him if he starts blabbing a lot of bullshit. And besides, he was drunk tonight.'

'I enjoy listening to people. I think it's fascinating to hear what they have to say. Your mother also talked to me before you arrived. My family were

166

never big talkers. Mum basically brought me and my sister up single-handedly. Even though Dad lived with us before the divorce, he was almost never home. Whenever he did come home, he was always furious because he claimed we'd touched his stuff. But he was an alcoholic. My mother was really crushed when she found out I wanted to be an artist. I guess she thought that's what had turned my father into a drunk. He wanted to do something great, but he never could decide what that might be; it was one of those impossible dreams that he carried all his life. I think my mother wanted me to be a doctor.'

For a moment neither of them spoke. Then Eva said, 'For as far back as I can remember, my parents have always encouraged me. Dad bought me art supplies when I was in middle school. An easel and everything.'

'But that's what I was saying. Your parents seem really great.'

'I suppose so.'

Eva thought that Russ might be right. Maybe she should talk to them about her situation. Was there any reason why she had to go through the whole thing alone?

She sat up and looked at Russ.

'How could you afford to fly here? Wasn't it expensive to get a ticket on such short notice?'

'I borrowed the money from my flatmate. Don't worry about it. He's got plenty of money.'

'What kind of work does he do?'

167

'He sells drugs,' said Russ, as if it were a perfectly ordinary profession.

'What kind of drugs?'

'To be honest, I don't really know. Party drugs, mostly. But it works out fine. My rent is cheap.'

Eva noticed how tired she was.

'Russ, mind if we turn off the light now? I need to sleep.'

'Okay, I'll do it,' he said and got up to switch off the table lamp.

Eva realised that he'd probably lie awake on the mattress, hoping that she'd crawl under the covers next to him. But she had no intention of doing any such thing. She was not attracted to him, and even if she was, she hadn't even considered having sex after finding out she was pregnant. She suddenly thought about a book she'd discovered in their summer cottage in Kristinestad when she was a kid. She and Helen had taken turns reading it. The book was titled *The Evolution of Human Sexuality*, with chapters on topics such as: 'The Female Orgasm: Adaptation or Artifact?' and 'Copulation as a Female Service'. She'd had an idea how an orgasm would feel long before experiencing it personally. That book made sex sound as if it caused people to revert to some sort of bestial state. The author claimed that the first criterion for making men attractive to women was good health – a flawless complexion, decent hair, straight teeth and symmetrical facial features.

Eva felt that the culture had truly surpassed

human evolution in that regard. She couldn't remember ever being attracted to a man who could be called 'decent'. She'd always had a weakness for slightly cruel men, those who looked like small-time criminals. And maybe that was what had attracted her to Malik – the sense that he was unreliable, so she didn't have to invest her own emotions in the relationship. It was different with Russ. He was like a little puppy. If she ever slept with him, he would consider it an act of great love, and a promise that they'd spend their lives together.

To Eva's surprise, she heard him snoring. She imagined Russ as a kid, standing on the Tube platform. She pictured a frightened little boy with dark hair. She had an urge to lean down and caress his forehead, but instead she put her hand on her belly. She knew there was no chance she'd be able to feel even the slightest movement inside, but she couldn't help pressing her hand to her belly, as if the tiniest sign of life might make her change her mind.

CHAPTER 14

When Eva woke the next morning, Russ was not in the room. She found him in the kitchen with Max and Katriina. They looked as though they were enjoying each other's company so much that she suspected it was some sort of trick, that the whole thing was a joke, like the one perpetrated in the *Truman Show* film. Eva felt sick, just as she had done every morning for the past two weeks, but she had learned that the nausea would subside if she had something to eat.

So she sat down at the kitchen table, pretending the scenario was the most natural thing in the world. And in some ways it was, since it was only a few months ago that she was living here at home. Back then she'd always eaten breakfast with her father before he left for work at nine thirty. Katriina never joined them for breakfast, since she got up at seven.

'I'm thinking of coming to London,' Max now said. He was wearing a T-shirt and pyjama bottoms, and his hair was tousled. He seemed pleased with life, even though he'd loudly protested about celebrating his birthday. At what age did people become content with their lives? At fifty? In that case, Eva longed to be fifty. She longed to feel carefree and not have to bear this ever-present sense of shame because she didn't measure up, because she was in somebody else's debt. When her father was her age, he'd already written his doctoral dissertation.

'What are you going to do in London?' Eva asked him.

'I'm going to demonstrate against capitalism and bankers. The same way we used to demonstrate against the Vietnam War.'

'You demonstrated against the Vietnam War? Really?'

Katriina glanced from one to the other and shook her head. 'Your father was busy chasing girls, not demonstrating.'

'I don't mean me, personally, but my generation,' Max explained.

Eva took a bite of flatbread and poured herself a glass of juice. 'Why is it that all of you guys who were young in the seventies always talk in such general terms about those days, but you can't remember any of the details? It's like you read about your youth in a book.'

'And that's presumably exactly what he did,' replied Katriina. 'Everything your father knows, he learned from books.'

'Nuclear power!' exclaimed Max abruptly. 'We demonstrated against nuclear power! Don't you remember, Katriina? We went to Stockholm to join the protest march. Not that it made any difference. These days they're building more of them than ever. Maybe we should chain ourselves to a tree.'

'I'm not sure you could smoke cigars if you were chained up,' said Eva.

Katriina laughed.

'The only thing I remember from that demonstration in Stockholm was that I bought a jacket at the NK department store. I think I still have it somewhere. Maybe it's worth something by now. Russ, would you like more coffee?'

'Yes, please,' said Russ.

Eva hadn't realised it would be full-blown winter weather in Helsinki. When she looked out of the kitchen window she could see how white everything was, and she thought how nice it was to have real seasons. In London the weather had stayed much the same for almost two months now.

'Mum, do we have any plans for today?'

'I told your sister we'd serve dinner at six. I don't know if she'll turn up or not, but I intend to cook, and anyone who's here is welcome to join us. How long are you staying, Russ?'

'Yes, how long are you staying?' asked Eva.

'I'm in no hurry. It depends on you.'

Katriina and Max both turned to look at Eva, as if they too wanted to know what she'd say. But she merely continued to eat her piece of flatbread. After a few minutes, when the awkward silence had settled into a more comfortable stillness, she poured herself a cup of coffee.

After breakfast, Russ and Eva went for a walk. They headed for Edesviken, following the shore to Sibelius Park. There was no wind, and Russ put his arm around Eva, which she found annoying. He was wearing a thick blue duffel coat, and he'd borrowed a pair of gloves from Max. She knew that she was going to have to send him back to London.

'Have you always lived here? It's so beautiful.'

'Mostly. But we lived in a smaller flat when I was younger. After my dad got more work, we moved to the place where they're living now.'

'Seems like your parents are very well-to-do.'

'I wouldn't say that. Well, I mean, they're doing okay. But my father has always said that nobody gets rich being a researcher. He says he could have made a lot more money as a statistician. I suppose it goes up and down. In the nineties he was really busy. These days he seems to spend most of his time at home in his dressing gown. When I was living at home, we used to play tennis every day, but whenever my mother asked what he'd done all day, he would tell her that he'd been working.'

They walked past the Regatta café and took the path up to the park. The huge monument made of steel rods loomed in front of them. Eva felt a cold gust of wind seep through her jacket.

'Russ, there's something I have to tell you.'

'Okay,' he said and waited for her to go on, as if he were a child who had just been taken into an adult's confidence.

'I'm pregnant.'

Neither of them said another word for several seconds. It was a terrible kind of silence, and Eva realised this was how it must have felt for Russ last night after he confessed his feelings for her. They kept walking, until they reached the monument and stopped.

'But how can you be pregnant?' said Russ. His complexion looked darker than usual, but maybe it was only in contrast to the white snow. Eva had such a sense of unreality as she looked at him. For once she felt herself inferior in his company. But she was also irritated.

'Do I really have to tell you how women get pregnant?'

'No . . . I just mean, how can you . . . Who's the father?'

'Malik.'

And she could almost hear Russ trying desperately to make sense of the situation as he allowed the information to sink in.

'I know it sounds weird. But it happened. Okay? I was really stupid, and I'd shoot myself if I could, but now there's nothing I can do about it.'

Eva heard her voice quavering, and her eyes filled with tears. Russ reached out and awkwardly put his arms around her as she wept. She hated herself

174

for crying. This was not how it was supposed to be, but once she'd started, she couldn't stop.

'Do you hate me, Russ?'

He didn't answer, just held her close. Nor did he speak as they turned to head back home. He remained silent as he packed his bag and as they stood in the front hall an hour later, waiting for his taxi to arrive. Katriina tried in vain to chat with Russ, who gave only one-word replies to her questions. She finally got the message and realised that something must have happened.

When Eva went to her room after Russ had left, Katriina stood outside for a moment and then knocked on the door.

'Sweetheart? Do you feel like talking? We could have a chat if you like.'

Eva didn't answer. She heard her mother go into the kitchen. But after a few minutes she was outside the door again.

'Eva, you don't have to go back to London. You can stay here if you want to. It's only three weeks until Christmas, after all.'

Eva lay on her bed and stared at the ceiling. The last thing she wanted was to stay here any longer than necessary. She'd wait until Wednesday, which was when her return flight left. But first she needed to see a doctor.

JANUARY TO MARCH

CHAPTER 15

During the first week of January it's light for only a few hours each day before the sun once again retreats from the world and leaves Helsinki to its desolate winter darkness. By the time the afternoon ferries depart from the south harbour, it's practically night, even though it's only a few minutes past five. The brightly lit vessels move slowly away from the dock, and like ancient animals they pass the fortress of Sveaborg and make their way along the channel, heading for Sweden.

Helen and her family walked along the corridors on board the *Silja Symphony*, looking for deck five, where they'd booked a cabin. Helen had picked up a brochure that listed the available activities during the crossing. The entire trip was planned out, down to the last minute, for families with children – from face painting in the Kidz Club at five o'clock to a pirate quiz game at five thirty, to a buffet dinner, children's bingo, and finally 'Dancing in Moomin Valley' at eight. It was actually a relief not to have to think up anything themselves. And the children were happy. Lukas ran ahead, looking for the right cabin. He'd been given his own card key and stuck it in the lock, but at first the door refused to open.

'Mum, the green light didn't go on. It's supposed to be green, isn't it?'

'Try again,' said Christian calmly.

Lukas tried again, and this time the door opened. Amanda stood next to him, waiting, and then followed him inside.

They quickly stowed away their things in the cabin. The children fought over the sweets that had been left for them on the table, but Christian solved the problem by putting them all away until after dinner. In the meantime, Helen put on her make-up in the tiny bathroom. The room smelled the same as all ship's cabins: an odour that was a combination of wall-to-wall carpeting and cleanser, with a vague undercurrent of old tobacco left over from the days before smoking was banned. When everyone was ready, they took the lift to deck seven to find the face-painting event. There was a long queue of families with little kids and grandmothers with their grandchildren, all of them eagerly looking forward to having a good time and exploring the entertainment options on board the ferry. Helen and her family moved on to the play-room across from the Duty Free shop.

After Helen had children, she abandoned the idea that travelling should be relaxing. Taking a trip meant making sure everyone had the maximum amount of fun together. It involved compromises, unexpected obstacles and challenges. It was an art to anticipate the pace and mood of everyone else. Should they stroll for another hour, or was it time to go back to the hotel and rest? Was anyone suffering from low blood sugar? Should they take public transport or attempt to walk? Should they keep going for a while? Were the children ready to visit a museum?

If they decided on the museum, they would dash through without really seeing anything, and as soon as they came out, they forgot everything they'd seen. The next day it was almost as though they'd never been there at all. Finally, they would go back to the hotel with aching feet to rest for a while, until it was time to go out and find something to eat.

When they ate out, it was important to choose the right place. They wanted to eat well, so that while they were eating they could conclude that the food really was excellent and that they'd made a good choice for a reasonable price. And they were already planning what they would say when they got home, how they'd tell their friends: 'Oh yes, we found this amazing restaurant, and it wasn't expensive at all. Such a pleasant atmosphere, and the waiters were so nice.' And if that wasn't the case, then they'd have to stretch the truth a bit in the opposite direction and exaggerate how bad the service was, since they couldn't afford to have any mediocre experiences. Taking a holiday wasn't really a 'holiday' at all, because they weren't really free; there were hundreds of variables that had to be constantly considered.

As in so many other places in the world, families with children had taken over the ferry. It was obvious that the playroom had once been a conference room. Here mid-level managers had spent their work days writing down company goals on little Post-it notes until it was time to delve into the buffet, and afterwards head for the bar with its polished dance floor. Very little energy or imagination had been invested in the transformation from conference room to playroom – there were a few Moomin posters on the walls, some sacks holding balls, several flat-screen TVs with PlayStation games and chairs where the grown-ups could sit while the kids played. At the back of the room there was also a bar that sold beer and pre-mixed cocktails to the parents, whose survival strategy was to numb their brains just enough to forget about the fact that the ball pit was actually a colourful smorgasbord of every kind of stomach-flu virus making the rounds that winter.

'You know what? I love you,' said Helen, going over to Christian and putting her hand on his shoulder. He was standing in front of a shelf holding bottles of red wine that clinked faintly with the movement of the ship. He pulled her close and kissed her hand.

Lukas was a couple of metres away, refusing to

let them out of his sight because he was afraid of getting lost. Amanda ventured further away and went over to look at the selection of sweets. When the family returned to their cabin, the kids wanted to eat some of their sweets, so Helen let them open the packages. Amanda had chosen several small packets while Lukas had bought a big pink bag filled with marshmallow treats.

Helen was feeling rested. It had been a busy autumn, as it always was at the school where she worked. This year she'd missed Amanda's Christmas party, but managed to attend the holiday show at Lukas's day-care centre. He was one of the three wise men in the Christmas pageant. He had only one line – 'Tonight we have seen the angels singing and speaking of the birth of the Messiah' – which he'd practised every day for several weeks, until it became a monotone litany, making it hard to distinguish a single word. When he finally stood on stage, he said his line so fast that it sounded like a monosyllabic mumble with a question mark at the end: 'Tonightwehaveseentheangelssinging- andspeakingofthebirthoftheMESSIAH?'

When they got home Helen had praised her son, telling him he was great. Lukas then concluded, apparently without any sense of irony, that he was 'born to be an actor'. He had a self-confidence based on his very own laws. He was both shy and incredibly attracted to being in the spotlight.

Helen now listened with half an ear as Amanda and Lukas, lying on the top bunk, compared the sweets they'd bought. After a while she looked up and saw that Lukas had already eaten half the bag. He had a wild look in his eyes. Helen quickly took the rest away as she put a finger to her lips, warning him not to say anything. Lukas understood what she meant. Helen and the kids often kept things secret from Christian.

'All right, let's go eat!' she said.

'Can we have hamburgers?' asked Amanda. She'd lined up all the little sweets packets and was now sucking on a piece of toffee.

'I'm sure they have meatballs and mashed potatoes in the café,' said Christian.

'I don't want any damn meatballs!' said Lukas. This winter he'd adopted the bad habit of cursing, and 'damn' was his favourite word. Christian would get furious whenever he swore, and they often waged long and bitter battles that ended with both of them feeling totally exhausted. It was like watching two characters in an old Western having a quick-draw duel, except that the only tactic either of them had come up with was to wear down his opponent.

'Hamburgers!' shouted Lukas now, as he jumped up and down on the bunk, his blood sugar level that of a diabetic who hadn't had his insulin shot. 'Hamburgers! HAMBURGERS!!!'

If there was one thing Christian hated more than allowing sweets before dinner, it was junk food: chips, burgers, greasy gravy, pizza, and, in particular, the Finnish speciality known as 'chicken basket'.

It was Amanda's and Lukas's favourite: a basket of fried chicken with chips, which was always on the menu in places popular with families who had young children. Helen had seen how that particular menu item could provoke an inexplicable sense of helplessness in Christian. According to him, there were few things more offensive than doing something unhealthy when it wasn't necessary – like taking the car when you could walk, drinking juice instead of water, sitting inside when it was good weather outdoors – or buying something expensive when there was a cheaper option. Worst of all, and what seemed to make him sink into an almost catatonic depression, was buying something unhealthy that was also expensive.

They went up to the so-called promenade deck. People streamed past them from all directions, coming from the lifts, the restaurants and the shops. Nowhere did a family seem so much like a family as on holiday trips – they went everywhere together, more like one body instead of four. Helen tried to see herself from the outside as she moved along next to Lukas and Amanda and Christian, but it felt as though they were interchangeable, and she might just as well have been walking with any of the other families she saw. Individual personalities were erased, and all the families looked exactly the same – as if they were figures in a computer game and the different decks on the ferry were various levels in the game. Two adults, two children, Tax Free, food, ball pit, sweets, face painting. It occurred to Helen that of course the kids wouldn't see things the same way. For them the ferry was still a new experience that was anything but anonymous; for them it had a meaning that would be added to other, similar experiences which, in combination, would shape them as individuals.

It was the middle of winter, but some passengers were wearing Crocs and T-shirts, as if it were summer, as if taking a mini-holiday on the ferry to Sweden was an opportunity to throw out all the rules, even those that applied to the seasons of the year. Two men, obviously from Stockholm, were studying the menu posted outside the café. There were hamburgers, pizza and a buffet offering meatballs, mashed potatoes and pork tenderloin. The latter was swimming in a congealed gravy that looked as if it had been there ever since the ferryboat was launched in the early nineties.

One of the men from Stockholm looked disappointed. Helen heard him mutter to his companion in a resigned voice: 'I was so in the mood for sushi.'

After dinner they went in search of the Atlantis Palace, which was where the rest of the programme for children was going to take place.

At first there was a dance performance with a pirate theme. The dancers were not Finns, or Swedes either. The group seemed to consist of a mix of Russians and Estonians, and the whole show was a bit half-hearted. Amanda seemed to watch without much interest, but Lukas was mesmerised, paying close attention to every single dance step.

'Mum, can we have one of those?' asked Amanda impatiently, pointing at a drink that a child at the next table was enjoying, something with a bright neon straw.

'Do you feel like getting her one?' Helen asked Christian. By this time she'd learned exactly what tone of voice to use so that he'd realise this was an Especially Important Request.

She used a variation of the same tone of voice – in a negative version – whenever he wanted to have sex and she really wasn't in the mood. She might have laughed about it if she wasn't so grateful that it actually worked.

Christian hesitated for a moment but then reluctantly got up to fetch a drink for each of the children.

By now the dancers had come to their final number. The music got louder, the lights flashed faster, and they were dashing around in a circle. The woman in the group had flung off her dress to reveal her short but incredibly toned legs. Two of the men, the most muscular of the group, grabbed her by the legs and hoisted her up so that she was standing on their hands. It was like a fireworks display of flexed muscles. The men stood as straight as they could, and their pirate trousers were stretched so tight that their genitals bulged.

There was something oddly feminine about the tableau, thought Helen, even though the men were clearly supposed to radiate a primeval pirate masculinity.

She glanced at her watch. It was eight thirty, which meant that it was late enough to retreat to their cabin and bring the evening to a close.

One by one the dancers broke out of the circle, but before anyone had a chance to get up to leave, even before the music had faded, a female staff member came on stage to say that the evening's programme would end with Moomin Disco with the entire Moomin family.

'Shall we go?' said Helen, and Christian nodded, but both of the kids protested.

'Just a little longer. Please?' said Lukas, his eyes shining with anticipation. Amanda didn't show the same enthusiasm as she sucked on the straw of her drink, but a sudden whim of big-sister solidarity made her add that she also wanted to stay.

'I can dance with Lukas. You can stay here,' she said, as if she were the third adult in the party.

The music had already started. Lukas seemed to be considering whether to go out on the dance floor, his whole body conveying contradictory feelings. Something in his brain seemed to say that the whole thing was a bad idea, that he'd be forced to do something that was potentially humiliating. At the same time, it might be fun, even character-building. Finally, he allowed Amanda to pull him out of his chair, and suddenly they were on the dance floor, waiting for instructions along with the other children as a shaggy and rather ungainly Moomin family appeared on stage.

The dance was led by a girl dressed up as Little My. Next to her stood Moominpappa, Moominmamma and Moomintroll. It was impossible to know whether they were men or women as they were all wearing white suits that were probably terribly hot and sweaty. As far as Helen could tell, the Moomin characters could see only through a black, net-like swathe near the snout, which meant that their field of vision had to be extremely limited.

The music started.

The Moomins bobbed and danced in time to a techno children's song with a fast 4/4-rhythm and a melody based on high-pitched voices repeating the Finnish words 'MUUMIHUMPPA SOI NYT KUULET MITEN MUUMIHUMPPA SOI'.

Helen and Christian stayed in their seats, their eyes on the dance floor. Helen watched to see how Lukas was coping. His eyes big, he was doing his best to imitate Moominpappa, who stuck one foot forward, then back. Amanda did the same, but with more confidence. She was a head taller than the other kids, and it was obvious that she was sticking close to Lukas so she could use the big-sister excuse if the whole thing got too embarrassing. Her body language clearly signalled that she was doing this only for the sake of her little brother, and for no other reason.

189

Little My stood back from the others, clapping her hands overhead. Now Moominpappa and Moominmamma were wagging their tails, and the children copied their movements as the song faded out.

Helen hoped that now they could all go back to the cabin, brush their teeth and climb into bed. She was tired, and she was looking forward to taking off these sticky clothes. But the programme director wasn't yet ready to let them escape. In a gushing voice she shouted: 'NOW IT'S THE PARENTS' TURN! LET'S HAVE ALL THE PARENTS UP ON STAGE!' Christian and Helen exchanged startled glances.

With flushed cheeks, Amanda came dashing over to their table and sat down to finish her drink.

Lukas was left alone on the dance floor. In confusion he looked for Amanda. Now that all the parents had been summoned, Helen watched one after the other step forward – Finnish mothers, their hair cropped short, wearing practical clothing; Swedish fathers, moving slowly after indulging in the *Silja Symphony*'s generous New Year's buffet.

Helen realised that she had no choice but to join Lukas and dance.

I love my family, she thought. I love them so much.

Helen danced the Moominhumppa. She was willing to endure whatever humiliation was needed;

that was what was required, after all, when signing the contract to become a parent.

Lukas watched her with awe as she came to the dance floor, as if she wasn't his mother but some stranger who had taken his mother's form. He nodded to her, as if confiding a secret.

The music started.

It was the same techno music as the last tune, but this time the choreography was apparently a free-for-all. The Moomins danced around the children, their movements totally uncoordinated, as the intensity of the music rose and the lights flashed even faster. Lukas clung to Helen's hand as Moominpappa – who apparently was having trouble with his motor functions – came staggering over to them, holding on to his tail. Helen clumsily flailed her arms about as she tried to smile, but it was a strained smile. The only thought in her mind was that she hoped the music would stop very soon.

Moominpappa was now turning pirouettes, which made him lose his balance. First he slid a few steps towards the right edge of the dance floor, so that some of the kids had to move out of the way. Then, as if the ship were moving through rough waters, he slid to the left until he came to an abrupt halt and fell to the floor, right on his snout. The music kept on thudding from the loudspeakers, and at first it seemed that Moominpappa couldn't get back on his feet. His snout had been knocked sideways so it looked as if it had twisted ninety degrees. It was a grotesque sight, like an animal that had been struck by a car. But finally he managed to get up, using one arm to push off from the floor.

Helen could see he was having trouble because the snout was so heavy and pulled his whole body off balance. When he was back on his feet again, he managed a few wobbly steps before Little My turned up and took him by the arm. But he shook off her hand and didn't seem to want any help, like a drunk who thinks he can make it home on his own even though everybody can see that he can barely stay on his feet. The other Moomins had now stopped dancing, but they were still on the dance floor, watching the commotion.

'Mum, what's wrong with Moominpappa?' Lukas shouted over the music.

Now the programme director appeared. She grabbed hold of Moominpappa's arm and gave it a good yank.

Only then did Helen look around and notice that all the other children and parents had stopped dancing to watch what was happening.

'I think it's time for bed,' said Helen. Then she and Lukas headed back to the table where Christian and Amanda were sitting.

She glanced over her shoulder to see the programme director dragging Moominpappa towards a room to the right of the stage. Moominpappa pulled off his top hat and head to reveal a little, balding head underneath. She could see that it was a man in his fifties who was so sweaty that his sparse strands of hair were plastered to his skull. But that was as much as she saw because then the programme director pulled shut the curtains to the room.

CHAPTER 16

During the spring Helen decided to assign Väinö Linna's classic novel *The Unknown Soldier* to her second-year class in secondary school.

'The book is about the Continuation War – commonly known as the Winter War – that was fought between Finland and the Soviet Union from 1941–44,' she explained as she stood in front of the class. 'As the story opens, the Winter War has just ended. Now what was it Linna wrote? That the Winter War was "the best of all wars so far, because both sides ended up as victors".'

The pupils fidgeted in their seats. Nobody said a word.

'Your homework was to read the first chapter, so you must have something to say. How does the author present his characters? Let's hear your thoughts. What is their attitude towards the war?'

'I just don't get it,' said Mårten, who was one of the biggest boys in the class. He was so buff that he seemed to have a hard time sitting at his desk. Every movement seemed stiff and slow, and he had to use his whole body because his arms were so bulked up.

'What is it you don't get?'

'I don't know,' he said, and some of the others murmured agreement.

'When do we have to finish reading this chapter?' asked Alex, a short boy who was one of the worst pupils in the class.

'I was thinking we should keep reading until the hour is over. How does that sound? I want you to write up a three-page paper about what you've read so far. I won't grade your work, but we can use it to start our discussion. I'll give you a few questions to use as a basis for your report.'

Several pupils sighed loudly.

'Okay then. Let's see how it goes. But you need to start now. We have twenty minutes left, so you should be able to write at least a page.'

After class, certain pupils complained that the book was hard to read because of the old-fashioned writing style. Helen had given them a textbook version translated from Finnish into Swedish by Nils-Börje Stormbom. The only part of the novel that was slightly outmoded was the dialogue, written in dialect, but even those sections couldn't honestly be described as 'hard to read'.

On the other hand, she wasn't really surprised by their reaction. Last autumn she'd asked her pupils to write a term paper on the subject 'Why do boys read far fewer books than girls do?' She didn't actually care for the topic, since the wording clearly steered the response so that the boys would have to defend themselves. But she'd taken the topic from a previous exam, and the point was for the pupils to use this paper to prepare for exams in their final year before graduation.

She hadn't known whether to laugh or cry when she read the papers.

One of them, written by a boy of perfectly normal intelligence, had begun like this:

'Ever since ancient times, women have read more than men. This is because men had to go out and hunt while the women had more time for reading.'

In her mind Helen directed a few harsh words at the parents who had raised these poor boys. Hadn't anyone ever told them what century they were living in? This was not the first time that Helen noticed how the home environment of her pupils was reflected in the papers they wrote. These days she avoided nearly all topics that dealt with integration and immigration; she found them just too depressing.

When she went to the teachers' room after class, she found Michael, the new history teacher, reviewing applications for the so-called 'Holocaust trip', which a group of pupils from the school made each year. Those who were interested in participating had to write a half-page essay to explain why they wanted to go. Only ten pupils would be accepted.

'Listen to this,' said Michael. He held up one of the applications and read aloud:

'I've always been interested in history and I think it would be *really fun* to go to Auschwitz.'

Helen laughed. 'Did you get a lot of applications?'

'About twenty. Mostly from girls.'

Helen knew that the great interest displayed by the school's female pupils was primarily because they all wanted to go on a field trip with the sexy history teacher. The fact that they'd have the opportunity to meet a guide who had survived a concentration camp was of lesser importance.

The school was housed in a large building constructed in the seventies when the municipality had expanded northward and also funded a new swimming hall, cinema and public library. During the autumn, the sun shone brightly through the big seventies-era windows in the back of Helen's classroom, but now that it was winter, the windows were transformed into blank, gaping mirrors.

All the classrooms and communal spaces were on one level, except for the outdated computer room, which had been set up in the basement. Next to it was the so-called lounge, conceived as a place where the teachers could take a much-needed cat nap. Helen couldn't understand how anyone thought they'd ever have time for that. She rarely had time even to sit down and read a newspaper, much less rest. Besides, the room was filled with stuff used for the school's annual bazaar: tennis balls, lottery tickets, wreaths, plastic flowers and a huge cardboard shape into

197

which the pupils were supposed to toss the tennis balls.

By the time Helen picked up Amanda and Lukas from school, it was usually close to six o'clock. Today was no exception.

'Mum, when are we going to get Blixten and Skorpan?' asked Amanda from the back seat of the car.

The kids had each been given a hamster when the house renovation was finished and they could move in. But just as Helen had predicted, she and Christian were the only ones who gave a thought to the hamsters when it came to feeding them and cleaning the cages. The latter chore took nearly an hour, and it was a thankless job, a Sisyphus-type task for the parents of young children. Katriina and Max had been taking care of the hamsters while the family was on holiday.

'I don't know. Soon. Maybe this weekend.'

'Can they live in my room?' asked Amanda.

'Will you be able to sleep if they do? You know how much noise they make at night.'

'But I go to sleep before they wake up.'

'Okay then. We can try it.'

'I want to have the hamsters!' Lukas shouted. Until now he'd hardly paid them any attention at all.

'We need to talk to your father about this when he gets home tonight. And besides, Grandma and Grandpa are taking care of the hamsters right now. Remember?'

Just as Helen finished getting everything out of

the car, her mobile rang. It was Katriina. Helen went into the kitchen and set her phone on the table with the speaker turned on so she could talk while she got dinner ready.

'Hi, I just thought I'd give you a ring to find out how things are going. How are my little darlings?' said Katriina.

'Everything's fine. How are the hamsters?'

'I'm not sure. I haven't really paid too much attention to them. They sleep most of the time.'

'Has the dog left them alone?'

'He was a bit curious at first, but now he's not interested in them at all.'

Christian and Helen had discussed whether they should leave the hamsters with Katriina and Max. They had the feeling that Helen's parents were too preoccupied with other things and might forget to feed them. Helen honestly didn't know how her parents managed to do so much, since she was having such a hard time handling all the demands of her own life. Whenever she phoned her mother, Katriina was always on her way to a meeting with some women's organisation or about to embark on a long trip, like now. Katriina explained that she was going to the Philippines.

'That sounds exciting,' said Helen.

'We'll see. You know how it is working with Asians.'

Helen had no idea what she meant by that.

'You know, everything seems great in the beginning, and people make all sorts of promises and smile a lot, but later on, when it comes right down to it, nothing happens.'

'Huh,' said Helen as she started chopping onions.

They had a big, white-painted kitchen. Christian had renovated the old house, doing all the labour himself except for the electrical and plumbing work.

Amanda was out in the garden. Lukas was in his room playing his favourite computer game – an online program called Moviestarz, which involved dressing digital paper dolls. Helen had seen the program labelled 'the world's biggest play community for GIRLS'. Amanda had noticed at once that her little brother was fascinated with a girls' game, and she made a point of teasing Lukas about this. His face took on an uncertain expression until Helen had countered by saying that there was no such thing as a girls' game or a boys' game.

For the past two weeks Lukas had been begging Helen to pay four euros so he could get a special membership in the game, which would mean more dolls to dress, including some boy dolls, along with so-called 'star coins' that could be used to decorate the doll's house. Christian, who had been following this whole negotiation from the sidelines, was vehemently against buying the membership. He viewed it as a waste of money, and he was also convinced that the program might infect their computer with a virus. His response prompted Helen to react as she always did: she bought Lukas a membership for ten euros. She also tracked down an email address for the game company and wrote a long email in which she criticised the game's gender bias.

Katriina was still on the phone.

'Mum, I have to go. I'm making dinner. Have a nice trip.'

'It's going to be so stressful.'

'Okay, well, give me a ring when you get back.'

'Kiss Amanda and Lukas for me.'

'I will. Bye!'

'Helen?'

'Yes?'

'Have you heard anything from Eva?'

'No, afraid not, Mum.'

'Okay. Bye.'

Helen went into Lukas's room. He was sitting at the computer, choosing clothing for a virtual paper doll. Helen stood watching him for a moment as he selected one garment after another, giving all his attention to the game.

He was tall for his age, and he had the same dark hair as both of his parents. He was clicking his way through the game as if he'd never done anything else – the malleable parts of his brain had apparently already adapted to life in front of a computer monitor.

'Mum, what does this mean?'

Helen read what he was pointing at.

'Star-mingle. Get to know your new friends!'

'Looks like a page where you can chat with other people. But you need to know how to write.'

'Oh,' said Lukas, who hadn't yet found the patience to learn his ABC's.

'It's almost time for dinner. Could you turn that off, please?'

'Can I play a little longer?'

'Okay. Ten minutes. Then you need to come to the table.'

Amanda was still outside in the garden. She was clearly the type of child who had the necessary imagination and self-esteem it would take to live in the middle of nowhere. Helen heard Christian's car pull into the driveway. Then she heard him talking to Amanda, and the two of them came into the front hall.

After dinner, Helen was sitting on the sofa in the living room, correcting more term papers. She hated the sofa, but she'd been forced to live with this piece of furniture because it was a present from Christian's parents. It was a family heirloom covered in worn brown leather and originally purchased by Christian's maternal grandmother. When she died, it was passed down to his parents. Helen suspected that she and Christian had inherited the sofa because her parents-in-law couldn't stand it either.

The springs were so worn out that anyone who sat down sank nearly half a metre. The sofa was also too small for the family. Christian occasionally oiled the leather with great care and effort, and he never allowed the children to eat anything when they sat there. He was afraid that might ruin the leather. As far as Helen was concerned, the leather upholstery could just crumble away, and the sooner the better.

'It's not even valuable,' Helen complained. 'Just because a piece of furniture has been in the family for two generations, that doesn't automatically give it antique status.'

'This sofa was in our summer cottage, starting in the early thirties. It was quite special in its day,' said Christian, speaking with the authoritative tone of voice that he reserved for everything that had to do with the idiosyncrasies of his family.

Helen had met Christian at a party for literature students in the early 2000s. This was at Vanha, and Christian had come with a friend who was a historian, although his own field of study was architecture.

They had sex for the first time in the cramped little room he had lived in. They didn't bother with a condom, since she thought it was a safe period in her menstrual cycle. Condoms made her think of the time when she was sixteen and went to the Roskilde Festival in Denmark with her friend Anne. Before they left, their mothers had made them sit down at the kitchen table and listen to a list of rules.

'We're happy that you're going. You'll have a great time. And you'll probably meet some boys there.'

Katriina had looked pleased, as if this was something she was actually encouraging.

'Mum, we're going there to hear . . .'

203

'Okay, okay, you're going there to hear some bands. I get it. But still, if you do happen to meet some boys – and that seems highly likely – then for God's sake, please, please, please use a condom.'

It wasn't until Helen became a teenager that she realised not everyone behaved like her mother. Not all women were born with that sort of flipped-out candour; some struggled all their lives to achieve it but never even got close. For Katriina, it was a completely natural part of her personality. She could instantly take over a room – in fact, an entire flat or even a whole neighbourhood if she so desired. Her voice could be heard everywhere, and there wasn't a single person she couldn't handle. She was not afraid of anyone.

But she could also go too far, and occasionally she failed to recognise situations when someone wanted to be left alone. She didn't understand that certain individuals constructed emotional walls around themselves. That was not something she had ever done.

Consequently, Katriina said whatever was on her mind; there were no taboo topics. Because why waste your life in silence when you could speak? This often presented problems, especially when Helen was young and Katriina would ask her friends all sorts of questions and tell them things most people considered private matters. For example, on the day Helen got her first menstrual period, her friend Frida was visiting, and Katriina immediately asked Frida if she'd also started menstruating. That was so embarrassing. At school Helen had noticed that she was bleeding, so she rushed home along Topeliusgatan. Katriina's first instinct was to celebrate. She suggested that the whole family should go out for dinner, but Helen had refused. Eva, who was three years younger, had no idea what menstruation was. But Katriina thought every event in life was worthy of a party.

On another occasion, she asked Helen's cousin Jonas from Österbotten, who was Eva's age, whether he thought Helen was sexy.

'Doesn't she look like a real bombshell?' Katriina asked. During the spring Helen had rapidly developed breasts, clearly visible under her tight sweater. Jonas was very embarrassed, managing only to stammer a reply. 'Er, yes, no, uh, I think I'd better be going home now.'

But it was dangerous for children to have a mother who made them think the whole universe revolved around them, that they were entitled to take centre stage in any situation, and that there was never any need to apologise for their behaviour. Such children began to believe that they actually deserved to be privileged. They began to think that the world owed them something.

Yet Katriina had never understood this. She didn't realise that she was the one – by constantly offering her daughters encouragement and talking about how they should be this or that – who had moulded them into adults who would never be satisfied with what life actually offered.

At least, that was how Helen saw it. And she wasn't thinking so much about herself as about Eva. She thought that her sister would have a difficult time of it if she didn't become successful.

Eva was braver than Helen, even though she was younger. When they were kids, Eva would go alone to the supermarket on Töölö Square to shop for groceries. Helen never dared to do that until she was eleven.

When Helen got her first job as a teacher, she was nervous about standing in front of the class. She was afraid that she'd lose her train of thought. And she'd never been the kind of person who wanted to be in the spotlight. But she soon discovered that she felt comfortable in the role of teacher. The pupils actually listened to her, no matter what she said; they even trusted her. There was something magical about that. Of course they often complained about the homework assignments, but she could deal with that. On the other hand, every Friday the full weight of the working week would descend upon her. All those noises and voices – the scraping chairs, the teenagers bursting with hormones – would echo in her ears long after she reached home.

Helen had been embarrassed by her mother's mention of condoms. Especially since she knew that Anne's mother would never have discussed the topic so bluntly. But also because at that point the whole idea of having sex had not even occurred to Helen.

Nor was she really thinking about it when she met Christian. She was simply very drunk. Two months later, she found out she was pregnant. But that wasn't a disaster, since they quickly discovered that they enjoyed each other's company. And so they got married before Amanda was born.

Christian's parents lived in Kyrkslätt, and occasionally they would come over to visit, but they rarely stayed long. They would dutifully eat whatever food was served to them, all the while casting suspicious glances about, as if they couldn't really believe that their son lived in a house like this – so modern and white, with children who were both so talkative and extroverted. His parents always seemed relieved when it was time for dessert. Christian's mother would bring cakes or chocolate to eat with their coffee. It was never easy to get any sort of conversation started. They were happy to have their grandchildren visit, but not overnight, since Christian's father complained that he couldn't sleep if they were there.

Right now Helen was trying to read *The Unknown Soldier*, but she kept dozing off. She glanced at her watch. It was already eight thirty, so she might as well get the kids to brush their teeth.

When that was accomplished and Lukas and Amanda had been tucked into bed in their own rooms, Helen decided to retire for the night. She tried to read some more, but she must have fallen asleep because after a while – it could have been five minutes or an hour later – she felt the weight of Christian's body sink down on the bed next to her. She noticed the smell of sawdust and winter as he tried to find a comfortable position. He put his arm around her, searching for her breast. His hands were cold, and she hesitated for a moment, not sure how she wanted to react.

Apparently he wanted to make love, but she was already half-asleep and had been deep in a dream world. It would require some effort for her to get into the proper mood. But he still had his arms wrapped lightly around her. She knew that she needed to indicate with her body language whether she was interested, and at the moment both options seemed possible. They hadn't had sex in . . . well, it must be two weeks, so she supposed there was a certain logic in having it now. But why couldn't he have come to bed before she dozed off?

'I don't think I really feel like it tonight,' she said.

He sighed, removed his hands and turned over.

Helen realised that now she was not going to be able to fall asleep. Did she regret her decision? As she lay there, silently weighing the pros and cons, the bedroom room opened and Lukas came in. He got into bed between them, moving quietly, like a little animal, and crept under the covers without saying a word. Then he reached up to touch her ear and fell asleep holding on to her earlobe.

CHAPTER 17

Katriina went to the Philippines in order to show her colleague, Heikki, who was in charge. When it was decided that they would start up a recruiting project for nurses in Manila, he had offered to supervise the entire operation, even though the responsibility was clearly Katriina's domain. Besides, she knew that she had better contacts and was a more experienced negotiator than he was. So she did what she'd always done: she made the decision to take on the job herself.

The day before her departure, a series of training sessions were held at the Scandic Hotel Continental in Helsinki, with colleagues from several different divisions within HNS. The day started with a lecture by a consultant, who used a metaphor about an ice floe in her speech. Everyone was supposed to imagine themselves as penguins helping each other from one ice floe to another. Then they had to walk around the room and picture what it was like to depend on the rest of the group; if one of them stepped outside of a specifically defined area, the entire collective would fall.

It was three in the afternoon by the time that session ended, and dusk had already started to settle in. The hotel faced Töölö Bay, just a stone's throw from where Katriina and Max lived. Katriina looked out of the window at the park. People were jogging around the frozen bay, as usual, even though there was a strong wind and the temperature had dropped to minus 10° Celsius. Several people were huddled together, waiting for the airport bus on the other side of Mannerheimvägen.

The mood from the training session hovered like a grey mist over the whole place, reinforced by the hotel's wall-to-wall carpeting, the young women in business suits dashing about, the group of people out in the car park smoking and gossiping, and all her other colleagues who were hunched over their coffee cups as they waited for the next item on the agenda.

'Two weeks in Manila. You need to go around to the biggest hospitals and drum up interest,' said Wivan. 'Collect names and contact information. They pay their own travel expenses, and we pay for an intensive course in the Finnish language, plus help them to find housing. It should be simple. All those girls dream of getting a job abroad.'

Katriina was supposed to make contact with the authorities and hospitals, and try to find nurses interested in coming to Finland to work.

This project was Wivan's baby, and she was the kind of boss who lacked all patience. She wanted everything to happen as fast as possible.

Katriina offered some cautious objections. She had a feeling that Wivan had no idea about the logistics required to make this project a success.

'There are thirteen million people living in Manila,' she said. 'We can't just go over there and gather up a bunch of nurses as if they were mail-order brides. At the very least, I'll need to set up some sort of liaison with the local authorities.'

A year earlier they had tried a pilot project that had proven quite successful. Sixteen Filipina nurses had received their certificates from a professional college in Helsinki, and the media had portrayed the venture as providing a solution to the demographic disaster that Finland would face when the Baby Boomers retired. In the future there would be approximately ten retirees for every working-age Finn. But the pilot project had involved only sixteen nurses. Wivan was now talking about a hundred ('or maybe more, if we can make a go of it').

'But there are companies already doing this sort of thing. Why can't we let them handle the recruiting process?' asked Katriina.

'We can't afford to do that. They're starting to stir up trouble within the profession, and it'll take for ever to work out all the details. It's better for us to establish our own programme with the Filipina nurses. That way we skip the middleman.'

Katriina tried to explain that there were a lot of puzzle pieces that would have to fall into place first. For instance, where would all the nurses live once they got to Finland?

'We'll solve that issue later. I think this is the way forward. You and I need to have someone who will take care of us fifteen years from now. And it's not going to be our children, I can tell you that. Do you really think your daughters will want to work as care-givers?' Wivan asked rhetorically.

When Katriina finally went home around five o'clock, she found Max sitting in front of the computer in his study.

'So, have you decided?' she asked.

Max had told his wife that his publisher wanted Laura Lampela to read his manuscript. Katriina thought it was almost touching to see how Max struggled to make up his mind. It was obviously difficult for his sixty-year-old male ego to accept the fact that a younger woman might be able to help him with his writing. Katriina also realised that Max was tempted by the idea. He was the type of man – maybe all men were this type – who would go to great lengths simply to win the admiration of a younger woman. His book was presumably just a small part of this effort.

'I don't know. What do you think? Maybe it's a stupid idea,' he said. A big pile of research notes was on the desk next to him.

'She seems very bright,' said Katriina.

'Uh-huh. She's no dummy, that's for sure. But I've got so much material,' he said, pointing to the stack of pages.

'Well, don't go and do anything crazy. If you're

thinking of working with someone else, the other person has to agree. And I hope you're smart enough to realise that if she starts flirting with you, it's not directed at you personally. She's young, and she's got nothing to lose.'

'Okay, okay,' said Max.

Katriina went over to him and put her arm around his shoulders. He took her hand. She leaned down and pressed her cheek against Max's unshaven face.

'Do you have a lot to do still?' she asked him.

'What do you mean?'

'How about coming to bed with me?'

Max looked from her to his manuscript, and then at her again. He kissed her hand.

'I'll be right there.'

On her way to the bedroom, Katriina passed Eva's old room, where they had placed the hamster cage on the desk. Katriina had fed the hamsters almost every morning and evening since Christmas, and also given them water. If she happened to forget a day, she compensated by giving them extra food the next time. They didn't seem to eat much, hiding most of the food in one corner or another of the cage.

Blixten and Skorpan always woke up around nine p.m. and then spent all night running in their exercise wheel, until they finally went to sleep about the same time that Max and Katriina were getting up in the morning. The cage had started out in the hallway, but Katriina couldn't sleep because of all the noise, so they'd moved it into Eva's old room.

When Katriina bent down to open the cage door, she saw that it hadn't been properly latched.

She looked inside, moved the sawdust around and also opened the little houses that the hamsters slept in. Max was about to walk past when he noticed her in the room.

'Are you coming?' he said.

'I can't find them,' said Katriina.

'I'm sure they're just hiding in a corner.'

Katriina gave Max a worried look. 'They're not here. They're not inside the houses or under the bridge. I shook the cage, but they didn't come out from anywhere. Was it you who left the cage door open?'

'Let me have a look.'

Max came into the room and peered inside the cage. Nothing moved, and he stretched out his hand to turn over the little plastic houses. He moved aside the straw-like bedding on top of the sawdust to see if the hamsters were underneath. They were normal-size golden hamsters, and it shouldn't have been easy for them to hide. So they really had disappeared.

'Max, I found the cage open. Did you touch the cage door today?'

'Why would I do that?'

'I'm not saying you did. I'm just asking.'

'No, I did not touch the hamster cage. I haven't touched it at all since it's been here.'

214

Katriina thought to herself that this was the last thing she needed to deal with right now. Could it have been Edvard? But how could a dog have unlatched the cage door? And why would he even be interested? He wasn't a predator. Not like a cat.

'What if they've run away?'

Katriina looked around the room.

'Don't make a sound.'

They stood there in silence, feeling ridiculous. Katriina tried to focus on listening for the hamsters, to see if they were still in the room. It couldn't have been easy for them to escape. The door was at least fifteen centimetres above the bottom of the cage, so they would have had to climb up on something. And then they would have been forced to get down from the desk, which meant they would have fallen about a metre to the floor, maybe a little more if they hadn't had the sense to hop down via the bed.

'Can we move on to the bedroom now?' said Max.

Katriina looked at him.

'You can't be serious. We need to find the hamsters before Helen and the children come over to get them. And I'm going to Manila tomorrow. If we don't find them tonight, you'll have to solve the problem somehow.'

'Can't we just buy new ones?

'Buy new ones? Don't you think they'd notice?'

'I'm not so sure they would. Isn't Helen always

saying that the kids have hardly paid any attention to the hamsters since they got them? Besides, don't they all look alike?'

'I don't know. But you'll work it out.'

Max sighed. Katriina knew that he was looking forward to working on his book while she was away. He'd also promised to take the bus up to Österbotten to visit his mother, since he hadn't seen her since last autumn.

Katriina kissed him on the forehead.

'I'm sure you'll find a solution,' she told him.

She spent the rest of the evening packing. Max went back to his study, emerging only to use the toilet or to get something from the kitchen. Later, Katriina sat at the kitchen table working, and she couldn't help feeling a certain tenderness towards him when she saw how he went over to the sink to get himself a glass of water, completely immersed in his own thoughts as he stood there for a moment without saying a word. She knew that this was how Max was whenever he was writing a book. She could tell that he was thinking about something, and she knew it would be useless to try to engage him in conversation.

She would try to be nicer to him when she came back from Manila. Maybe they could do something together, maybe take a trip. If only he could make some progress with that book of his, she thought. Maybe then Max might show an interest in something other than himself.

CHAPTER 18

After Christmas, Russ moved into a green two-person Occupy London tent outside St Paul's Cathedral. He had a mobile phone, a laptop, a small mattress, a sleeping bag and a set of winter clothes. Eva first heard about his move when she went back to art school in the New Year. She had sent Russ home on a cheap Ryan Air flight via Riga. After that, she wandered around Helsinki for two days, getting her feet soaking wet because she had brought only party shoes with her. She tried to spend as little time as possible at home because her mother talked nonstop about how stressed she felt and how depressing it was that nobody wanted to celebrate Christmas with them. Eva had visited Helen and Christian in Esbo as well. The whole time she kept thinking about how much she longed for the anonymity of London.

She decided to go to a clinic in Helsinki. She was surprised at how easy it was to get an appointment, and how quickly everything proceeded after that. A nurse did an ultrasound and told her that she was nine weeks pregnant. Eva was given several pills to take, along with some sort of hormone solution. Soon afterwards, she began to feel sick. She had abdominal pains and started bleeding. There was something other-worldly about the entire experience, something that made her think of science-fiction films, about horror and splatter movies, even though the foetus was still only a tiny lump, and even though there wasn't yet any consciousness or individual to speak of – maybe that was exactly why she had such thoughts. Worst of all was that she felt so incredibly sorry for herself. If the father had been anyone but Malik, she might have kept the baby. But now was not a good time for her to be pregnant. She couldn't finish the art course with her stomach growing; she couldn't turn up for class with a baby getting bigger and bigger under her sweater. 'Oh, hi, Teach. This is your child.' So she chose the only option open to her.

When she'd left the clinic, she had such a sense of unreality that she had to sit down for a while in the glassed-in seating area outside Tin Tin Tango before she could return to her parents' flat. It was snowing hard outside the windows as she huddled under a blanket and drank a glass of *glögg*. The next day she left for London while her parents were both at work. She took the bus from Hesperia Park to the airport and had a glass of wine to celebrate – mourn? – her newfound freedom, having chosen not to have the baby.

One evening a few days into the New Year she

was walking along the Thames feeling lonely. On Christmas Eve she'd spent the last of her money on a takeaway from a Nepali restaurant on the corner and then watched TV all evening. Several days earlier she had gone to Harrods with Natalia to try to get into the Christmas spirit, but instead had ended up feeling depressed as she watched her flatmate buy expensive gifts for all her relatives. At a particularly low moment Eva had pictured herself jumping into the cold river – it was so hypnotic, beautiful and sad at the same time, like a painting done with thick, dark-green brush strokes.

Under all the self-pity, part of Eva actually appreciated the whole experience, even felt a certain thrill at the misery she was going through, since she knew that sometime in the future she might write it all down, memorialise it, so that it would become part of *The Story of Eva*. She saw herself as one of those modern, big-city people who might look perfectly ordinary, but – if asked – could recount a fascinating personal history.

Eva was surprised to hear that Russ had moved into a tent. She hadn't thought he was political enough to join the Occupy movement. Ben was the one who told her about Russ on the first day of class after the holidays. The morning newspapers were filled with articles about how the City authorities wanted to drive out the demonstrators because they had taken up position in an area that was in part privately owned. Eva had sat on the Tube reading about the whole thing and wondering how long the demonstrators would be able to hold out, how long they'd be willing to stand the cold, the lack of showers, listening to the jeers of the passers-by and never really managing to get anything concrete accomplished. Eventually the media would tire of reporting about Occupy London. At that point, the motivation of the participants would be put to the real test.

Eva had read about a theology student who quit the university to become an Occupy spokesperson. The radical priest Giles Fraser had declared his support for the demonstrators, saying that he 'could very well imagine Jesus being born in a tent camp like the one outside the cathedral'. In another article one of the demonstrators pointed out that the apostle Paul, for whom the cathedral was named, had been a tent maker. It actually made sense that Russ would be enticed by the movement, latching on to a specific purpose, in the same way he had apparently become attached to Eva.

'I hear he's been out there since late December. It must be freezing,' said Ben. 'We'll see how long he lasts. I mean, Russ isn't exactly the outdoors type. It can get very cold with nothing but a sleeping bag as a blanket.'

Ben was in the studio, using Adobe Illustrator to make a checked pattern. Eva had come to the college mostly because she needed company. She made herself coffee as she watched what her class-mates were doing.

Eva hadn't heard from Russ since Max's birthday party. She hadn't wanted to phone him because she needed time to think. Malik was also out of the picture for now. After the holidays the students were supposed to spend time working on their own. Eva knew that Malik and his wife had a house in northern England, and that Malik had relatives elsewhere in the world, so she assumed he'd spent Christmas in some exotic place where he wouldn't have to worry about getting wet feet. But she turned out to be wrong.

'Malik says we're supposed to meet here next week. He wants everyone to report on how their work is going,' said Laurie.

'You've talked to him?' asked Eva in surprise. She was sitting in a corner of the room.

'Uh-huh,' said Laurie, with a secretive expression that provoked a mixture of contempt and jealousy in Eva. Was Malik now sleeping with Laurie? What did that mean for Eva? Had they talked about her art, just as she and Malik – mostly Malik – had talked about the other students in the class?

'He wants us to put on a show at the end of March. We're going to have the entire ground floor of Sarah's gallery,' Laurie went on.

'You mean that feminist gallery? That's a shitty venue,' said Ben. 'There are plenty of better places in the city.'

'Really? Like where?'

Ben kept his eyes on the computer screen as he worked.

'Like . . . I don't know. But there are lots of places. That gallery is just for lesbian artists who paint pictures of their own sagging breasts.'

Winter had arrived in London, but it was a raw and damp winter that did nothing for the city's appearance. The parks were transformed into gloomy plains with naked trees and patches of frost-damaged grass. The sun refused to shine, leaving a sky that was as uninspired as the art Eva was trying to create. At night the temperature dropped below freezing.

Eva was still painting, but the composition seemed all wrong, and she was unable to capture any feeling in the light; the work lacked any sense of depth.

When the Occupy protests first began in October, many ordinary Londoners had participated at the weekends and after work, helping out by demonstrating or by contributing money and food. But after a few weeks the number of tents decreased by half, until now there were about a hundred remaining. The Occupy movement had opened up a schism within the Church. There were those who thought the movement deserved support, while others wanted the tents to be removed from the vicinity because they might present a health and safety risk. Some people also worried that the demonstrators would scare off visitors to the cathedral – an argument that Eva found especially stupid since tourists thronged the area whatever the weather.

She read in the newspaper about the long-drawn-out dispute over who actually controlled the land. The Church owned part of it, and the City of London Corporation also owned part. The original plan was to put their tents outside the London Stock Exchange, but that had proved impossible because the City of London was so in thrall to big business.

Russ didn't answer his mobile when Eva rang him. She tried in vain for two days and then decided to go over to St Paul's to find him. This was on a Wednesday, and she had no trouble locating him. He was standing in one of the communal tents, making sandwiches.

'Hi,' he said as he kept his attention focussed on his task.

'How long have you been living here?' asked Eva. She was surprised at how happy she was to see him again.

'I don't know. A few weeks.'

'So how's it going? Doesn't it get cold at night?'

Russ shrugged.

Eva had a feeling that she had hurt his pride, and that now he was putting on an indifferent front to show how unmoved he was by her presence. He was slicing tomatoes, cucumbers and salami, moving with great care, as if even the smallest details were important for the revolution to occur, as if he were preparing the ground on which the entire revolution rested. Or else he was just trying to look busy so he wouldn't need to talk.

The whole Occupy area was littered with anti-capitalism banners, pamphlets and flyers from mobile-phone companies. The wind had scattered them everywhere, spreading them all over the ground.

Inside the tent an announcement on a sheet of A4 paper promoted a capoeira course that was being organised. Eva picked up a flyer and read about: 'THE LOBBYING ACTIVITIES OF BIG BUSINESS, THE GREED OF BANKERS AND THE TOTAL ARSE-FUCKED STATE OF OUR PLANET.'

There was a steady coming and going in the tent. Most people seemed to know each other. Some gathered in small groups to talk, while others sat with computers on their laps. The whole place seemed marked by quiet activity. Eva had the general impression that everything was clean and orderly – at least more so than she'd expected. A woman came in and asked Russ if it would be okay for her to charge her mobile.

'Sure, but pull out the cord when you're done. Otherwise you'll be wasting electricity,' he told her.

Eva thought that Russ looked thinner, even though it was only a few weeks since she'd seen him. He reached out to take an apple from the pile on the long table where all the food had been set out.

'Would you like one?' he asked.

'Where does all this food come from?' she asked.

'Donations. People bring food every day. Ordinary people who want to support us and help out however they can.'

'So what are you actually doing? I mean, how do all of you spend your days?'

He sighed.

'Do you really want to know? Or are you just being polite? Because you don't need to pretend that you're interested.'

Eva felt hurt. What had she said wrong?

'Of course I'm interested. Are you busy right now, or could we go somewhere else? I'd like to get a cup of coffee.'

The bells in the cathedral tower chimed twelve thirty. Even though they were inside the tent, she could feel the January wind seeping under the sides and tugging at the canvas, but Russ didn't seem to notice. He had stopped shaving, which made him look even more gaunt, and he was wearing a corduroy jacket with a grey hoodie underneath. He wore gloves, and she could see that he had on at least three pairs of socks. There was almost a Zen-like calm about him, a self-confidence that he hadn't previously possessed.

'The thing is,' she said, 'I had an abortion.'

She caught a glimpse of something, a slight hesitation in his eyes, but it was gone so swiftly that she barely registered it was there before he began making another sandwich. He turned his head away so that she couldn't see his face. After a moment he went to the other end of the tent to get a bottle of water. Then he came back to where she was standing.

'I'm sorry, but I'm afraid I've got more work to do. The City wants to drive us out of here, as I'm sure you've heard. I have to collect 250 names on this petition before the day is over. If you want to help out, you could sign your name here,' he said, handing her a stack of papers that lay on the table nearby. He gave her a pen, and Eva signed her name.

When Eva got home she lay down on her bed and listened to Natalia walking around the flat, trying on various outfits before going out to another dinner with some of her clients from work. She'd been away between Christmas and the New Year, and Eva had hardly seen her since she'd returned. She wondered if she should tell Natalia that Russ had joined the Occupy movement. When the protests started back in October, Natalia had reacted strongly. She thought the demonstrators were directing their energy at the wrong people, and she seemed to feel an endless need to defend her own choice of career.

'I never planned to work for the Stock Exchange. But I needed to find a job, and this is London! It's expensive to live here. And it's not like it's my fault that the world is the way it is. I'm just doing my job.' That's what she'd said one day when she came home from work after being stopped by a demonstrator who wanted to give her a hug. Apparently it was common for demonstrators to use that particular tactic. Instead of shouting jeers, they tried to humiliate bankers by showing them love. Natalia had reluctantly submitted to being hugged, as if to display her open-mindedness, even though the guy 'hadn't taken a shower in at least three weeks'.

Now Eva heard Natalia knock on her door.

'Yeah?' said Eva without getting up. It occurred to her that this was exactly the same scene that took place whenever she was at home in Helsinki, except it would be her mother standing outside the door instead of Natalia.

'Just wanted to know if I could borrow some lipstick. I can't find any the right shade.'

'Sure, that's fine,' said Eva, swallowing a lump in her throat.

Natalia opened the door and came in. She was wearing a dress and trailed a cloud of perfume. She was tall, beautiful, happy. Eva thought she was probably the least neurotic person she'd ever met. Natalia seemed supremely comfortable in her own skin, as if every day she acknowledged with gratitude the pleasure that her body gave her.

Eva had tried to explain to Natalia that the Occupy protests were primarily of symbolic significance. Even though political decisions were required

227

to regulate the markets, it was the people who worked at the Stock Exchange who were the face of capitalism.

'But they're talking about the one per cent,' Natalia had replied. 'And that's not us! We don't earn especially high salaries. If I did, I'd buy my own flat and I wouldn't need to have a flatmate – no offence intended. The wealthiest people don't work in some office in the City. They probably don't work at all.'

Eva had told Natalia she was right about that, and later they both agreed that the protests would undoubtedly fade away, since the demonstrators didn't seem to have a list of realistic demands. Eva still had no idea what Natalia actually did at the London Stock Exchange, but she seemed to go out a lot with people she called her 'clients'. Right now she was again all dressed up to step into that world.

'Eva, is something wrong?'

'No. What do you mean?'

Eva shouldn't have been surprised by the question. Her hair felt lank – when had she last washed it? – and she was lying on the bed, wearing her dressing gown and staring at the ceiling. Her room was a mess.

'I wasn't going to say anything, but you spent Christmas here alone instead of going to be with your family. And when I got back, you hadn't taken out the rubbish and the fridge was completely empty. When we went to Harrods you seemed depressed. After the holidays, all I found in the kitchen were four empty wine bottles.'

Eva wanted to say something, she wanted to explain how hard it was to work out what she should be doing – how impossible it was when all her life she'd heard her parents say that she needed to accomplish something, but she'd never understood why. And how insecure she felt about what she was doing. How depressed she felt about life.

She tried to look as lively as she could. 'I'm just a little stressed out right now. I've got a lot of work on at college.'

'But you're not doing anything.'

'How do you know that?'

'We live in the same flat, so of course I know what you're doing. I've seen you lying in bed all day. And I know it's none of my business, but you really should eat something besides pistachios.'

Eva sighed. She would have preferred to sleep the whole month away, but there was something about Natalia's puppy-like loyalty that made Eva feel she needed to reply.

'So what do you think I should do?' she asked.

Natalia tilted her charming head to one side.

'Come with me.'

'What? Where?'

'Come to dinner with me. Wash your hair and put on something nice. I'm going to a cocktail party, and there'll be lots of people, including some cute single guys. It would do you good.'

'You want me to go to a party with a bunch of bankers? No, thanks.'

'Oh, come on. There'll be all sorts of people. Fun people. Not everyone who works for the Stock Exchange is stupid, you know. On the contrary.'

So Eva agreed to go. She let Natalia choose what she should wear, pay for the cab ride and introduce her to lots of people whose names she would never remember. As Eva moved through the crowd at the party – it was held in an enormous flat – she thought she recognised a few people from TV. And after a few glasses of the drink that was served from a big punch bowl in the middle of the main room, she slowly started to feel life returning. Just past eleven o'clock, she was invited to have some cocaine in the kitchen, and she decided she might as well say yes. After that, she talked to an interesting American man about the Occupy movement, listening to herself spout opinions that she didn't even know she had. ('England may be a class society, but at least we dare to talk about it, as opposed to you in the US'; 'I don't think I'll ever have any children. Don't you agree that it's irresponsible for people to have children?')

She had a wonderful feeling in her body. At times it seemed like the rush was better than anything else – to be totally 'in character' and focussed, to be the person that everyone expected her to be, sociable and extroverted, an individual with an interesting perspective on life. It was so easy in this state.

When it was almost one in the morning, Natalia wanted to go home, but Eva didn't. Not now, when she was finally enjoying herself. She couldn't bear the thought of going back to their flat; she wanted to keep partying, and it didn't matter where. But Natalia said she had to work the next day. So when several people in the kitchen suggested going to a nightclub around the corner, Eva chose to join them instead of taking the cab home with Natalia.

Two hours later she was sitting at the bar in the forgiving dim lighting of the nightclub, just before closing time. She was glad that she didn't need to think about anything. All she had to do was listen to a long story that culminated in a description of the amazing consistency of the snow in the mountains of Japan – one of the Australians who was into extreme sports was telling the story. A few minutes later, Eva found herself moving closer to the guy until she was practically leaning against him, wanting nothing more than to feel his beard against her cheek.

When she woke the next morning, she looked out of the beautifully glazed window of the balcony to see the sun shining for the first time in three weeks, an utterly horrible sunlight. And she realised that she'd ended up on the other side of town. It would probably take her more than an hour on the Tube to get home. She'd had too much to drink, and they'd taken a cab to his flat. She remembered teasing him about the snowboarding posters on the walls. She still felt drunk, and she broke into a cold sweat as she stared at the posters. Why had she behaved so badly?

She got out of bed and turned to look at the man lying there. He was still asleep. What was his name? Brandon? Brendon? Something with 'r'? And now she saw what he looked like in daylight: hairy, and shorter than she remembered. He was snoring loudly – the sound of a guy who had brought home plenty of women in his life and had learned that it never paid to be the first one to wake up. Eva looked for her clothes and found everything except her knickers. They were in the bathroom. She recalled with nervous gratitude that Brandon/Brendon had fumbled with a condom during the night. She wondered if she ought to leave him a note. But what good would that do? What would she write?

On her way home on the Tube, she thought about Russ.

CHAPTER 19

Max was a realist when it came to infidelity. He had no illusions that there was some other woman out there who would make him happier. In fact, this was a thought that often occurred to him when he met women. He would think to himself: that laugh would be annoying after a while; that particular facial feature is something I couldn't stand for very long; or, it would be awful to have to look at that chin every day.

From a purely neurological point of view, it was said that the sensation of falling in love had a life span of twelve months. Brain scans of people at various stages of love showed wildly varying results. A person who has newly fallen in love displays increased levels of dopamine and lower levels of serotonin. Genuine affection – which occurs after a couple has been together for a longer period of time – is associated with oxytocin in women and vasopressin in men.

The percentage of dopamine in people who have fallen in love is comparable to the level produced by drugs such as cocaine. Love is also similar to drugs in the sense that the user continues to crave stronger doses, until finally the need can no longer be satisfied. One year of fire is followed by thirty years of ashes, as someone once said. But in reality, wasn't one year plenty? And well worth it?

Max had begun to understand why some people took up extreme sports. They could get the adrenaline rush they wanted and still be a good and virtuous person. It was so strange, when he thought about it. Risking your life by jumping off a cliff was considered acceptable within the realm of social conventions. Yet falling for a woman who was not your wife was deemed a cardinal sin. But loyalty was one of those things that was deeply ingrained in human DNA.

He had agreed to show his manuscript to Laura Lampela, even though he wasn't sure it would do any good. She sent him an email the very next day and invited him to come over to her flat to discuss the text. Max was surprised that she didn't suggest a more neutral meeting place, but he offered no objections. Instead, during the two days before their meeting, he played better tennis than he had in years.

Without mentioning it to Katriina, he had already sent Laura a big section of his manuscript: about three hundred pages from the beginning of the book, recounting Westermarck's first visits to England. There he'd made contact with many of the intellectuals in London, including the Couplands – who were Goethe scholars – and twenty-year-old James

Sully, who moved in the same circles as Darwin, Huxley, Robert Louis Stevenson and George Eliot. During that same year the World Exposition was held in Paris. At the age of thirty, Westermarck found himself in the centre of all the major cultural events of the day. It must have been the very pinnacle of intellectual interaction, and yet England was also a dirty, grey and gloomy place. How was Max going to describe all of that? How could he make his readers fully appreciate that era?

'I hope you like steamed mussels,' Laura said as she opened the door.

'Hey,' said Max. 'Are you planning to offer me dinner?'

'Sure, if you're hungry.'

She was dressed up more than was usual for a casual first meeting to discuss work. Max was glad that he'd worn a blazer.

'Is that saffron in the sauce you're making?' he asked. He had noticed the honeyed and spiced aroma as soon as he entered the stairwell.

'A little saffron, a little white wine, some shallots and parsley. It's a recipe I learned from my mother,' she told him.

He paused in the doorway to Laura's tiny kitchen – it was more of a kitchenette – and wondered whether he ought to sit down.

'Do you like garlic?' she asked.

'Who doesn't?' replied Max, looking around the

room as he discreetly rubbed his calves with his feet. His muscles ached from all the tennis games he'd been playing. Laura's place was a cramped flat in the Rödbergen neighbourhood, dimly lit and slightly dreary, with walls that had been carelessly painted. Max hadn't expected her flat to be so unattractive, considering her age. This was more like a student's lodging than a flat where a woman would invite men to visit.

A mobile lying on the table began to ring. Laura didn't seem to hear it as she continued to cook.

'Your phone is ringing.'

She looked up in surprise.

Max nodded at the mobile. Laura put down the ladle she was holding and came over to look at the display to see who was calling. Then she switched off the phone.

'Okay, now we won't be disturbed.'

Laura was wearing a white blouse that was so sheer it was almost transparent, and Max could see the white bra she had on underneath. She had pinned up her hair, loosely, using some sort of clip, and it looked as if it might come undone at any second. And she wore red lipstick. It was all a bit too much. Did she always dress up like this when she cooked on Friday evening?

Max knew there was something in the social contract that prevented him from asking. He had been invited here on her terms, so he was not allowed to make any demands. All he could do was follow Laura's lead and try to interpret her

236

signals. Right now she was signalling self-confidence and sensuality, as if she was in charge, and she seemed to relish that role.

'So, have you had time to read any of my text?'

'Of course I have. But maybe we should have dinner first. I didn't know if you'd be hungry, but I made enough for the two of us. I've printed out your manuscript and made a few notes. We can discuss them later.'

'Whatever you like.'

She didn't seem to be in any rush to get to the text. Does that mean she thinks it's good or bad? Max wondered. Maybe she was offering him dinner in order to lighten the shock when she later tore his work apart with her criticisms. He went into the small living room that also served as a bedroom. It was clean and tidy, but equally simple and minimalist in appearance, as if Laura had neither the budget nor the space to acquire anything that might make the place more pleasant. Or as if she were on the verge of moving away at any moment.

'So what's your wife doing tonight?' asked Laura from the kitchen.

'She left for the Philippines yesterday.'

'Oh. Will she be there long?'

'Two weeks.'

Two weeks, thought Max. Two weeks that he could spend working with Laura every day. Two weeks that he could use to get closer to her. Provided that was something she wanted. Was it such an unreasonable idea?

'All right then. Dinner is ready,' said Laura, inviting him to sit at the kitchen table.

There was a brief, awkward moment later in the evening when Laura went to the bathroom and Max was left sitting at the table. He wasn't sure whether he should make a motion to leave or not – had he already stayed too long? She hadn't said anything to give him a clue as to what might happen next, and she hadn't said a single word about his manuscript. They'd talked about other things instead. And he had enjoyed himself; he found it easy to talk to Laura.

When she came back to the kitchen, she turned on the lamp in the corner and suggested that they sit on her bed since she didn't have a sofa. A TV and coffee table stood in front of the bed.

Max noticed that she had touched up her lipstick.

'So,' he said, raising one eyebrow.

'So,' she replied and smiled, showing her dimples. 'I've never done this before. Shall we get to work?'

Neither of them spoke for several seconds. Max was trying to think of something sensible to say, but his cheeks were bright red – probably because of the wine. He felt like a fumbling seventeen-year-old. And he couldn't for the life of him remember what his manuscript was about. Had he actually written something?

'I . . . er . . . I mean . . . all those pages I sent you, well, that's not the final draft, but I thought it might give you some idea of where I'm going with the book . . .'

'Yes, it did,' Laura said. 'Very impressive. I think what you've written is really good, particularly about Westermarck's personality, if you know what I mean. He seems nice. Spoiled and clever and perhaps a bit boring, but nice. I especially liked the part about how he was forced to give up his piano lessons because of all the croquet games he'd been playing.'

Max tried not to show how relieved he felt.

'It's funny you should mention that, because I thought that was amusing too. These days mothers worry about their sons playing too many computer games. But in Helsinki in the late nineteenth century, they were afraid their boys would get addicted to playing croquet.'

She laughed and touched his arm. Max didn't know what to do with his hands.

Laura had placed the manuscript on the coffee table. He looked at the words he'd written and suddenly they didn't look as shabby as he'd thought they were. All those sentences that he'd agonised over for so long now seemed to have come alive.

'That's really nice to hear, Laura.'

Without thinking about it he'd said her name, but now it hovered in the air, as if laden with significance.

'To be honest, I don't know why you would need my help. This is essentially a finished book. It might need to be tightened up a bit, but otherwise

I think it's fine the way it is. It's not supposed to be a scholarly treatise, is it?'

'Not at all. That's not my intention. But I've just . . . I don't know. I've been working on it so long, and I know that Westermarck is a major figure, a real giant – and how do you write about someone like that? How do you do him justice?'

Laura ran her fingers through her hair. She leaned forward so that her necklace hung over the manuscript pages like a pendulum.

'I've made a few notes that might interest you. Not a lot, but they may be of some help. Shall we have a look?'

Max nodded with a contradictory feeling of relief and indifference. Now that she had given his book her blessing, he didn't think he needed any more help. He would have much preferred to kiss her.

Two hours later, Max strolled home along Manner-heimvägen. The street was deserted, and the wind blew the snow across the black asphalt; the snow piled up in small drifts against the lamp posts and traffic markers. The whole area looked like a tundra landscape.

He had decided against getting a cab, since he felt the need to walk and sort out his thoughts. He slipped and slid. He wrapped his coat tighter and hunched his shoulders, feeling the cold shoot like rays straight across his scalp, since he wasn't wearing a cap. He hadn't thought he'd need one when he left home to go to Laura's place.

The weather had a sobering effect on him. His teeth were chattering, so he clenched his jaws and thought about making a decision, although he didn't know what that entailed. The more he tried to formulate it, the faster it slipped away. Maybe he didn't want to formulate it. He could have been twenty, or even nineteen. Seventeen. Not sixty. Once again he had that feeling, that obstinacy in his mind, an attempt to steel his consciousness, partly because he wanted to think about her – yes, he did want to think about Laura – but also because he was freezing, and it was easier to withstand the cold if he kept his thoughts focussed the way a marathon runner did as he approached the finish line, doing his best to fix his gaze several hundred metres ahead.

Off in the distance he could see the Opera House and the huge crossroads where the wind was blowing from all directions. A taxi drove by, a tram screeched past. All he had to do was turn left and he'd soon be home, so now he was able to direct his attention to one topic: Laura.

What did it mean? Where would this lead? He tried not to let his thoughts wander too far ahead, since that would soften his brain and then he'd again start to freeze; then he'd become aware of the raging winter weather all around him. Finally, he blotted out all other thoughts and focussed solely on her image, the way she looked. He pictured her breasts, her bum, her lovely bum. And with that picture in his mind – her bum, now bare – he trudged through the tundra-like Helsinki night until he came to the door of his building and stepped inside the stairwell. It was quiet in the flat. Katriina was far away, and Edvard was asleep. He took off his blazer, went into the kitchen and drank a glass of water. Then he went to the bedroom and sank on to the edge of the bed to take off his socks. The heat in the room burned on his icy hands and on his cheeks. Then he crawled under the covers, stretching out to take up nearly the whole mattress, and felt asleep, with Laura's naked bum still in his thoughts. During the night he dreamt of Edvard Westermarck and Marrakesh. But this time, Laura was there.

CHAPTER 20

Katriina landed in Manila on Tuesday. A hazy light had settled over the afternoon, and she felt groggy from jetlag and the little bottle of wine that she'd had on the plane flying between Hong Kong and Ninoy Aquino Airport. She'd been wearing the same clothes for almost forty-eight hours, so the only thought in her mind was to take a shower and get a few hours of sleep. In the arrivals hall a chauffeur welcomed her and then escorted her to the car, where she was greeted by a man who had apparently been assigned to show her to the university's guest quarters. He spoke elegant English but with a heavy accent.

Katriina was sweating. She felt huge, as if she were a head taller than everyone else, and she wished that she'd worn a different pair of shoes instead of the high heels she had on. The flight had taken twenty-two hours, with two stopovers, first in Amsterdam and then in Hong Kong. She thought about going to the closest shop to buy a pair of flats as soon as possible, maybe even right after unpacking and taking a shower.

The drive from the airport seemed to last for ever. When they got closer to what looked like the centre of town, the car had to stop at every traffic light. Katriina looked out of the window, but was too tired to take in much of what she saw. It was hot and humid, and she could smell food and exhaust fumes. She felt as if she were sitting inside a space capsule, an alien vessel, separated from the reality outside.

Finally, the car pulled up outside an enormous walled property with a beautiful, black-painted iron gate that opened on to a garden with sprinklers and a nicely kept lawn. They continued on towards a rectangular concrete building that had to be the place where she was going to stay. The man who was her guide got out and opened the door for her.

'Mrs Paul, we hope that you will be pleased with your room. We have put you in one of the university buildings. That is where our visiting professors stay.'

'Thank you. I'm sure it will be splendid,' replied Katriina.

A long narrow corridor with terracotta floor tiles led to a staircase. They made their way up to a hallway on the top level that was lined with a number of doors. The man went over to the third one, took out a key and unlocked the door. Then he waited for Katriina to enter first.

There was a bed, a TV, a small desk and a toilet with a shower. It looked much like every other room of its type she'd stayed in before.

'If you need to use the Internet, we have WiFi here. You'll find the password on the desk. Are you hungry?'

'No, I think I'll just rest for a while.'

'Okay. I need to get back to work. Our driver will come to pick you up in three hours. We're going to have dinner with the head of the university and one of the personnel managers at the university hospital. I'll leave you to rest now. I hope you will be comfortable here.'

The man left the door open as he left. Katriina closed it and then went over to look out of the window. The courtyard was deserted, but she was overwhelmed by a floral scent – there must have been thousands of flowers. Then she sat down on the bed. The sheets were newly pressed and felt a bit scratchy. She took off her shoes and stretched out on the bed, feeling cool relief in her feet, though she didn't dare look at them. She was sure she must have blisters. Should she sleep for a while? She'd never been good at taking short naps; she was too restless for that.

The tropical air pressed against her temples even though the room was apparently air-conditioned. She had to visit at least five different hospitals and three schools, but she was glad to be travelling alone. She wouldn't have to maintain a certain image of who she was. She lay on the bed, listening to her own breathing amid the silence in the room. The sun and the heat rested on her eyelids, and she relaxed. The red colour that she now saw led her far away, back to her childhood, to her room on Högbergsgatan one morning at the start of the summer holidays. Her mother was at home, and Katriina was ten years old, lying on her bed and trying to hold on to the dream she was having when she heard her mother talking to someone in the hall.

The memory lasted only a second, maybe two or three seconds, before the scent of the flowers erased the scene and reminded her that she was on a business trip.

After dinner that evening she had no energy left for anything else. She got undressed and crept naked under the clean white sheets, trying to picture how the week might proceed. She awoke around five in the morning and spent the early hours walking around the area. There was a park nearby, and there she sat for a while, watching the Filipina mothers with their children and the ageing retirees going through their exercises.

Katriina's chauffeur was in the courtyard waiting for her when she came out of the building. The official work day started with a sumptuous lunch. The main course was lobsters, which sat on the serving platters, waving their antennae as everyone dug in. It must be some sort of reflex motion, thought Katriina. She listened with interest to a discussion led by a female researcher from the university hospital. The topic was the effect that the export of workers was having on the Philippines, and how this had led to a shortage of doctors, since even physicians were leaving the country to work abroad as nurses.

'There are two sides to this issue,' the woman said. 'On the one hand, young people gain new opportunities for their lives, and they may return home to improve the medical practices in our country. On the other hand, many of these young women are much too optimistic. They may leave behind their families and children for an uncertain life abroad. They send money home, but they can't afford to come back for a visit. There are a lot of children growing up here who are being cared for by their grandparents.'

The woman's name was Maria. She was petite and serious and regarded Katriina with suspicion, which was evidently due to her scepticism about Western nations importing Filipino workers. When she revealed more about her personal story, it turned out that she was not only a doctor but had once been a political prisoner. She had served time for offering medical treatment to suspected terrorists and rebels. Katriina was surprised by what she heard. In her experience, people in Asian countries generally didn't discuss anything that might be considered political.

That afternoon they were scheduled to visit one of the hospitals. They drove for almost an hour. The traffic was horrendous, with cars honking nonstop, and the humid air was heavy with exhaust fumes. People of all ages swarmed around them and crowded the streets. They drove through a shanty-town district where Katriina saw people praying, groups of kids running around and people riding bicycles loaded down with sacks and rubbish.

At last the car stopped outside a big building surrounded by a wall. When they went inside the hospital Katriina felt everyone's eyes fixed on her. She was probably the only white person in the whole place, and the patients, in particular, stared at her as she walked along the corridors.

It was a run-down hospital. Katriina glanced into one of the rooms and saw what looked like a coconut being used to hold an IV container. Nurses were everywhere. In some of the rooms people were praying, and the whole place was hot and damp with a strong hospital smell from cleaning agents and medicines, disease and bodily fluids.

They stayed for two hours, getting to know the staff and some of the patients. As usual, little time was spent on the real reason for their visit. Instead, they talked in general terms about the differences between Europe and the Philippines, about the disparities in standards and practices, and about training and procedures. It was frustrating, since Katriina knew that her primary goal was to establish contact with the recruiting offices and educational institutes that attracted interested nurses. But she also realised that some of the work would have to be done from Finland, after she returned home.

For now it was enough for her to meet as many people as possible, hoping that they would remember her later.

When the visit was over, she was driven back to where she was staying. In the evening she decided to take a walk. Waiting outside the iron gate was Danilo, the chauffeur who had driven her around all day. He was shorter than Katriina, a man in his forties with a somewhat boyish appearance, which made her constantly aware of how she spoke to him, enunciating her words slowly and carefully, as if he might have a hard time understanding.

As soon as he saw her, he rushed over to the car and opened the door.

'No, no, I'm just going for a walk. You don't need to drive me anywhere,' she told him. She stood there on the pavement, wearing a blue dress that felt so cool after spending all day in the car and inside the sweltering hospital.

Danilo closed the car door. They conversed in English. He had a decent command of the language, speaking in short, somewhat staccato sentences.

'Mrs Paul, I can drive you if you are going out . . .'

'No, no, that's not necessary. I'm just taking a walk in the neighbourhood. Are you here every day?'

'Not every day, Mrs Paul. Sometimes I drive other people. But they told me that I should be ready. If you want to go somewhere.'

'But surely you're not expected to sit and wait

for me all day? Didn't they give you a schedule of my meetings?'

'I am sorry. All I know is that I must drive you if you need to go somewhere.'

'I'm the one who should apologise. I'm not planning to go anywhere else tonight. So you don't have to drive me. And if there's somewhere else you need to be, please feel free to leave.'

Danilo looked at her for a moment, as if he were pondering whether to believe her or not. Then he thanked her, got in the car and drove away.

He was her chauffeur for the rest of the week. After a while Katriina had the feeling that he was the only person with whom she had any real contact, the only one with whom she'd reached beyond the chit-chat stage, even though he was not especially talkative and gave only terse replies to her questions. She found out that Danilo lived on the outskirts of town, that he was married and had one child, and that he'd been a chauffeur for five years. Before that he'd worked in the restaurant business, but he preferred driving – or maybe he was simply stating the fact that driving was now his job. Katriina didn't always understand his English. He drove her to the hospitals, to dinners, to the university. Every evening she would go straight to her room and to bed because she was so worn out from the strain of maintaining the courteous facade that was required during all the meetings with strangers.

★　　★　　★

On Friday when Katriina came out into the court-yard, she found Danilo standing next to the car. He was having a smoke, his eyes fixed on the ground. When he saw her, he quickly tossed the cigarette away and opened the door. She hadn't asked him again why he never went home in the evenings. It didn't seem right to question him. Maybe he was paid an hourly wage to stand out here all day, waiting for her.

Today she was attending yet another luncheon. One course after another was brought to the table; the amount of food seemed endless. Katriina drank only water with the meal, and she did her best to discuss in concrete terms the work required in the months ahead. Everyone at the table seemed in high spirits, a mood that she recognised from business dinners back in Finland. No one really wanted to talk about work; they just wanted to enjoy the food and drinks, since somebody else was paying for them. The guests included people from the local unions and the university, as well as government officials. Katriina had the sense that she was treading water. How was she supposed to get anything done if she couldn't get these people to discuss details? She was still feeling jetlagged, or maybe she was coming down with a cold. She was having a hard time breathing, and she found herself picturing what would happen if she suddenly fainted. When the meal was finally over and Katriina was once again seated in the car, Danilo asked if he should drive her home.

It was dusk, with an amazing sky filled with clouds gathering in the most astonishing shapes.

'Would it be possible to drive around a bit to see some more of Manila? A little detour? It doesn't have to take very long. I'm sure you want to be getting home to your family.'

'There is no hurry, Mrs Paul.'

'Is there some area that's not so touristy? Someplace you'd personally go if you weren't working?'

Danilo paused to think about this. Katriina was just about to say that she'd changed her mind and they could drive straight back when he started up the car.

'It is a bit of a drive. But I think I have an idea what you mean,' he said.

'Thanks,' said Katriina, leaning back. It didn't really matter where they drove. She just didn't want to return to her lonely room. She realised that she missed Max, but it was too expensive to ring him, and besides, she had no idea what time it was in Finland.

They drove for ten minutes, maybe fifteen. First through the city's wide streets with all the neon lights, then on the motorway, until finally the traffic thinned out, and they were driving along the coastline with a good view of the sea. The water was a gleaming deep blue and purple. The night got darker as they drove, and Katriina had no idea in what direction they were headed, but she decided to simply sit back and enjoy the drive.

After half an hour they reached an area that looked like one of the shantytowns they had previously driven past, although here she saw more signs of an infrastructure: a few shops open for the evening, people gathered on the street corners, music coming from car windows. A town. They kept driving, entering a neighbourhood with very narrow streets. Danilo didn't say a word, and Katriina began to feel slightly uncomfortable. This wasn't exactly what she'd had in mind, not this sort of complete isolation, this unfamiliar district in the middle of nowhere. She'd pictured a brief detour before returning to the building where she was staying. There were hardly even any streetlights here.

Danilo stopped the car and turned off the engine. Katriina didn't say anything.

'This is my neighbourhood, Mrs Paul. I grew up here. And I still live nearby. My sister has a restaurant here. If you like, we could go in and have a look. So you could see how the local people live.'

The restaurant didn't resemble any place that Katriina had ever visited, but she felt as if she'd seen it in pictures, maybe in a travel brochure, or in a dream. It was small but packed with people of all ages: women in tight dresses, older men having a drink and young men who were already well on their way to becoming just like them. A waitress wound her way between the tables, and customers shouted their orders. The place smelled of beer, food, sweat and cigarettes. In one corner a small band was playing some kind of salsa music. People turned to look at Danilo and Katriina when they came in.

Danilo went over to the bar and shook hands with the bartender. They exchanged a few words, and he nodded in Katriina's direction. After a moment he came back with two beers, telling her 'this is on the house'. He seemed happier than when he was driving, more self-confident, at home in his own daily milieu.

They sat at a table for a while without saying anything. Danilo looked around the room before fixing his eyes on two big-busted women wearing neon-coloured tops. They were standing near the jukebox in a corner of the room, watching the band. Danilo noticed that Katriina saw what he was looking at, but that didn't seem to faze him. Unperturbed, he continued to stare at the women.

'So this is your sister's place?'

'Yes,' he said. 'She is in the kitchen. Working. She might come out in a little while.'

They each drank a beer as they waited for the food Danilo had ordered.

'Do you have a lot of brothers and sisters?'

'Five.'

He leaned across the table so she could hear him above all the noise.

A woman who had to be Danilo's sister came over and set plates of food in front of them. She looked like her brother and was about the same height, but twice as wide. She also had childish features but her face was round, which made her look older. She was probably Helen's age, in her thirties, or maybe closer to forty. Katriina ate some of the chicken, which tasted strongly of garlic, and the soup that was flavoured with ginger. She was already very full. Danilo ate as if he hadn't had a meal in a very long time. When he saw that she didn't intend to finish her chicken, he ate that too. After he was done, he excused himself and went out to the kitchen.

Katriina looked around the room. No one seemed to be paying much attention to her. The young women over in the corner were dancing, and two men at the bar had turned their chairs around and were trying to get their attention. There was a hot and sweaty atmosphere, voices came from all directions in a rising and falling cacophony.

When Danilo finally emerged from the back room, Katriina could hear him yelling, his words terse and staccato, exactly the way he normally talked, but angrier. Without understanding what he said, she could tell that he was shouting insults at the kitchen. He slammed his fist on the bar as he walked past. Then he turned around and yelled something else.

'I am going to drive you home now, Mrs Paul. Now you have seen a little of the real Manila,' he said, sounding almost aggressive.

Katriina nodded, and they went back to the car. It had started to drizzle. As they drove away from the area, she realised she would have to make a real effort to stay awake on the way home.

They left the town behind, and the whole time Danilo kept his eyes fixed on the road, without saying a word. All Katriina wanted now was to get back to her room. She longed for the white sheets on her bed, wanting nothing more than to rest after the heavy meal and the loud music.

They were approaching the sea. Danilo was driving fast. Katriina didn't dare lean forward to look at the speedometer, but she guessed they must be going over 120 kilometres per hour.

It was just as they came over a small hill, in a curve with poor visibility, that she felt the thud. Not enough to stop the car, but strong enough to make Danilo react. A few seconds later he stomped on the brake and slowed down until they came to a halt. He turned off the engine.

A heavy silence settled over them.

'What was that?'

Danilo didn't answer as he opened the car door and looked back. The only thing Katriina could see in front of them was the small section of road illuminated by the car's headlamps. On one side was the sea, on the other a darkness that could be a forest or a field; it was impossible to tell. Danilo didn't speak as he turned the key in the ignition. The engine coughed, then reluctantly started up again, and he backed up a few metres.

'What do you think that was? An animal?' asked Katriina.

'I do not know, Mrs Paul. We hit something.'

He backed up further. Twenty, fifty metres, and then parked the car on the verge.

'I am just going to see what it was. Will you wait here?'

Katriina was now feeling nervous. Wait in the car? She didn't want to do that. She was in the middle of nowhere in a foreign metropolis, and she didn't know a soul. It was dark and anybody might drive past.

'I'd rather come with you. Is that all right?'

'Okay,' he said. She got out of the car and followed him through the beams of the headlamps, which lit up the rain.

Katriina thought about how she'd tell this story to Tuula once she got home. ('And then we ended up in the middle of nowhere, and I mean really nowhere, and he could have been a rapist or a psychopath . . .') But her thoughts were interrupted when she saw Danilo stop. He was looking down at the ground as he lit a cigarette.

'What is it?' she asked.

When she came up beside him, she saw what it was. They had run over a dog, medium-sized, with grey fur, or at least it looked grey in the dark. The body looked intact, but the snout had been crushed. The animal had been tossed into the air, and it was now lying on the other side of the road. Its tongue, ear and nose were covered in blood. A dead heap of flesh and fur.

'What bad luck,' said Katriina, and Danilo

glanced up at her. 'But it must have happened fast, don't you think? I wonder if he belongs to anyone.'

Danilo shook his head and continued to smoke his cigarette.

They stood there for a moment, and Katriina thought about something she'd read regarding the functioning of consciousness. If you turned off the light so there was only darkness and silence, the brain still worked just as much as it did in daylight. The consciousness was always active, even in complete darkness. The closest you could come to extinguishing consciousness was by administering anaesthesia. That was a state resembling death.

'I have a dog,' Katriina said now. The whole situation seemed so absurd, and she decided the only natural thing to do was to start up a light conversation.

'Dogs are stupid animals,' replied Danilo. 'Run right into the road. Trust everybody.'

Katriina felt a vague uneasiness, a slight nausea. The food she'd eaten was making her queasy. It occurred to her that no one knew where she was. She hadn't spoken to anyone in her family all week. It seemed unreal that only a few days ago she'd been in wintry Finland. She leaned down and took off her shoes because her feet were aching. The asphalt was still warm, but little streams of water were running along the road towards the culvert.

'Should we move it somewhere else?' she asked.

'Not much we can do,' he replied.

The dog didn't seem as repulsive when she looked at it now. She had a sudden urge to bend down to get a closer look. She knelt down and ran her hand over the animal's damp abdomen. It was still warm. She felt a slight movement, as if the dog was breathing.

'I think it's alive,' she said. A shudder passed through her body.

Danilo leaned down to touch the dog.

'What should we do?' asked Katriina, looking at the chauffeur.

When they were back in the car, neither of them spoke. Danilo pulled on to the road, and Katriina thought for a moment that he was driving back to the city, but all of a sudden he made a big U-turn, accelerated, and aimed straight for the dog's head. Katriina screamed, but Danilo said nothing.

Half an hour later he dropped her off outside the gate to the building where she was staying.

'It's awfully late,' she said.

'Yes. Sleep well, Mrs Paul. I am driving home to my son now.'

'How old is your son?' she asked.

'Five.'

'So he must have gone to bed long ago.'

'No. He is waiting for me. His mother works at the restaurant at night.'

'Your son is at home alone?'

'Yes.'

She thought of saying something, but he seemed to have read her mind.

'He is fine. He is often alone when we are working.'

She tried to find something to say to conclude the conversation. 'I have two grandchildren. Amanda is amazing. I miss her. I wish I could spend more time with my grandchildren. I also have a grandson named Lukas. Someday I'll take them travelling with me. Maybe even come here to the Philippines.'

'That sounds good, Mrs Paul. Good night.'

CHAPTER 21

On the day after his dinner with Laura, Max bought himself a new shirt and jacket, played tennis and then phoned Stefan to ask him about the breathing techniques he'd mentioned during the dinner party at the Keskinens' place before Christmas. Max was feeling very anxious. What if he took this leap with Laura? And what if he made a fool of himself? What if he failed to measure up to the demands of the day? He felt like a rusty old car, the kind that people drove only for nostalgic reasons, or because they hadn't noticed that these days there were significantly more beautiful, more streamlined and less fussy vehicles on the market.

'I'm so happy you rang,' said Stefan in his gentle, almost feminine voice, which made Max regret having made the call.

Max didn't know whether he could manage being with a younger woman from a purely physical perspective. The mere thought was somehow paralysing. What if the sheer stress of it all made him impotent? He might not even have a chance, but he imagined pleasures that were greater than the intellectual triumphs he'd experienced in his career, which, if he were completely honest, had occurred much less frequently in the past few years.

'I promise that Katriina will thank you afterwards. Come over and I'll take you through the basic exercises. Then you can practise on your own at home.'

'Okay. But, Stefan, would you mind not saying anything to Katriina about this? I don't want her to know.'

'Ah, so you want to surprise her in bed? Great.'

'Well, something like that. How long do you think it takes . . . I mean, to master it?'

'That's impossible to say. Two weeks, two months. It all depends on you and your attitude. It's ultimately more of a mental thing than physical. It has to do with learning to control your blood flow, relaxing, getting your sexual energy and aura moving.'

'Is it hard to do?'

'No, not at all. That's the whole point. It's supposed to be easy.'

Max took the bus out to Kottby, where Stefan and Gun-Maj lived. Fortunately, Gun-Maj wasn't at home. Max took off his jacket in the front hall and hung it on a hook that looked as if it was a souvenir from Africa. He couldn't really tell whether it was meant to be a clothes hook or a decoration, but Stefan didn't protest.

'Are you planning to do yoga in those clothes?' he asked as they went into the kitchen.

'Did I wear the wrong thing?'

Max had on a shirt and a pair of brown corduroy trousers. He now realised his attire might not be the best yoga outfit.

'No worries. I've got clothes you can borrow.'

Max saw no option but to accept the offer. This was not a moment for vanity. Stefan told him to wait while he went to get the clothes.

'Would you like some tea? Just put on the kettle,' he shouted from the bedroom as Max sat in the kitchen, looking around. The room was filled with plants, but was otherwise surprisingly minimalist. Max had expected a hippie-style flat filled with Indian ornaments. Instead, it was quite plain, with white-painted walls and lamps that emitted a kind of fluorescent light. Max was cold. The temperature had dropped during the week.

Stefan came back to the kitchen with the clothing. 'This should do. You can change in the bathroom.'

He handed the clothes to Max and showed him the way.

In the bathroom, Max was confronted with a full-length mirror and a wash-basin made of dark imitation wood. He took off his trousers and shirt and draped them neatly over the edge of the tub.

What the hell are you doing? he thought as he looked at himself in the mirror. Max had generally been satisfied with his body, but now he saw it the way a thirty-year-old woman might see it: the drooping stomach, the baggy underpants that hid his hairy groin and shrunken penis. His chest sagged, and his body was slightly pear-shaped, especially when viewed from the side. He stood in front of the mirror and tensed his arm muscles as he sucked in his stomach, which instantly made him look stronger and more fit. He wished he'd done something about his belly when he was in his thirties, or even in his forties, but now it was too late. On the tennis court he'd seen men of his age who had six-pack abs, men with bodies like athletes, some of them even older than Max. It was a mystery to him how they'd managed to keep themselves so fit.

He looked at the clothes Stefan had given him. A grey T-shirt that was luckily big enough. That wasn't the problem. The trousers were made of a soft, white linen, but they were too short, so when he pulled them on, they ended just below his calves, and they also felt tight across his thighs.

'Stefan?' he called. 'These trousers are too small.'

'Can I see?'

Max was startled to hear that Stefan was standing right outside the bathroom. The door was slightly ajar. Had he been there the whole time? Max opened the door.

'They're fine. Next time you can bring your own clothes.'

Max sighed. Why on earth had he decided to come here? They went into the living room, where Stefan had pushed aside several armchairs and spread two yoga mats on the floor.

'Normally I'd recommend a proper yoga room. But this will do for today. The point is that you should be able to do this anywhere.'

Stefan sat down on a mat, and Max followed suit.

'Okay. First we're going to do some simple, basic exercises so you'll get a feeling for things.'

They did that for about fifteen minutes. It was harder and more strenuous than Max had anticipated.

'So the goal is for you to learn to control your blood flow. Sex has a lot to do with being relaxed. For instance, if you're stressed, you're not going to enjoy sex as much. If the body isn't sufficiently relaxed, the blood collects in the middle of the body instead of in the arms and legs. Relaxation automatically leads to greater arousal, since the arteries carrying blood to the genitals open up, and the blood is pumped directly into the penis.'

Max had always found it comical when anyone talked about 'the penis' in such a clinical way. He tried not to laugh because Stefan was taking the whole thing so seriously.

'In women, relaxation causes greater sensitivity around the clitoris, and it makes them wetter.'

Max assumed that Stefan had discussed these things many times, and that was why he could speak with such calm authority. He tried to relax, but couldn't help thinking that he'd been incredibly indiscreet. What if Stefan should mention this session to someone?

'Where's Gun-Maj?' asked Max.

'She's out of town. At a conference in Östersund in Sweden. She won't be back until Sunday.'

Max didn't ask any more questions as he tried to imitate what Stefan was doing. It was difficult, not only because his body was going numb, but also because the linen trousers were cutting uncomfortably into his crotch.

'Now we're going to do a position called the chair pose. Put your arms at your sides, like this.' He showed Max how to place his arms. 'And lift your chest up as you squeeze your thighs together and hold your arms straight, raising them over your head and pointing your fingers in the air.'

Max did his best. He was surprised how good it felt, even though it was so awkward that he couldn't hold the position for more than thirty seconds.

'Remember that this is supposed to feel good. If it's uncomfortable, then you're not doing it right,' said Stefan. 'Does it feel good?'

'It's fine,' said Max.

They practised a few more times. Then Stefan demonstrated a series of poses: the cobra, cat, camel, the standing fan. There were so many that Max couldn't remember them all.

After a while Stefan went to the kitchen to get them some water. Max was stretched out on the floor, feeling how his whole body ached, but it wasn't entirely unpleasant.

Stefan came back and handed Max a glass of water.

'When it comes to sex,' he said, drinking some water, 'there are some areas that men, especially those of us of a certain age, need to pay attention to. Number one is breathing. If you feel like you're about to lose your mojo, there's a lot you can do by breathing properly.'

'Mojo?'

'Yeah. You know. If it gets limp. If you notice that happening, you can try to breathe rhythmically with your partner. It might also help to try to increase the blood flow to the penis by tensing and releasing the abdomen.'

'Got it.'

'Another problem that men have, especially younger men, is premature ejaculation. This is one of the most important things that yoga can help with. Some people say that you should reach orgasm only about every hundred times you have sex. Touching should be enough. It can be just as powerful as a regular ejaculation.'

Max didn't reply. What was he supposed to say?

'But if you ask me, I don't really believe in that theory. Have you tried going around for several weeks without getting any release? I've tried it, and it doesn't work. You end up having wet dreams. But there *is* something to that theory. When you feel yourself about to come too soon, you can try to force the energy back into your body. In the best case scenario, you'll have a physical orgasm that is closer to what a woman experiences – in other words, your whole body will come. That's very rewarding, let me tell you. I wish I'd known about that when I was young. On the other hand, it's lucky that this is a secret only old guys like us happen to know. We need to have some way to compete, don't you think? And that's our endurance level.'

Max nodded. 'So how are we supposed to be able to do that?'

He couldn't believe he'd actually asked that question. Was it even true? Or was it an illusion caused by lots of yoga exercises?

'It takes a little practice. And it's not something I can teach you. I mean, you have to practise at home. Preferably with Katriina, but you can also try it on your own. You can masturbate if you like, and right before you come, try to slow down and focus on gathering all the energy inside your body instead.'

Max nodded. 'I'll give it a try.'

He couldn't actually picture himself doing that. This whole session was a mistake, but at least it was over now, and he could go back home.

'So, are we done for today?'

'Yes, I suppose we are. If you get confused and can't remember these poses, there are some excellent instruction videos on YouTube. Just try Googling "ustasha yoga" and you'll find lots of the most common poses.'

'Could you write that down for me?'

'Sure.'

In the sex study that Max had done in the nineties,

the missionary position was still by far the most common among Finnish couples. Clearly a lot had happened since then. Maybe it was time to do a new study.

Stefan got up to write everything down for Max on a scrap of paper. Then Max went to the bathroom to change his clothes. He folded the clothing he'd borrowed and gave them back to Stefan, who smiled with his tanned, leathery face – the way only a man who has frequent and satisfying sex can smile.

'I'm glad you came over. I have to admit I didn't think you had it in you.'

'It's good to try everything, don't you think so?'

'I totally agree.'

'Do I owe you anything for the session?'

'Absolutely not. Just consider it a friend helping out another friend. Say hi to Katriina.'

Max thanked him and went out into the winter darkness. He got out his mobile phone and rang Laura.

'Hi, Max. I was just thinking about you.'

That was more than he'd hoped. She was thinking about him. Max felt a new sense of confidence, as if he definitely could do this.

'Hi. Listen, I was just wondering about something. Feel free to say no. But would you like to come with me to Österbotten? We could do a little work over there.'

'When?'

'Well . . . I was thinking we could take the bus

in the morning. If that's not too short notice, of course. I need to visit my mother. But we have a cottage we could use before we head back home. Maybe we could get some work done.'

'That sounds like fun. If you like, we could drive my father's car. I can borrow it.'

'I don't have a driving licence.'

'You don't?'

'No. You know . . . protecting the environment, et cetera.'

'That's no problem. I can drive.'

CHAPTER 22

Amanda had inherited the boldness of the Paul family, along with a feeling of entitlement, a sense that the world existed for her sake. She was not afraid of unfamiliar situations; instead she viewed them as challenges that were meant to be handled. By the time she was four years old, she already knew how to swim, and when she was six she was diving from the three-metre board at the Swimming Stadium. The next summer she was diving from a height of five metres in the Gumtäkt district.

Helen allowed her to climb the tower and dive. She knew it was dangerous. She knew that Amanda might do a belly-flop, which would knock the breath out of her. But she let her try it because the fact that Amanda even dared attempt such a dive fascinated mother and daughter alike. Helen never would have tried anything like that when she was a child. So Amanda, who was half the size of the other kids, climbed up the tower. She waited for her turn and then took up position at the very edge and dived off. Without a trace of fear.

Lukas was different. He hesitated, carefully

271

weighing things before doing them. He didn't want to subject himself to any risks or land in unexpected situations.

Helen thought that life was like the game they used to play as kids. After placing ten sticks on a board, someone would kick the board and make the sticks fly in all directions. Everyone ran off to find a hiding place while one person picked up the sticks and put them back on the board before going in search of the other kids. The real challenge was for someone to come out of hiding to kick the board before everyone had been found. Those who were timid stayed in place and let someone else do the kicking. Helen thought that Amanda and Eva were the sort who would always run out to kick the board.

She viewed herself as the one who picked up the sticks and searched for the others. Life was an endless process of picking up sticks. There was always something that needed to be done or cleaned up, and as soon as Helen felt that the biggest job had been taken care of, as soon as the kitchen or hallway had been tidied, one of the kids would come running inside and toss their dirty shoes on the floor, so she had to start all over again.

By the end of the week, she felt as though she'd been working overtime after an extra-long shift, counting the minutes until she could crawl into bed. She just needed to make the last steps up the mountain, pick up the clothes from the floor, fill the washing machine, gather up the Lego pieces, take out the essay books to grade, cook dinner and then clear away the dishes. She had to push aside all thoughts other than the tasks at hand and try to make sure that everything went smoothly for the remaining four or five hours before the whole family went to bed, exhausted from the winter fatigue and darkness and the children's minor but vexing fights about completely trivial matters.

Now it was Friday, and Helen was sitting in the teachers' lounge listening to everyone plan their weekend. There was a Friday mood in the air, a feeling of loosening their ties – even though Niklas, the mathematics teacher, was the only one actually wearing a tie. A feeling that they'd soon be free.

'What are you doing this weekend?' asked Marit, who was Helen's closest friend among her colleagues. They were seated across from each other, sharing a desk. They often worked together and helped each other correct papers.

'I don't know. Nothing special.'

'Would you and Christian like to come over for dinner tomorrow? Do you think you could get a babysitter?'

'Just the two of us?'

'I was thinking of inviting Michael too.'

Michael was the new history teacher, and Helen knew that Marit had been looking for some excuse to socialise with him outside of school. The problem was finding a babysitter. Katriina was out of town, and Helen doubted she could persuade Max to come to Esbo to spend the night at their place. But maybe she could drive the children over to her parents' flat in Helsinki.

'I'll have to ask my father. Maybe.'

'Try. I was thinking of making *bœuf bourguignon*.'

'Great.'

'I promise it'll be worth it.'

Helen considered accepting the invitation without Christian, but it wouldn't be much fun to be the third wheel. She decided to ring her father after the next class.

The work week had been longer than usual because they'd attended training sessions every evening. Gunvor, who was the principal, had gone to a continuing education course somewhere in Sweden and had brought back new ideas that she wanted to put to use at the school.

Helen suspected that Gunvor had misunderstood half of what she'd learned at the course, which supposedly dealt with equality in schools.

Instead of discussing how they could make the school less gender-segregated, Gunvor had spent four hours talking about the differences between boys and girls – and doing it in a backhanded and peculiar way that was presumably completely unintended. In an attempt to show that she was politically correct she ended up saying things like: 'Boys have more energy and that means we need to be more attentive to their needs.' Or: 'Girls like to work together because then they're better able to focus.'

Gunvor had asked the teachers to come up with concrete goals for improving the atmosphere in their classes.

Niklas had suggested they start by 'getting Erik Hulkkonen to take off his cap during class', which made everyone laugh.

Erik Hulkkonen was in the third year, and Helen could understand why Niklas detested him so much. The boy, who was from a wealthy family, had blonde hair and a buff physique. He seemed to regard the teachers in his school as nothing more than riff-raff. Niklas, with his little mobile-phone holster, was the sort of person that Erik and his ilk ate for breakfast. But Niklas was an adult and able to exert authority over Erik, and he did so as often as possible.

Gunvor was not particularly old, just over forty, and it was clear that she still viewed all new trends as potential ways in which to elevate the school's image. She drove a Volvo big enough for a large family, even though she had no children. Her life revolved around her dogs, and there was a certain kennel-like smell about her. Helen thought Gunvor herself was a little like a dog: eager to take on new things, but also suspicious about anyone she regarded as threatening. She enthusiastically displayed her Gunvor nature, or what Marit and Helen had labelled her 'psycho laugh'. They had also settled on the term 'old-man shui' for the way

Bengt, the German teacher, wore the same jacket to work every day and reeked of tobacco. Occasionally Helen had to use a computer where he'd been working, and the smell he'd left lingered for several minutes.

After the last class Helen phoned her father. Marit had told her it was crucial that she find a babysitter because Michael had already accepted the dinner invitation.

Max sounded anxious on the phone. Helen hated asking for help on those occasions when she was certain her request would be denied. It was so humiliating to listen to all the excuses.

'I'd like to come out there, but I'm afraid I can't. I'm going to visit Grandma tomorrow. If it was any other day . . .' Max said.

'That's okay, Dad.'

'What about next weekend?'

'No, it has to be tomorrow. But that's all right. We can skip it. Say hi to Grandma for me.'

'What about Christian's parents?'

Helen had thought about asking them, but she knew they wouldn't want to spend the whole evening at their flat. So that meant driving the kids over to their place in Kyrkslätt. Christian's mother was willing to babysit, but there was always a feeling that it was a lot to ask. They would agree to do it, but preferably not overnight. Besides, for some reason Lukas had a hard time sleeping there, and Christian's mother would always phone if he gave the slightest indication that he wanted to go home. That meant they would end up sitting through dinner with their mobiles close at hand.

So when Helen got home she was surprised to hear Christian offer a third option.

'What about ringing Marit and this Michael guy and asking them to come here for dinner instead? Then we won't need to find a babysitter.'

That was actually a great idea. Helen was amazed because Christian rarely suggested inviting anyone over. But it might be a good compromise.

'But are you planning to cook? Or do you want me to come over and help you?' Marit sounded sceptical. Helen realised that moving the dinner to another location represented a certain downgrading in Marit's eyes. If she wanted to seduce Michael, it would be easier in her own flat than in a home with young children in Esbo.

'You do realise that *bœuf bourguignon* has to be prepared a day in advance, right? I was just on my way out to the supermarket.'

'I'm sure I can manage. Or I'll make something else.'

'Okay, okay. But let me know if you need help. I'll come over early and bring a salad and dessert.'

After Helen ended the conversation, she went into the kitchen and Googled the recipe. It turned out that she'd need mushrooms, bacon, beef and red wine. Christian came in.

'So, are they coming?'

'Yes, they are. But unfortunately that means you now need to go food shopping.'

CHAPTER 23

Edvard had apparently discovered that the hamsters were loose in the flat, because right now he was standing in the front hall and barking. Max tried to get the dog to show him where they were, but Edvard just stood there, looking upset.

Max didn't have time for this. He needed to pack if he was going to drive to Kristinestad with Laura in the morning. He decided that the hamster problem would have to wait until he got back. Surely two hamsters could survive for a few days without food.

He let Edvard sleep in his study, closing the door so he wouldn't start barking in the middle of the night. In the morning he packed some last-minute items, attached the lead to Edvard's collar, and walked over to Laura's place.

Max was in a dream-like state; he had a feeling this wasn't really happening to him. It was all going so fast, like a film rolling before his eyes. He thought this was how it was supposed to feel: living in the moment, noticing every little detail of his surroundings, every individual smell – not just a conglomeration of smells, but being able to separate out each of them from the rest. He felt acutely aware of the moment he was experiencing.

Laura opened the door with the phone pressed to her ear. She had on a T-shirt and pyjama bottoms, and she wandered around the flat as she talked. Max wondered if this was how she opened the door to everyone. Maybe he was just one in a series of men who had crossed this threshold. She seemed to be having a conversation related to work, because he heard her say things like 'deadline' and 'five thousand characters', and she laughed before saying something like 'No, no, I can make it, I need the work right now.' Then she ended the call. She came into the living room where Max was sitting on her bed.

'Hi, Edvard! The two of you are early.'

'I know. I thought it would be a good idea to get started before rush hour. Are you still willing to drive?'

'Absolutely.'

The fact that Laura had borrowed a car, a trim little Toyota, had opened up whole new possibilities. They wouldn't have to bother taking a taxi out to the house in Sideby. Usually Katriina or Helen drove when they went to visit; otherwise Max was forced to take both a bus and a cab.

Half an hour later, Laura's mobile rang again when they were in the car. She took the call, and Max could hear she must be speaking to a friend because of the way she was giggling and teasing, almost flirting. She talked for twenty minutes, and Max tried not to listen too closely.

'Sorry, that was my father,' she said, after ending the call. She kept her eyes on the road and seemed to be an experienced and confident driver, much like Katriina.

Max stared straight ahead. 'What kind of work does your father do?'

'A bit of everything. He has a consulting business, and it's been going really well.'

Max merely nodded. He wasn't particularly interested in finding out anything about Laura's father. Was he older or younger than Max? And which was worse?

Earlier that morning, Max had gone to the shop on the corner to buy food for the trip. Then he'd phoned his sister to say he was going to visit their mother. Elisabeth lived in Närpes, a half-hour drive from Kristinestad, but he knew he needed to ring her in advance or she'd hear about his visit later from their mother.

Every time Max went to Österbotten, he wondered whether this might be the last time he would see her. She wasn't seriously ill, but she was old, and there was always the risk she might suffer a stroke, since she'd already had a few minor blood clots in the past. During the past few years she'd been confined to a wheelchair, and Max was grateful that his sister lived in Österbotten (which Elisabeth had nicknamed 'Gloomy-bottom').

After their father died, Max had sold their

childhood home, to their mother's great sorrow, especially when it became necessary to empty the house so she could move to a flat in Kristinestad. She loved collecting all sorts of things and found it impossible to throw anything out. Her room in the nursing home was also filled with papers, stacks of old newspapers and various items she didn't really need. When the house was sold, Elisabeth had, true to form, already selected what she wanted to keep: Arabia porcelain, glass candle-holders from Iittala, a bookcase from Asko. Katriina had many times pointed out to Max that he also had a right to those things.

'I can't understand why you let her just take everything that had any value.'

But Max hadn't felt like fighting with his sister over a few plates.

'So where does your mother live? Is it a nice place?' Laura now asked.

'I suppose you could say that. It's run by an association. The buildings have been designated historic structures and all that. The oldest is from the 1800s. Very grand. The Österbotten associations are good at that sort of thing.'

Max thought that when he got old he wouldn't mind living in that sort of place. They didn't have the same problem recruiting nursing staff in Österbotten as they did in Helsinki. Yet he could see where things were headed. In fifteen years the area, which was now sparsely populated, would be overflowing with retirees.

Dusk was setting in as they arrived in Kristinestad. They drove round the small bay and entered the town, which stretched out invitingly in the dim light before them. Christmas lights still shone in many of the windows. In another lifetime Max could have imagined living here, yet he felt sad every time he came back because nothing ever seemed to change.

After crossing the bridge they drove towards the central square. Max knew every cobblestone of this place, every street corner, and every crevice in the facade of every building. They were all stored inside of him, like a dormant form of basic knowledge that he could take out at any time. His father was buried in nearby Lappfjärd. It was said that when the church was built, metres were mistaken for cubits, and so the structure had ended up eight times larger than planned. It could hold more than three thousand visitors and was the second-largest provincial church in Finland. It looked more like a cathedral, towering over an area with so few inhabitants.

'I think it's best if we stop here in town and park near a café. Then you can wait for me there while I walk over to the old folks' home. It shouldn't take long.'

Max had given this some thought as they drove and decided it was what they needed to do. Under no circumstances did he want his sister to know that he'd come to Kristinestad with someone other than his wife. The mere fact that they were driving through town like this was a risk – Max knew people in every neighbourhood, and they might easily give him away. Gossip spread like wildfire through the communities of Österbotten.

The home was not far from the centre of town, about a kilometre away, but Max wasn't properly dressed for the weather. He wore no cap, and his toes were freezing. January in Kristinestad: the candles shining mutely from hundreds of windows decorated for Christmas, the piercing wind sweeping around the corners of the buildings, a lonely lamp post illuminating the sign that identified the street as Kattpiskargränd, a hint of the sea somewhere close by.

After his father died in the early eighties, Max's mother had lived alone, but in some ways it seemed as if that was when she first began to live. She got involved in various clubs and took a more active role in her job. She worked at the social welfare office in Kristinestad, and if the child protection services had trouble placing certain children in foster homes, she often let the kids stay with her. That would never be allowed in present-day Finland, but at that time it was still possible. Max knew that he'd inherited a sense of solidarity and social consciousness from his mother. During the nineties, when the first refugees from Yugoslavia arrived in Finland, she had offered to hide a family at their summer cottage in Sideby. By then she had retired. The authorities were looking for the family and posted their names in the newspaper. Ebba, along with her daughter Elisabeth, managed to hide them for a week before the police tracked them down.

Max went inside the home and shook off the snow from his shoes. Then he plodded along the linoleum floor towards his mother's room. His wet shoes made a slurping noise, the sound of a son taking a temporary break from his stressful life out in the big world. An old grandfather clock ticked steadily in one corner, and a woman who worked in the kitchen was wiping off a table.

'Hi,' said Max.

The woman looked up. She was young, maybe thirty-five, with her hair cut in a trendy style and dyed purple and blonde – maybe the work of one of the students at a nearby beauty school.

'Hi, Max! We didn't know you were coming.'

She recognised him and knew his name. So why didn't he know hers?

'I was thinking I'd drop by to wish my mother Happy New Year.'

'It's a little late. She usually takes an afternoon nap about this time. Would you like some coffee?'

'Sure. Thanks.'

He sat down to wait, looking around the room. A stuffed wood grouse adorned one wall, a vitrine containing Lions Club banners stood in the corner, and the whole place was neat and clean, with not a speck of dust in sight. Somewhere further along the corridor he could hear the unmistakable sound of a pair of shuffling slippers – an old person taking a walk.

So was this how life ended? In a building smelling of linoleum, with stuffed birds and lace tablecloths and women with new haircuts speaking the southern Österbotten dialect? It could have been worse.

Max finished his coffee and then headed for his mother's room. Quietly he pushed open the door and went in. A small lamp was on, standing in the corner next to her bed, casting a halo over her. She was lying on the bed under a blanket.

Her hair was as white as the pillow. A few years ago she was still colouring her hair, but she had stopped doing that now, and there was something almost mystical about it, as if she'd already crossed over to the other side. Max touched the blanket and tried to wake her up.

'Mum?' he said, giving her arm a little shake.

She opened one eye, just one, which looked so strange, as if she were performing some sort of trick. Then she opened the other eye too and slowly turned her head towards him. When she recognised Max her whole face lit up with a smile.

She tried to say something, struggling to get the words to come out of her throat. At first he heard only a hoarse sound, and her smile changed to a concerned expression as she swallowed hard. Finally, she got control of her vocal cords.

'Max,' she said. 'You're really here?'

'Yes, I am. Happy New Year, Mum!'

She stared at him with a gentle expression that was hard to read.

He helped her to get out of bed, holding on to her waistband as he moved her over to her wheelchair standing near the bed. Then he rolled her to the middle of the room, over to the sofa and coffee table, which was covered with newspapers. There was also a bouquet of flowers in a vase – he glanced at the card attached to the flowers and saw that they were from a former neighbour – and a little box of cough lozenges.

Max picked up a tube of some sort of hand cream. 'Dr Oppolzer's AFRO-Schlamm contains an African clay that has both antibacterial and antiseptic properties at the same time as it heals skin problems. Daily use of this clay has also been proved to have beneficial effects on heart ailments and vascular disease.'

'What's this?' asked Max. 'Something that Elisabeth sold you?' But his mother didn't reply, and he decided to drop the subject. Elisabeth sold natural remedies to people crazy enough to believe that anything labelled 'natural' had to be good for them.

The bookshelves and bureaus in the room were filled with photographs of Max's daughters and Amanda and Lukas, of Elisabeth and her three children and grandchildren, of other relatives' kids, and a wedding photo of Max and Katriina, taken in 1979. Max looked so young and thin, with a little downy moustache.

He took off his jacket. 'So Elisabeth has been over to visit?'

It took a moment for his mother to answer. Over the last ten years Ebba's health had been up and down, but it was her moodiness that had been the major problem. These days she took antidepressants, a dozen pills with names like escitalopram and mirtazapine. Max didn't know much about medicines, but she had seemed happier during the past two years, so apparently the pills helped. He had a feeling that she wasn't the only resident of the nursing home who took pills for depression. He assumed that he would end up doing the same when he got older.

'Yes, she was here . . . when was it? Last week? Was it Christmas last week?'

'No, two weeks ago.'

She nodded.

Max felt a pang of guilt. If he'd had a car he could have brought his mother home for the holidays and let her celebrate Christmas with the girls and with Amanda and Lukas, but it was too late for that.

'The grandkids came over for Christmas. They're getting so big.'

Ebba didn't respond, so Max searched for something else to say.

Suddenly she asked, 'Does Amanda still play the piano?'

'I think so.'

'I'm glad. It's good to play music. It's good for your health.'

Max nodded. For a few minutes neither of them spoke, and he thought how good it was that she was able to live here.

'I'm thinking of staying overnight at the cottage.'

He spoke louder than normal, even though he knew there was nothing wrong with her hearing.

'How is Katriina?'

She was looking at him intently.

'She's fine. She's on a trip to the Philippines right now. For work.'

'Oh,' she said. 'The two of you travel so much.'

Max turned away and stared out of the window. Then he picked up the tube of hand cream, unscrewed the top, and sniffed at the contents. It smelled pleasant, like the sea. His mother had always had cosmetics at home – hand creams and suntan lotions – and in the sixties she'd even worn a fur coat, since his father had been so adamant about keeping up with the bourgeois customs of a provincial town.

Max remembered that as a child he would wrap his mother's fur coat around him after she'd hung it up. It was a good hiding place because it reached all the way to the floor, and it became almost a daily retreat for him, embraced by its warm darkness. As a grown man he was struck by what a Freudian image that was, practically a parody. His mother had meant everything to him when he was a child, since he never felt comfortable with his father's passion for sports and physical strength. Vidar wanted his son to take up skiing and orienteering, but Max preferred to read books. At most he might kick around a football, and later on he rode a motorcycle to various parties in the Österbotten region.

If Laura hadn't been waiting for him in town, Max would have stayed longer. But after half an hour, or maybe forty-five minutes, he couldn't help glancing at the door.

'Well, I think I'd better get moving.'

He knew that for Ebba the most important thing was that he'd turned up at all. She had other things to keep her occupied here, other people she could talk to, various activities and visits. A couple of years ago, Max had received a phone call from one of the staff. She told him that his mother and one of the other patients, a man named Harald who was close to ninety, had started up some sort of relationship. Harald had his own car, so their plan was to drive down to Helsinki to visit Max and his family. Harald also had relatives in the city. But after multiple discussions with the staff and with Elisabeth, everyone had agreed that it would be a bad idea, since Ebba would have a difficult time getting from her wheelchair into a car. Both Ebba and Harald vigorously protested this decision, and in an outburst of almost adolescent rebellion, they threatened to make the trip all the same. But Max managed to persuade his mother to take the train to Helsinki instead, accompanied by Elisabeth.

Harald passed away only a few months later, and since then Ebba had not mentioned any more car trips.

Now she nodded as she looked at her son. Max wondered whether he ought to help her back into bed, or leave her where she was.

'Would you like to go to the dining hall?' he asked.

She stared at him for a moment without speaking. Then she said, 'I think I'll just sit here and read the paper.'

'Okay, Mum. I've got to go now.'

'All right. Take good care of Katriina,' she told him.

'I will, Mum.'

Then Max got to his feet and picked up his jacket. He went over to his mother and gave her a hug. She smelled the way she always did now, of medicine and the food that they served in the home. Her cheek felt cool, and her hair was so soft, like that of a young child. Max's parents had been married for decades, but how happy had they really been?

He went back out to the corridor. The woman he'd spoken to earlier was setting the tables for dinner.

'So, you're off, are you?' she said.

'Uh-huh. I've got to head back home.'

'How was she?'

'She seemed fine.'

'She's a very special lady. You have a very special mother.'

'Thanks.'

★   ★   ★

When Max stepped outside, he found that the wind was blowing hard. As he started walking towards town, he rang Elisabeth.

'Okay, I saw Mum and I'm just leaving now.'

'What are you going to do next?'

'I'm going to spend the night at Råddon.'

'Isn't it a little cold for that?'

'It'll be fine.'

'How are you going to get out there?'

Max paused for a moment before replying. What should he say? As far as his sister knew, there was nobody who could drive him out to the cottage.

'I suppose I'll take a cab.'

'I can come and pick you up in the morning if you like. And drive you to the bus. You're taking the bus home, right?'

'No, that's not necessary. I'd like to do some writing, so I'm not sure when I'll be leaving.'

'Okay. If you think you can afford the expense of a taxi.'

Max had no desire to listen to his sister's reproaches about how he squandered money.

'Elisabeth, do you think Mum seems a little more . . . tired than usual?'

'I don't know. I see her so often, so I'm not sure I'd notice the difference. When was your last visit?'

Max tried to remember. 'In September, when we came to visit you. But I talk to her on the phone all the time.'

'Well, maybe she is more tired. But she's getting

older, you know. Can you picture Dad living in a place like that?'

'No,' said Max. 'I think it's good that he didn't even have to consider it.'

'Me too.'

Half an hour later Max rejoined Laura. By then it was three thirty, and she looked a little worn out.

'Sorry it took so long.'

'That's all right. Are we ready to leave now?'

'Definitely.'

A thick layer of snow covered the yard in front of the cottage. There was a damp smell in the air, and autumn leaves were piled up against the stairs. Max hadn't been out here since August. Back then it was warm and sunny, with lots of birds everywhere. Now it was almost four o'clock and already dark, but it was a lovely, aching kind of darkness with pines towering behind the cottage and a dignified silence hovering over the entire property.

Max was hoping that Laura would find the setting romantic. He was expecting to find firewood stacked up inside so they could light a fire, and maybe then one thing would lead to another.

'Has the cottage been in your family a long time?' Laura asked.

Her cheeks were pink from the cold. Max thought she looked like Snow White, dressed in her black coat as she walked beside him.

'I took it over from my parents twenty years ago.

The girls spent a lot of time here when they were kids. We call it Råddon. My mother had a tendency to use it as a sort of extra storage place when she was still able to get around.'

'It looks nice.'

'I just hope we can warm it up a bit. We don't have to stay long if you're tired. But it might be nice to have a cup of coffee before we drive back.'

They went inside, and Max immediately made a fire. Laura sat in a chair to watch. She took out her mobile and tapped on the keys.

'The coverage isn't great out here.'

'I can see that,' said Laura. 'I can't get online.'

For Max, the cottage was filled with memories. On the windowsills were white and black stones that his daughters had collected. The shelves held books that had once completely captured his attention – though it felt as though that was in another lifetime. And it was in the bedroom that they'd always believed Eva was conceived. There were folders with newspaper clippings that his mother had saved from early in his career, and occasionally he'd find himself paging through the articles with a certain perverse pleasure.

It was not a large summer cottage. It had two bedrooms, a bathroom, a living room with a tiled, wood-burning stove, and a small kitchen. In the yard was an outbuilding where they'd put in a sauna and shower. Max had also built a veranda, and it was there that the family ate their meals in the summertime. Actually, he hadn't built it on his own – he'd had help from his son-in-law one summer when Helen and Christian had come to visit, just after Amanda was born. Max had felt like an idiot, since he seemed to be constantly getting in the way whenever he tried to help. Finally, he allowed Christian to take over most of the project, and that made both of them happy.

In the summer the cottage was airy and filled with light. With the windows open, a breeze could blow right through, and the sun shone on the kitchen table every morning when they had their breakfast. Now the place was closed up like a cocoon. The view from the window revealed nothing of the world outside. It was like staring at a blank wall. The cottage could just as well have been floating in space.

'This is so nice. Do you come here every summer?' asked Laura.

'The girls don't come out here much any more. Sometimes Helen brings the kids, if they feel like making the drive. We'll have to see what happens with the cottage when . . . well . . .'

He stopped in mid-sentence. It wouldn't be very erotic to start talking about getting old and dying.

'Max?'

'Yes?'

'Are we really going to do some work, or did you bring me out here to seduce me?'

There were plenty of ways Max might have answered that question – after the fact he came up with several different options that would have been better. But he had no time to think, so he did the only thing that came to him, the only thing he could possibly do: he pretended not to have heard her. He simply got up and went into the kitchen and opened a tin of tomato soup to heat for dinner, wondering if he'd ever be able to muster enough courage to go back into the living room. He thought about the yoga exercises he'd learned. He thought about Katriina. He thought about his daughters.

Did you bring me out here to seduce me?

He thought about adding some fresh chilli peppers, garlic and diced tomatoes to make the soup taste better.

The problem is that I wasn't thinking at all.

He thought that if he simply failed to answer her question, she might not ask him again.

When he went back to the living room, he set two bowls of soup on the coffee table and sat down. He was just about to say something, when Laura spoke first.

'Is there any bedding here? Because I think I'm too tired to drive home tonight. Could we sleep here and drive back tomorrow?'

Max would have been lying if he claimed that the same thought hadn't already crossed his mind. He had hoped that Laura might suggest this change in plan. He'd even brought along a DVD they could watch if they got bored. It was the British film *Brief Encounter* from the forties. Max had watched it with Katriina back in October when they both happened to be home and had no other plans for the evening. But she had fallen asleep halfway through, even though she'd later insisted that she'd enjoyed the film. Max had accused her of being shallow, and they'd ended up having a row about it.

This time things were different.

The minute they put the DVD into Max's computer, Laura was so immersed in the film that she almost seemed to have forgotten he was there. He thought it was pleasant to watch a movie that way, with someone who was truly into the whole mood. Yet Max found it difficult to surrender himself to the story. When Laura set her feet on his lap ('Is that okay?') he suddenly felt as nervous as a teenager, worrying that he might get an erection – something that would have been unthinkable only a couple of weeks ago. The whole situation, being out here in a remote place with another woman, and for once not knowing what direction the evening – or even his life – was going to take, made him feel both restless and terribly self-conscious.

It got so bad that he had to count backwards from a hundred just to focus his mind on something else.

When the credits began to roll, Laura kicked her feet into the air as nimbly as a gymnast and then reached for the wine bottle to pour herself another glass.

'Oh, that was great. It's been a long time since

I saw a black-and-white film. I especially liked the scene at the train station in the beginning, when the man starts talking about what it's like to be a doctor, and she says that he reminds her of a little boy. It made me think of you.'

'That's Trevor Howard. One of the best British actors. It was good, wasn't it?' replied Max as he straightened his trousers, which had hitched up and felt tight across his crotch. They discussed the movie some more, and Max was able to show off how much he knew about British talkies from the 1940s, and about the background of this film in particular.

'I brought something too, if you're interested,' Laura told him. She went over to her handbag and took out a small plastic bag that contained something Max quickly realised had to be marijuana.

'It's been ages since I smoked dope,' he said, looking at the plastic bag and then watching as Laura rolled a joint.

'But you have tried it before, right?'

'Sure, just like anybody who was young in the seventies. But maybe things are different these days. I'm not going to develop a liking for techno music or start wearing latex outfits, am I? Because I haven't got time for that sort of thing.'

'No. Ha, Ha. You must be thinking of ecstasy, or something like that. The dope I brought isn't that strong. At the most, you might start giggling a bit.'

Max was sceptical. Yet he'd surprised himself

lately with so many other things. What was keeping him from trying something new? He needed a distraction, something that would make him stop thinking about his mother and would put him back in a blissful, dreamlike state. He wanted to release those forces in his brain that would make him feel like he didn't have a care in the world.

'Okay. What do we do?'

Laura showed him, and a sweet fragrance quickly spread through the room.

'What would my daughters say if they saw me now?'

'Do you think they'd be surprised?'

'I can't believe they've tried this themselves.'

Laura laughed.

'You think they have?' asked Max. 'Wait, don't tell me. The less I know, the better.'

After smoking one of Laura's joints, they sat in silence for a while. Max was waiting to feel something. Back in the seventies he'd tried cannabis at a party in Berkeley, but he didn't really know how to do it properly. This time Laura had shown him how to hold the smoke in his lungs.

He'd never felt a greater urge to kiss someone, but he sat there as if turned to stone. A shiver raced through his body when Laura leaned back and stretched.

'My mother seemed so frail today, so vulnerable,' he said.

Laura looked at him and then reached out to take his hand. 'How old is she?'

'Eighty-five,' said Max.

Laura settled herself more comfortably on the sofa. Max stayed where he was, staring at her. In his fantasy they moved into the bedroom, where Laura took off her clothes. He imagined how they would pull the covers over themselves, the sheets cold and stiff, but quickly warmed from their bodies as they pressed close to each other. Her breasts were incredible, of course, the most exquisite breasts he'd ever seen in his life – and he felt euphoric at the mere thought of touching her breasts, of being allowed to do that.

'Do you feel anything?' asked Laura.

It took a few seconds for Max to remember where he was. She was still sitting next to him, fully dressed, giving him a crooked smile.

'Maybe a little,' he said and suddenly had a strange feeling that she was there but not there, as if he were dreaming the whole thing. As if the entire room was about to disappear. A dream from which there was no awaking.

Max got up and stumbled to the bathroom, thinking it might help to splash a little water on his face. Laura's make-up bag was next to the sink. It held a toothbrush, contact lens solution and a familiar-looking tube: 'Dr Oppolzer's AFRO-Schlamm contains an African clay that has both . . .'

He turned on the tap of the large water container that they'd brought along and splashed water on his face. It was fresh and cold, and made him feel better. He looked at himself in the mirror and saw a face grimacing at him.

Max knew that he needed to go outside and breathe in some fresh air. So he put on his shoes and coat and opened the door to the yard. Edvard, who'd been lying on the floor in front of the fire all evening, got up to follow him out. A strong gust practically blew them off their feet and made Max's coat flap in the wind. It was snowing. In fact, it was more than just a snowstorm – it was a blizzard, bending the bare gooseberry bushes towards the ground and changing the shape of the entire landscape. What struck Max the most was the noise: the roaring of the wind. It was as if he could hear every nuance: the low rumbling at the bottom, the rushing sound at mid-level and the high-pitched whine on top of everything else that cleared his mind of all thought, making it impossible to think of anything whatsoever. He stood out there in the yard for a long time. It was great to feel at one with nature, to let the wind sweep him up. Then he moved further away from the cottage and leaned on the wall of the sauna building to listen. Edvard ran around in circles, and Max tried to follow the snowflakes as they fell, but there were too many to distinguish one from the other. He walked down to the shore and stopped to look out across the ice, thinking that this might be the most beautiful sight he had ever seen.

★   ★   ★

By the time he went back inside half an hour later, Laura had fallen asleep on the sofa. He felt elated, happy. Nothing had happened tonight, nothing that he needed to feel ashamed about, but he had a feeling that now he could do some writing on his book. If only it wasn't so late, if only he was sitting at his desk back home instead being here at Råddon. He sat in the living room for a long time, staring as if hypnotised at the glowing fire. Finally he went into the chilly bedroom and lay down on the bed. He was ravenous but didn't have the energy to get up, so he simply pulled up the covers and tried to sleep.

'Have you been up a long time?' asked Max when he went into the kitchen the next morning.

Laura was already there, and he didn't dare meet her eye.

'A couple of hours. I had to send off a column that I'd promised to write,' she told him. 'I'm sorry I fell asleep last night. Did you go out with Edvard? I don't know what happened. Suddenly I was just so tired that I couldn't keep my eyes open.'

Max felt like an idiot. Apparently he didn't have what was required to take advantage of the situation. He tried to see this in a positive light: maybe it was because he was a good person. Maybe he wasn't the type of man to commit adultery.

He made breakfast and they drank coffee, then washed the dishes from dinner. Laura checked her phone, answered a few text messages, and kept on working.

When they were ready to leave, they found the car buried in a snowdrift, and they had to dig it out before they could even get in.

They listened to the radio as they drove towards Highway 8. The newscaster reported that the storm was not about to let up, and everyone was advised to stay off the motorways. Max thought how ironic it was that nothing had happened on this trip, nothing that would require him to lie or make him feel guilty, but now they were about to get stuck in bad weather and if that happened, he'd be forced to explain.

'I wonder if we should stop somewhere,' said Laura. 'I'm not sure I want to drive in this kind of weather.'

'You're right, it doesn't look good. But maybe we should try to get home.'

Just as they were about to enter the motorway, Max's mobile rang. It was Elisabeth. He didn't answer. But when he put the phone back in his pocket, it rang again.

'Why aren't you taking the call?' asked Laura.

'It's just my sister.'

'But what if it's important?'

CHAPTER 24

When the four of them sat down to dinner on Saturday, Helen heard nothing but praise for the food. She had lit candles and served the children their meal in the living room. Michael and Marit had arrived together in a cab.

'It's very, very good,' said Michael.

'Yes, it really is. What kind of spices did you use?' asked Marit. She had on a red dress, and Helen noticed that she'd put extra effort into her appearance, wearing lipstick and a strong perfume. Her attire was almost too much for a simple dinner with friends. But Michael laughed when she did, and he kept giving her looks that boded well for later on. When he said something amusing, Marit put her hand on his arm, as if they were an old married couple.

'Just wine, vegetable bouillon, thyme and a few bay leaves. Nothing special, really.'

'Impressive,' said Michael in between bites.

Why didn't they invite people over more often? Right now it seemed crazy that they never did. But then Helen remembered: she and Christian were often way too tired during the week to even contemplate something like this. And they had no close neighbours, which normally would have led to more socialising.

Everyone took a second helping. Helen served the beef with jasmine rice, and Christian ate a huge portion as he eagerly talked about some project at work that Helen hadn't heard about before. After he'd been going on for a good twenty minutes, she gave him a look to signal that he ought to change the subject.

'Sweetheart, do you think everybody wants to hear every single detail?' she asked.

She was thinking about Michael, who sat there listening so politely. Was he actually interested in any of this? Wouldn't he rather move to the sofa and sit next to Marit?

But he didn't seem bored at all. On the contrary, he was listening attentively to Christian. It was strange to see people she knew in different roles, to see how others viewed them. They couldn't know that everything Christian was now discussing got extremely tiresome after a few years. Helen sat at the table and looked at her husband until all she could see was his mouth, and out of it came disconnected phrases that had no meaning whatsoever.

'. . . and you know how hard it can be to get a building permit for an old house. I mean, just putting in a ramp for a wheelchair requires a ton of paperwork . . .'

He went on and on. After a while, his monologue shifted to other topics – the expansion of the city of Helsinki out towards Busholmen, the lack of low-priced housing, the segregation in urban areas, and the district of Berghäll – all flowing together into one long, enthusiastically delivered speech. Then Christian got up to put on some music, and when a Neil Young tune came on, it turned out that Michael was also a big Neil Young fan. At that point Helen stood up and began clearing the table, scraping the food left on the plates into the rubbish bin.

'Now wait . . . there's something I really have to show you,' said Christian.

Helen saw him run up the stairs, almost tripping on the way, but at the last second he regained his balance and raced on. Michael could then turn his attention back to Marit.

Helen knew that Marit was planning to take Michael home with her that evening. She stood next to the kitchen worktop, surreptitiously studying them. Marit had probably pictured the two of them sharing a cab ride, and then that red dress of hers would be shed the moment they stepped inside her flat. Maybe she'd also imagined going to bed together, the glances exchanged in the teachers' room on Monday, and the whispering of their colleagues, which would lead to gossip among the students. Michael was no Brad Pitt, but no one else at the school was either.

Helen turned around to look out at the yard,

but she could see only darkness through the window. What was taking Christian so long? She could hear him rummaging about in the storage room upstairs. She pictured him hauling out the items she had so carefully arranged on labelled shelves, how everything would come tumbling down, and all the Christmas decorations would be scattered over the floor for her to find in the morning.

When he finally came back downstairs, he was carrying a stack of vinyl LPs.

'I know I've got a record player somewhere up there too, but I haven't had a chance to set it up since we moved. There's been so much to do with the house and the kids . . . but I just had to show you these albums.'

It occurred to Helen that Christian had no idea what the real purpose was behind this dinner party. He didn't realise that Marit was here with Michael, that the whole evening was just a pretext for the two of them to socialise outside school. Instead, he was directing all his attention to Michael. Helen thought he was worse than the girls at their school; Christian seemed totally infatuated with this stranger who had suddenly appeared in their home and showed an interest in listening to all his stories and looking at his old LPs.

Helen hadn't seen her husband so exuberant in a long time. He was usually very reserved and proper, the one who stopped drinking first, who was a bit boring but always polite, who put the children to bed and calmly whiled away the evening. Now he was pouring more wine for Marit and Michael as soon as their glasses were empty, and Helen thought: what if it's my fault? What if I'm the one who makes him seem boring?

After dinner Marit and Helen sat on the sofa in the living room while Christian and Michael stood outside on the front steps to have a smoke. Christian conjured up a pack of cigarettes from one of the kitchen cupboards. Helen hadn't even known it was there.

When the men came back in, they had a lengthy and intense conversation about British pop music in the eighties – Helen heard them mention the names Billy Bragg and Lloyd Cole – which ended with Christian getting out his laptop and setting it on the kitchen table. Then they both started shouting names to each other like 'Bill Drummond!' and looking up video clips on YouTube.

Marit and Helen sat in the living room, struggling to find something to talk about. Marit kept glancing towards the kitchen with a frustrated and restless expression. At one point she reached for her handbag and touched up her lipstick.

Christian offered Michael some Calvados, and of course he accepted.

'What about us?' said Helen, and at first Christian didn't seem to understand her remark. Then he nodded and got up to set the bottle of Calvados on the coffee table.

'You can use the same wine glasses, can't you?' he said.

At ten thirty Marit took a cab home. Christian insisted, with a silly grin on his face, that Michael should stay for a while. Helen didn't want to say anything, since it seemed so unnecessary. So she simply excused herself and left the room to check on the kids while Michael and Christian continued talking in the kitchen.

By midnight Michael was still there. Helen had been forced to ask them to turn down the volume on the computer, so as not to disturb the children. The two men had finished off the bottle of Calvados by the time she came back to the kitchen, feeling sleepy and worn out. She had almost fallen asleep in Lukas's bed. They were now drinking beer.

'I promise to clean up tomorrow, but I've got to find that record player. We're thinking it'd be great to have a vinyl evening here sometime,' said Christian.

'Sounds fun,' she said. She was too tired to talk.

'Doesn't sound like you really mean it.'

'Of course I do. Sure, I do.'

He gave her a hurt look, but there was also something blank about his expression, combined with a comical grin. Michael looked more sober, and now he got up.

'Well, I think it's about time for me to get going.'

'You don't have to,' said Christian.

'Yeah, I do. It's getting late. Do you know the number for the cab company?'

'Leave it to me. I can send a text to order you a cab,' said Christian. 'Now where did I put my mobile?'

Helen went to the bathroom to brush her teeth and take out her contacts while Christian and Michael waited for the taxi.

While they stood outside, she took off her clothes, put on her nightgown, and climbed into bed. She set a glass of water on the bedside table and got out her mobile. She heard a car pull into their driveway and a door open and close. A moment later Christian came inside and seemed to be doing something in the kitchen. Helen had already cleaned up from the dinner party, but now she could hear him opening the fridge, taking out food and opening a beer. She decided to give up waiting for him and instead started listening to her audio book.

Much later she saw the bedroom door open, letting in light from the living room. She felt the bed sag as Christian sat down next to her. She smelled cigarettes and alcohol as he took off his socks and then practically fell on top of her. He was searching for her breast. His hands were cold, and for a while she lay there without moving.

Then she took out her earbuds and switched off her mobile in silence. Christian's hand, limp and motionless, was still on her breast.

'I'm not really in the mood tonight,' she said.

He sighed, removed his hand and turned over. He didn't say a word.

'Sorry, but I'm too tired. You shouldn't have stayed up so late. Couldn't you come to bed earlier next time?'

'Okay,' was all he said.

'By the way, I thought it was nice that you and Michael hit it off so well.'

'Uh-huh.'

'But didn't you realise that Marit is interested in him? She didn't have a chance with the two of you carrying on a bromance like that.'

Christian didn't reply.

'I mean, it's great you liked each other. It's always good to meet new people.'

He got up and went into the bathroom, turned on the light in there, turned it off again and came back to bed.

Helen lay awake for a while, thinking about something she'd once read in a story by Alice Munro, about how people in their thirties sometimes had a hard time acknowledging that they were living their own lives. That was it exactly, and she realised that it could hardly be expressed in a more mundane way: life was happening right now. It was not something that would happen later.

'We made plans to go out some evening,' said Christian suddenly.

'What?'

'Me and Michael. It's been a long time since I had a night out.'

CHAPTER 25

Eva went over to St Paul's one day and found Russ in the process of rigging up a sound system for a political rally that was apparently going to take place later in the evening. It had snowed all week, and big drifts were piled up outside the tents. A man wearing a Guy Fawkes mask was shovelling snow in the small square. Eva had walked all the way from Piccadilly Circus to Fleet Street, and several times she'd been forced to jump aside to avoid being sprayed with slush when the big red double-decker buses roared past.

'Back again?' said Russ.

He was standing inside the white tent that had been dubbed the University.

Eva didn't answer as she looked around, thinking it was funny that even a global grassroots movement would have such obvious accessories. Hanging on the wall was a rainbow-coloured flag with the word PEACE on it. A Palestinian shawl had been wrapped around the microphone stand. On a black, hand-painted board she read: 'BANKERS, POLITICIANS, THE GLOBAL ELITE AND

THE MASS MEDIA ALL LIE, STEAL, BRAINWASH AND DESTROY YOU AND YOUR FAMILY.'

For the past few nights the temperature had dropped below freezing.

'Don't you get cold sleeping here?' Eva asked.

Russ was wearing a cap, and he'd exchanged his corduroy jacket for a down coat. He seemed to be in good spirits.

'It's not so bad. The snow is worse. Last night I had to shovel the snow off the roof or the whole tent would have collapsed. And since the wind has been so strong we had to work out some way to anchor the tents in place. We can't stick stakes into the cement, so I brought over some sandbags.'

Eva wondered how long Russ was going to last in this place. He seemed determined and involved, like someone who enjoyed what he was doing. Russ picked up a pile of cables and began untangling them.

A young guy came into the tent to ask Russ if he felt like 'coming with us'.

'Are you leaving now?'

'Yeah. In about five minutes.'

The guy was wearing fingerless gloves, and he had a long scarf wound loosely around his neck. He was properly dressed for the winter weather, with multiple layers, almost as if professionally outfitted.

Russ hesitated. He looked at Eva.

'No, I think I'll pass. You go ahead. I can catch up with you later.'

'Okay.'

After he'd left, Eva asked Russ what the man wanted.

'The water pipes to the tap we've been using froze. So now we have to go around to the nearby shops and local businesses to get water. But I have enough for a while,' he said.

Eva couldn't picture herself sleeping here. She wasn't sure why. But she didn't understand how these tents, and these people with their flags and Palestinian shawls, were going to accomplish anything concrete, anything that would make a difference in a fundamental way. She wondered if it was her attitude or theirs that was the problem.

Suddenly she saw a familiar face appear in the tent opening.

It was Malik.

Eva hadn't seen him even once since Christmas. His only communication with the students had been through Laurie. He'd also assigned them what he called 'inspiration weeks', which meant they were supposed to work on their own until it was time to gather for group critique sessions again. Some of the students had lost patience and claimed they weren't getting their money's worth from the course and should demand a new teacher.

In three weeks it would be Eva's turn to show what she'd been working on. Nothing was finished yet; in fact, she'd started over several times, scrapping ideas and painting over pieces that she'd spent weeks working on.

Now Malik was standing right in front of her, wearing a little woollen cap on his head. Maybe it was meant to make him blend in with the Occupiers.

'If you've come here to persuade Russ to go back to class, you're wasting your time. I've already tried, and he's not budging. I think this is his calling,' said Malik as he went over and put his hand on Russ's shoulder.

There was something about the body language between the two men – something new compared to the way Malik had treated Russ in class during the autumn. Eva was so surprised to see Malik that she couldn't think of a thing to say. She had never before felt excluded from male company, had never felt threatened by it. The guys' jargon was surprisingly easy to comprehend. But right now it was like arriving at a party only to realise that she hadn't been invited.

'I'm not going back to college,' said Russ as he wound several cables around his elbow.

When he was finished, he hung the cords over the back of a chair and took out a tobacco pouch and papers. Then he sat down and rolled himself a cigarette, focussing all his attention on what he was doing.

When Eva studied Malik more closely, she saw that he'd completely changed his style of clothing. He was wearing high boots and a green military jacket. He was also unshaven. She wondered whether Malik had tried to seduce Russ. She didn't really want to think about that, but she couldn't help herself, and she pictured Malik's big arms wrapped around Russ's slender body.

Eva turned to Malik and asked, 'So, have you moved out here too?'

She couldn't really imagine Malik living here – not this man who showered four times a day, who changed his clothes twice daily, who was dependent on full-length mirrors, who started each morning with a double espresso, who claimed that he 'hated nature' and thought that 'a traffic jam is more beautiful than a fucking symphony orchestra'. Would he really choose to live in a tent?

'There's something big happening here, Eva. I don't know what it is yet, but it's big, and it's fucking fantastic to be living in a time when we get to experience it.'

He seemed manic, high on something.

'There's so much adrenaline here, you can almost touch it.'

He waved his fist in the air as if to show how he was touching the adrenaline.

'Do you sleep here?' asked Eva.

He shrugged. 'I still have to correct tests and shit like that. But I come over here every day. It's electrifying, all these bloody people – anarchists, communists, hackers, environmental freaks. You should stay out here. It might all end tomorrow, but right now it's fucking magical,' Malik said, and then he left the tent as abruptly as he'd entered.

Russ raised his eyebrows. 'I think he's high.'

Eva was relieved to hear him say that.

'Have you eaten yet?' she asked.

'What time is it?'

'Almost three.'

Russ seemed to consider whether he was hungry or not, as if he had to remind himself about his own body and its needs. He tossed his cigarette on the ground and stamped it out. Then he lit another one.

'I suppose I could eat something.'

As they came out of the tent, Eva looked up at St Paul's. The sky had clouded over again, and the dome seemed to disappear in the haze. She was freezing.

Russ noticed her looking at the cathedral.

'Have you ever been inside?'

She shook her head.

'If you're not in a hurry, let's go in,' he said. 'I need to use the toilet, and I prefer the one in there.'

On the revolving mahogany door Eva noticed a Bible quote printed in big white letters: 'This is none other than the house of God; this is the gate of heaven.'

It was warmer inside the cathedral, which was pervaded by a great sense of calm, as if they found themselves somewhere other than the centre of London in January, as if they had travelled back in time. A few tourists stood in the small corridor that led to the desk where visitors paid an entrance fee.

Russ nodded to the cashier, and she let them slip past.

'I'm just going to make a quick stop at the loo. You can go in and look around. Take as much time as you like.'

The cathedral was enormous and so beautiful that it took her breath away. Eva walked further in and sat down in a pew. She studied the details of the dome, the dark brown space glittering with gold. She looked at all the paintings on the ceiling and the intricate patterns of the windows. She didn't notice when Russ joined her.

'Pretty impressive, isn't it?' he asked, as he hugged himself to warm up his hands.

'How long has Malik been coming here?' she asked.

'A fortnight. He's driving me crazy. But he has money, and if there's one thing we need, it's financial support. It's expensive to keep the whole place running, especially now that people keep turning up who are hungry and have nowhere else to go. It's become something of a refuge.'

'We haven't seen him at college in two weeks.'

'I think Malik just wants to be in the thick of things. I think he sees this as a way to collect some kind of cultural capital or good karma. But to be perfectly honest, I don't think we're going to be here much longer. Things have got tougher since the holidays. More vandalism. A few nights ago somebody cut up a couple of tents.'

'Do you think they're going to give up?'

'It's not just that. The thing is that this anti-hierarchical model isn't viable. Everyone's been trying to set up a sort of horizontal democracy, with no one acting as the leader or making all the decisions, but it just doesn't work. People still let themselves get manipulated away from their original goals. And somebody has to be the face of the Occupiers, somebody has to talk to the media and guide the movement forward. You can't have everyone going off in different directions, because nothing gets done. I mean, it's a little like a family. Not everyone gets to decide, and it's not always possible to come to a consensus. It doesn't work. Someone has to make the decisions.'

'So you're thinking of coming back to college?'

'No, definitely not. If there's one thing I've realised here, it's that I need to be working. Actually, I think that everybody needs to feel that they're doing something that has meaning. The work itself is what's important. Doing something and having a reason to get up in the morning. The whole Occupy movement is a kind of workplace for people who can't stand ordinary jobs. So it's ironic that we get criticised for being lazy and not working, when in reality we're working really hard. The problem is that so many other people don't see it as work. But we're trying to stir up questions and bring issues to the forefront – and that can only be useful to society. The people here are simply trying to show that there's another way of living, based on other things than constant growth and unregulated capitalism. I've met people here who have spent most of their lives living in tents,' said Russ.

For a moment neither of them spoke. Sitting in the cathedral reminded Eva of Österbotten. She thought that if she ever got married, she would want a church ceremony. It was ridiculous to be thinking of that now, but she couldn't help it.

'Did you say something about getting food?' asked Russ.

Eva treated Russ to lunch in a nearby café, and afterwards they walked back to St Paul's. That afternoon a meeting called the 'General Assembly' was being held. Everyone used various hand gestures to indicate what they wanted to say, so as to prevent all the participants from talking at once. If someone rolled his hands forward, it meant that he wanted the discussion to move on; if someone waved one hand in the air, it meant that he agreed with whoever was speaking. The participants included all age groups. The youngest attendees Eva saw must have been seventeen: two girls with cloth bags and close-cropped hair who held hands or rolled cigarettes as they listened.

One of the items on the agenda had to do with stolen valuables. Someone had nicked a portable stereo. One woman repeated that everybody had to take responsibility for their own things. Then they discussed how they were getting electricity.

Someone suggested they ought to get rid of the generator since it would be more environmentally friendly to rely exclusively on solar panels. The subject caused a lively discussion, but ultimately they all agreed that it was more important for people to be able to use their computers so they could tweet and blog directly from the Occupier site. It was also decided that it was 'a lesser of two evils' to pay for the electricity out of the general, shared account rather than force people to go to nearby capitalistic businesses in order to use their laptops.

That evening a vicar and a professor were scheduled to give speeches, but Eva was too cold and tired to stay. She stood with Russ outside his tent, trying not to shiver as she talked to him.

'Russ, if you ever have time, I'd like to see you again. Maybe someplace else. I've thought a lot about you ever since you came to visit us in Finland.'

'I've been thinking about you too. But I decided not to call because you didn't seem interested before. I just don't have the energy to compete with someone else. If nothing ever happens between us, I'll survive.'

'I know, I know. I'm sorry.'

He scratched his moustache.

'I was thinking of asking you something,' he said.

'What?'

'Could I come over to your place and take a shower? If your flatmate wouldn't mind, that is.'

CHAPTER 26

The lights switched off in the plane. The passengers had been served food and wine and then coffee. A fat man sitting next to Katriina had already started snoring loudly as she tried to find a more comfortable position in her seat.

She'd settled all the practical arrangements. She'd had a meeting with a local organisation that had a lot of experience in sending young women abroad to be trained as nurses. And Katriina now had some sense of the big picture regarding the logistics required if HNS was going to start importing nurses and staff on a large scale.

Katriina opened the *Helsingin Sanomat*. Reading the newspaper after a long trip was a way of getting back into her daily routines, a way of coming back home. There was nothing better than sitting on a plane with a long flight ahead of her and just letting the articles sink in, reading every single paragraph. After finishing with *Helsingin Sanomat*, she continued on to *Iltalehti*.

Every Friday one page of the evening paper was allocated to a guest columnist, and now a photo of Laura Lampela caught Katriina's eye. There was something about Laura's face in the picture that revealed an alarming self-confidence, something about the way she was standing with her hand on her hip. The expression and pose of someone who knew that her interpretation of the world was the prevailing view, someone who knew that she represented a generation that would soon take over, of which she was clearly the voice.

Her column had been given the headline 'Chance Meetings', and it had to do with her reaction to the film *Brief Encounter*. From the very beginning Katriina thought the whole thing sounded familiar, for instance when Laura described the film's subtle innocence, the fact that the heroine, who had fallen in love with another man, could not leave her husband and children because the story was set in the late 1930s in Great Britain, 'long before the sexual revolution'. Laura wrote that morals had changed – 'today we would laugh at the repressed emotions of the main characters' – and then she described how the film had nevertheless become a classic because of Celia Johnson's superb acting, her 'desperate looks and unceasingly controlled narration'. The point of the article was that Laura was making a connection with the present era. Today the film offered the audience a 'titillating sense of pleasure' with its innocent and virtuous story because our moral compass regarding relationships was so very different. 'At a time when more than half of all marriages end in divorce, an adulterous affair is as original as a litre of milk. But the dream of a great passion is as prevalent as ever.'

For about two minutes Katriina sat there in the dimly lit aircraft with a feeling that she'd been duped, not just as a wife but also as a reader. She had an urge to get up and ask her fellow passengers how anyone could behave so shamelessly – but everyone was sitting quietly in their seats, as if nothing had happened, as if Laura's article had not been a direct invasion of Katriina's personal life. She glanced at the passenger to her left, across the aisle. The woman, who was close to Katriina's age, gave her a smile, as if she were somehow involved in the whole thing, as if everybody in the world were actually involved, and they all knew about it except for Katriina.

What time was it? She looked at her watch and saw that she still had four hours before landing. She read the column again, fixating on certain phrases – they were the exact same things that Max had said when they watched the film together, and there was also something about the entire argument that was so typical of Max. Maybe he'd thought that Katriina wasn't really listening, but she was; she'd heard that part about the desperate looks and the dream of a great passion. She'd heard Max praise the screenplay by Noël Coward, and she'd heard Max point out that the film could be viewed as an archetype of the repressed emotions of the British middle class.

It couldn't be coincidence. There were too many things that sounded familiar.

Katriina closed her eyes.

She felt the plane bounce up and down, a slight turbulence. She asked for a little bottle of red wine. After she'd finished it, she asked for another.

There were certain moments that Katriina would remember for the rest of her life. Brief moments, specific incidents – like when the girls lay on her stomach for the very first time, newborn and utterly vulnerable; or when she watched Max defend his doctoral dissertation; or when she was fourteen and won the silver medal in the regional competitions in diving at the swimming hall.

The same was true of those last four hours on the plane from Manila, but instead of feeling like a moment, they seemed to last an eternity, as if she were in some sort of limbo state, a world in which all possibilities were still open to her. She felt like the cat in the paradox known as Schrödinger's cat: she was both alive and dead at the same time. As long as she sat in the plane, both possibilities existed: Max had been unfaithful, and he hadn't. Because until she got home and confronted him, she couldn't know for sure. And as long as she was on the plane, unable to phone or ask anyone, her whole life, her whole future, was still completely open.

It was close to four in the afternoon when Katriina opened the door to their flat. It was Monday, and

Edvard came racing towards her, jumping up to greet her. Katriina called Max's name. She could hear both the agitation and the alcohol in her voice.

'In here,' he answered from the bedroom.

The first thing she saw was Max standing next to the bed, holding the phone in his hand. The TV was on, showing scenes from an American crime show, as if everything in life was completely normal. Katriina thought he must be talking to her – and if so, there was no longer any doubt.

Yet she had a strange feeling that everything was the same as always. This was her old bedroom, and there stood her old bed and the TV, and on the wall hung the watercolour that she'd received as a gift on her fiftieth birthday. There was the book she'd left on the bedside table before her trip. And there stood her husband of the past thirty years, looking as if he'd just eaten a sandwich, since there was a spot of mustard on his worn-out old T-shirt.

Max said goodbye to whoever he was talking to and set the phone on the table.

'Hi,' he said.

'Hi,' said Katriina.

'My mother had a stroke.'

Katriina had pictured a lot of different scenes as she sat in the taxi on her way home from the airport. She'd imagined how she would throw the entire contents of the refrigerator at him – as she once had done when they were newlyweds and had a terrible fight. How she would scream shrilly and punch him in the stomach so hard that he slammed against the wall. She had pictured herself hauling all his clothes out of the wardrobe, stuffing them into a backpack, and then tossing it into the stairwell. But she had not predicted this scene. She hadn't imagined that her mother-in-law would have had a stroke and that suddenly there was an entirely different topic to discuss. Katriina felt overcome by shock, sorrow, a feeling of helplessness in the face of death, but she tried to push those emotions aside.

'It's just by chance that I'm home. I have to go back out there tomorrow,' said Max, taking her in his arms.

Katriina leaned her head against his chest and saw how the whole quarrel she'd built up in her mind had now vanished. She felt Max's hands stroking her hair in an attempt to console her, and how he pressed his face against her neck. But in an attack of fury she pushed him away. She was not going to let it go, he was not going to be allowed to have the upper hand emotionally.

'Max, are you having an affair with Laura Lampela?'

The TV show continued on as if nothing had happened. For a few seconds the only sound in the room was the dialogue, the well-oiled repartee, the stereotypical way in which the characters communicated by firing off one-liners. And Katriina knew that Max would have to say something quickly, because it was no longer possible to take anything back, now that she'd said it out loud.

'I don't know what you're talking about,' he said as he went over to the table, picked up the mobile, and stuck it in his pocket. He turned to the wardrobe and started taking out shirts.

Katriina's anger returned. She was surprised at how fast it erupted. It began almost unnoticed, like a slight pain in her stomach, but then it grew, creeping up to her chest and into her throat, to settle like a pounding heat in her temples. She was sweating, an annoying and ungovernable part of getting older.

'Then how do you explain that article Laura wrote in today's *Iltalehti*?'

Max turned around. She'd caught his interest, and he almost smiled.

'Laura borrowed the DVD from me, and I told her a little about the film. I took the bus out to Österbotten. Mum had a stroke yesterday when I was on my way home. They're not sure she's going to make it. Elisabeth is over there now, but I need to go back tomorrow. They're probably going to move her to the big hospital in Vaasa.'

Katriina started to cry. The tears poured out of her, and there was nothing she could do, no way she could control her feelings. Her sobs were the only sound in the room except for the TV. She wasn't thinking about Max, and yet she was – he couldn't very well be making up this story about his mother having a stroke.

'I'm tired and I need to rest. It's been a busy day, and I have to get up early,' he said.

'Do you love her?'

He sighed. 'I don't know what you're talking about.'

'If you love her, I want to know,' said Katriina.

Max paused before replying. 'What do you want me to say? Nothing happened. I met with Laura a few times. She told me that my manuscript is good. But nothing happened. What do you want to hear?'

'Don't ask me what I want. What do you want? Do you want to move in with her?'

Part of Katriina felt like laughing, and she almost did – but she realised that if she laughed, that would be the totally wrong response, considering Ebba.

Max touched her cheek and gave her a hug, which was what he always did when she was sad about something. She pressed her face closer to his chest, let his hands stroke her hair, let him kiss her on the head. She reached up to caress his beard.

Max reacted instinctively by hugging her harder, running his hand over her hair, and then down her back to her arse. He was tired, worn out, but paradoxically enough – as she now noticed – not too tired to get turned on. Maybe it was the only logical way of handling this situation, the only emotion that wasn't split in two and could still be understood. She responded to his caresses by tipping her head back to look up at him. She closed her eyes, leaned closer and kissed him. Then she took his hand and led him to the bed.

His hands were moving all over her body. Now he shifted his weight and began kissing her neck, then her breasts and she felt his hands trying to get under her dress. Somewhere deep inside her a titillating sensation stirred. She moved higher up on the bed and he followed, then slipped down and began pulling off her clothes.

Several seconds, or maybe several minutes later, they were lying on the bed, wrapped in each other's arms.

She felt his tongue, so soft. She moaned faintly, and he went on. Everything ran out of her, all her fear, all her anger. She felt so safe in this situation. This was her life. And yet it seemed new, as if something had changed in Max's behaviour. Maybe it was the tension, the not knowing, so that in a way she was sharing her bed with a stranger.

It was dark in the room, with Max's body on top of hers, the familiar salty taste of his skin. When he entered her, it felt thrilling in a way it hadn't done for years.

'Oh, Max . . . what are you . . .'

In the midst of pure ecstasy she turned her head and opened her eyes.

Her reaction was so strong – and her scream so loud – that her knee rammed into Max's head before he could pull off the covers. He looked at her, confused and alarmed.

'What's wrong? I'm sorry, I was just trying something new.'

Sitting on the bedside table right next to Katriina was one of the grandchildren's hamsters, staring her right in the eye. On the floor next to the bed, Katriina's knickers were moving about. They must have landed on the other hamster when she took them off, and now the little creature was trying in vain to get out.

CHAPTER 27

The sequence of events happened so fast that the outcome was inevitable. When Max thought about it later, he realised that nothing could have been done to save Blixten.

Max jumped out of bed, planting his right foot on the floor. When he set down his left foot he felt something soft, something moving next to Katriina's knickers. He heard a strange and awful – but also extremely brief – squeak from the floor. When he lifted his foot, he saw the squished and shocking result of what he'd done.

Katriina was still sitting on the bed, peering nervously at Skorpan, the other hamster on the bedside table who was staring back at her.

'Have they been missing all week?' she now asked.

Max leaned down to inspect the damage.

It was bad. Blixten lay on his back with his mouth open, and the tiny paws hung lifelessly at his sides.

Katriina got up and went into the bathroom to put on her dressing gown. Max picked up his clothes and got dressed. He lifted the crushed hamster off the floor and placed it on the bed. He didn't have time for this right now, didn't have time to deal with this sort of problem.

Edvard came into the room and sniffed at Blixten.

'We need to catch the other one before it disappears again,' said Max.

Katriina came out of the bathroom and went over to the bedside table. Skorpan was sniffing at the lamp, moving back and forth across the table. Katriina bent down and picked up the hamster in both hands. Then she went to Eva's room and put it inside the cage.

Max went to the kitchen to get a glass of water. Edvard followed.

'*Do you love her?*' Katriina had asked.

Max had never been the sort of person to take a stand. He'd never felt any desire to adopt a specific position regarding an issue simply for the sake of argument. This might be considered cowardly – a way of avoiding controversy – but he'd also seen so many people of his generation get locked into specific opinions that marked them for the rest of their lives.

Of course there were moments in everyone's personal life when he or she was forced to heed what might be called an internal compass. Was it certain actions that shaped who a person became, or did people act in accordance with who they were from the very outset?

He thought about the trip back from Kristinestad.

Elisabeth had phoned just after they'd got on to the motorway. Laura and Max had had to turn around and drive back to the hospital. Once they arrived, it was clear there was very little they could do. Elisabeth was crying as she sat in the waiting room, and she didn't ask any questions when Max turned up with Laura. By then it was close to lunchtime, and they were both hungry. The snow-storm was still raging, and nobody knew how long they would need to stay in Kristinestad.

'You drive home if you like. I can take the bus,' Max told Laura.

'Don't worry about me. I'll stay,' she said.

Max didn't really want her there, but he couldn't very well force her to go home. He and Elisabeth went to their mother's room and had a talk with her doctors.

'Cerebral haemorrhage,' said the female doctor in charge. 'She's old, and she's had a blood clot before. This one was quite severe. If she manages to pull through, she'll still be at risk for more strokes. She might do fine, but I don't want to get your hopes up.'

Their mother looked peaceful as she lay in the hospital bed. Her face was only slightly distorted – something about her mouth, something about her features that was oddly unfamiliar. Elisabeth continued to weep. Max gave his sister a hug. They sat down, then got up to pace the room as they waited for the doctor to come back and tell them the results of the blood tests.

Max went out to speak to Laura again.

'You can drive home if you want. Looks like I'm going to be here for a while.'

'I don't need to go home.'

'But I'm sure you have better things to do.'

'Not really.'

They found a café on the square where they could have lunch, and afterwards they got back into Laura's car. She'd changed her mind and was going to drive home. That's when it happened. Max leaned over to kiss her, and it all happened so fast. She willingly took off her trousers and knickers and let him come inside her. It was sex of the mechanical sort, sex as a way of warding off everything that was frightening – sex because the world around them, with all of its conventions, no longer existed. The only thing left was a great white roar. Sex that was cramped and awkward, sex in the midst of a snowstorm with Radio Vega playing in the car. When they'd finished, Laura put her clothes on again, and Max said 'thank you'. Then she drove off, and he went back to the hospital.

As he sat next to his mother's bed, he thought that maybe some sort of proviso allowed a person to be unfaithful under certain circumstances, for instance if a state of shock made the man in question not responsible for his actions. Ebba lay in bed, breathing quietly. As he looked at her, Max felt a darkness spreading through him, a feeling of loss. It was somehow incomprehensible that he should find himself in this situation right now, that he'd reached this point, a moment that he'd imagined many times over the course of the years, though it had always been something abstract and remote. It was true that Ebba had never lived nearby – visiting her required a drive of several hours – but she had been there the whole time, like an awareness in the back of his mind, a constant presence in his life. And now he would be forced to carry all their shared memories alone, his memories of his mother and father, of his childhood, and one day they would cease to exist altogether. When that happened, what would be left of the life he'd lived?

He fell asleep on the bus ride home. Now, as he stood in the kitchen, he doubted that anything at all had happened with Laura. It felt like a memory that didn't fit in.

'Do you love her?'

When Katriina came into the kitchen, Max avoided looking her in the eye. It was like they were juggling several balls at once. He felt guilty, and yet he didn't. He couldn't muster any real regret about what he'd done. The situation had simply demanded it.

Right now Max was doing what came easiest to him. He was packing a bag with his tennis gear. It was still lousy weather outside, with the temperature around minus 20° Celsius. The icy wind bit at his cheeks, his whole body, as he ploughed his way through the world. He could have used a pair of skis.

He opened the doors to the tennis hall and breathed in the familiar smell of linoleum, sweat and sports drinks. It was Monday evening, and when he went into the locker room, he said hello to Jorma, who – from what Max understood – worked in a small theatre in Berghäll. He'd often heard Jorma talk about the difficult directors he worked with, about actors who drank and about scandals in the Finnish theatre world. Max didn't know much about that world since he rarely went to see a play unless Katriina made him go. But he liked listening to people in different professions to his own; it gave him a new perspective.

Standing at another locker was Juha. Max knew he'd been diagnosed with cancer a year ago, but he'd regained his health and had now married a young woman from Belarus. It was common practice for everyone who came to the tennis hall to gossip about anyone who didn't happen to be present. In that way, all the information circulated in an eternal loop, so that no one could ever be sure whether he might be the current subject of gossip.

Juha never talked much, but he was a hell of a tennis player. He had the unusual gift of being able to deliver a backhand shot that was nearly as perfect as his forehand. And his physique gave no clue that he could move so fast. He also had a powerful serve. Max could see why a young woman would be attracted to him; maybe his physical prowess was not limited to the tennis court.

A highly physical and aggressive game of tennis didn't always mean that the player had an aggressive personality. On the contrary, many people seemed to reserve their aggression for the tennis court. But if an individual displayed a fierce, competitive streak when he played, it was likely that he was equally competitive in his personal life. An unscrupulous attitude could carry you a long way in a tennis game, but in Max's experience, the best players had it in their blood. They played tennis as if they were performing a ballet, approaching every aspect of the game intuitively. Those kinds of people were often good at everything they did, as if they possessed a certain musicality. Max had seen it in some of the younger men with whom he occasionally played tennis, a sort of natural superiority that also managed to come across as generous.

When Max played, it was a matter of endurance. Of refusing to give up, even though the lactic acid in his legs made him want to lie down on the ground from pain and exhaustion. Of never missing a shot, but at the same time not taking any unnecessary steps. That was what had carried him through thousands of tennis games. Staying on the court in all situations, until his opponent finally gave up.

'Do you love her?'

CHAPTER 28

Russ stayed the night at Eva's flat. When he went back to his tent in the morning, she went with him.

'Looks like there's a lot to be done here,' said Eva as she looked at all the Occupiers who had just got up and were starting to go about their daily routines, whatever they happened to be. Snow had covered Russ's tent in the night, and he began shaking it off. She felt sorry for him, even though she realised he didn't want her sympathy.

'I'll manage,' he said, as if reading her mind.

He lifted the tent poles and kicked at the sandbags, which were piled high all around the tent. A man came over to Eva and asked her for change. She dug through her pockets and found a few coins to give him.

They ate breakfast together in the tent University. There were about a dozen people inside, discussing the ongoing battle with the City and the property owners. The City still wanted to remove the Occupiers, saying that they were interfering with traffic. Another claim was that the tents were responsible for an increase in crime in the area and for hurting local business.

'The ironic thing is that we're taking care of people the City hasn't been able to help. That's why it's important we never leave this spot. And it doesn't really require a lot of us. What we need are tents. The tents are our most important symbols, they show that the area is occupied. That this is a place where people live,' said a woman wearing a knitted cap with earflaps and a wind-proof winter jacket. She was holding a cup of tea in her hands and looked as though she was in her early forties. Eva thought the woman seemed used to this kind of meeting, like a professional grass-roots activist.

'But what principles are we going to follow?' asked a guy who Eva recognised from her previous visit. He was the one who had stopped by the tent when she was talking to Russ.

'I know we've discussed this many times before, but we should have some sort of general rules. Should food for the homeless be given a higher priority than paying expenses? Should we really put all our energy into keeping the soup kitchen running? That's not why we're here. That's not why this whole thing started. The question is whether there's a more effective way to get out our message.'

Everybody had turned their attention to him. The woman with the cup of tea shrugged.

'No manifesto.'

The others seemed to agree with her. They waved their hands about in a manner that Eva now knew was their way of expressing approval.

When she got home to Bethnal Green an hour later, without Russ, Eva found Malik waiting outside the door. He had his finger on the button to the intercom and was letting it ring nonstop. His head was pressed against the wall.

'Hi, babe,' he said, slurring his words.

'Stop that. Don't you know that if I don't answer, I must not be home? What do you want?' she said.

'Just wanted to come over and see you. Can't I drop by to see a friend?'

He was high, or drunk, or maybe just nervous. He scratched his neck and seemed to be having a hard time staying upright, even though his whole body was now leaning against the door.

'Why are you here?' asked Eva. 'The last time you came over, you called me a cunt.'

'I just need a place to sleep.'

'Is that why you've been hanging out with Russ? Because you're homeless? Why don't you go home?'

Malik looked at her as if he didn't understand the words, or as if she'd asked a question that was incredibly stupid and funny. It seemed weird to her that Malik – who had so much money – didn't just get a hotel room if he couldn't go home. On the other hand, and this was something she'd

340

noticed during their affair, he was the kind of person who craved company. Despite all his talk about art history and 'fucking Saatchi' and bragging about his wild life, when it came right down to it, Malik didn't seem to have any friends outside college. Was that why he acted like such a tyrant in class? Because he had no idea how to behave normally with other people?

Reluctantly Eva opened the door and let him in. She knew that Natalia wasn't home; otherwise she never would have invited Malik in.

He headed right for the fridge and took out a beer, drinking half the bottle in one gulp. Then he sank on to a kitchen chair and stared at the table.

'Eva, I need to tell you something. And you have to listen closely. There are maybe five – no, three – artists in my generation who really mean something, who have it in them, who have what it takes. I'm one of them. I could have shown at the MOMA and sold out the whole fucking second floor. I could have lived in that fucking building in Lower Manhattan with that whole Julian Schnabel clan if I hadn't been so fucked over by the establishment. One mistake. Just one! A guy makes a fucking little mistake and it's all over.'

Eva was still standing in the hallway. She hadn't even had time to unbutton her coat. She was just about to ask 'What mistake?' but he spoke first.

'You know what it is?' he asked. 'You know what it takes?'

'No,' replied Eva. Slowly, she took off her coat and hung it on a hook as she tried to think how she could get Malik out of the flat.

'It takes adaptation,' he snarled, his eyes fixed on the table. 'Simple Darwinism. You have to adapt! Remember that! And another thing. That fucking auction house . . . millionaires who get bored with stocks and reserves and shit and want to own some fucking unique object that will keep its value. Do you know what auction houses are, Eva?'

'No.'

'They're funeral homes. The art dies. Why do you think artists want nothing to do with them?'

He got up, went into her room, and flung himself on to her bed. Eva wanted to throw him out. She'd never seen him in such a pathetic state.

He leaned over to look at her art books and picked up the thick volume on the Pre-Raphaelites, flicking his index finger through the pages. He licked his finger and leafed through more pages until the book suddenly fell out of his hands. It landed on the floor with a bang, which for some reason made him giggle uncontrollably.

'All women are whores. Do you know that?'

Eva had never been so afraid of Malik before. Right now she was alone in the flat with him, and there was no one she could call to ask for help. She shouldn't have let him in. She closed the door to the bedroom and left him lying on the bed.

After a while, as she was sitting in the kitchen and thinking about phoning her mother, she heard a sound from the bedroom. Was he crying? Was the great Malik Martin crying?

She listened carefully. Yes, it really did sound as though he was crying. Several minutes passed. He was moaning, sobbing, mumbling something, and then he fell silent. She stayed where she was in the kitchen, not knowing what to do.

After a few more minutes of silence, she went over to the bedroom door to listen. Not a sound. When she opened the door and looked inside, she saw him lying on the bed, motionless. He was a big man, his back was enormous, and his hair was sticking out all over.

She noticed a faint odour. Had he farted? She took a step forward, and now she saw a dark pool spreading out across the blue sheet. When she got closer she noticed the stench.

'Malik?'

No answer. He just lay there, on his stomach, heavy as a deer that had been shot, a body that didn't seem to belong to its owner, just a big, foul-smelling black lump lying on her bed.

She went into the kitchen and rang Russ.

When he didn't pick up, she really started to worry, wondering whether she could come up with a Plan B. Who should she call? Who would be able to help her with the situation? How was she going to explain this to Natalia?

She rang Russ again, and finally he answered.

'Hi, it's me,' said Eva. 'I've got a problem. A really big problem, actually.'

'What the fuck!'
'I opened the window. Do you think he's dead?'
'No, he's still breathing.'
'What should I do?'
Russ went over to Malik and poked him. He stirred, just a little, and seemed to mutter something.
'Well, at least he's still alive. Barely. Fuck.'
'Do you think he's overdosed?'
'Who knows. Maybe he just had too much to drink. My dad used to shit himself sometimes after drinking all night. When I got up to have breakfast I'd find him stretched out on the floor in the front hall. My mum had to clean up after him.'
'We can't exactly send him home in a cab in this condition, can we?'
They went into the kitchen to consider the options. A cloying smell of excrement hovered over the whole flat, and Eva was worried her neighbours would be able to smell it out in the stairwell. She knew that the number one priority was to get Malik on his feet.
'You'll have to go in there and get him to stand up,' she said, feeling more angry than scared.
'You think I can do that? If this wasn't your flat, I'd just leave him lying there. He must weigh at least fifteen stone.'
Eva was sure that he weighed a lot more than

that. 'But since this is my flat, he can't stay there. Natalia will be home later tonight.'

They went back to the bedroom and poked at Malik. He responded by turning his head before sinking back on to the pillow and scratching at his filthy trousers.

'Time to get up!' Russ yelled, trying to sound authoritative as he tugged at Malik. 'Fucking hell,' he added. 'This really isn't how I was planning to spend my day.'

Next to Malik, Russ looked like a baby brother, a thin little hipster trying to shake some life into a rhinoceros. At first, Malik waved Russ away, but then he opened his eyes and looked up.

'You need to have a shower, Malik.'

Russ pulled at him, and Malik seemed to be trying to cooperate. He propped himself up into a sitting position, but the look on his face told them that he was still completely out of it. He was staring at the wall. Eva looked at the two men and could suddenly picture Malik as a child – a pitiful, lonely and confused little boy who woke in the night, having peed his bed. With a great effort he stood up, leaning on Russ.

'We need to ring his wife. Do you have her number?'

'She's probably at the gallery. Should we try there?' said Eva.

'Sure. Can you do it?'

Eva nodded. She knew that's what she had to do.

In the kitchen she noticed that her mobile was vibrating. It was her mother.

'Hi,' said Eva. 'I'm in the middle of something right now. Can I call you later?'

'Well, okay, um . . . it's about your grandmother. She's had a stroke. I just wanted to know if you could come home.'

CHAPTER 29

Katriina was busy cleaning. That seemed to her the most sensible thing to do in this situation. She went through the fridge, throwing out everything that wasn't fresh; she scrubbed the toilet; she even got down on her hands and knees to wash the area around the rubbish bin.

If there was going to be a funeral, it would take place in Lappfjärd. And that meant that Katriina would have to take care of the practical arrangements. She was good at that sort of thing. She knew what kind of food to order, and she would make sure there was a certain level of sophistication about the memorial service, even though it would be held in Kristinestad and even if there weren't very many mourners. Elisabeth would be there, along with her boys, and Katriina and Max with their daughters, as well as Amanda and Lukas, Ebba's brother, a few cousins from Kristinestad, maybe some of Ebba's former colleagues from the social welfare office and a few surviving veterans who would attend because they'd known Vidar.

Katriina liked seeing Max look so helpless. She liked the fact that he had no idea what to do, that he was so silent, that she still had a certain hold over him. For the past few hours they hadn't discussed Laura Lampela, but Katriina had amused herself by calculating that she had been twenty-six when Laura was born, which meant that Max had been thirty, which meant that Laura was ten years old when Max was forty, and that was exactly the period of time when they were living in the United States. Katriina went through all these calculations while she was on her knees in the kitchen, scrubbing at the worn surface of the cupboard doors. When she'd finished, she went into the bedroom, still wearing her rubber gloves, and found Max lying on the bed. He had finished packing.

'Have you talked to your sister?' she asked.

'Uh-huh. No news. Mum is sleeping.'

Katriina rubbed her forehead. The wet glove felt cold and unexpectedly pleasant.

'Max. I'll help with anything that's needed. I'll make the funeral arrangements. But after that, we need to talk.'

'There's nothing to talk about.'

'Don't you think I know what you're like? How charming you seem to other people? How charming and loving and wonderful you are to everyone except me?'

'I don't know what you're talking about.'

'I'll go with you tomorrow,' Katriina now said.

'You don't have to do that.'

'I know, but I want to. I want to see your mother one last time while she's alive. So of course I'm going. And Helen is too.'

'What should we do about the hamsters?'

'You'll have to deal with that. Early tomorrow. Go out and buy another one that looks the same.'

'What did you do with the one I stepped on?'

'I put it in the freezer.'

'The freezer?'

'I couldn't exactly just flush it down the toilet, could I?'

'No, I suppose not,' said Max.

So it was decided. At nine in the morning Max took the tram over to Stockmann's department store. Inside, he walked past the perfume counters and took the escalator up to the sixth floor. The place was deserted except for the sales staff, some Russian tourists who'd arrived in Helsinki early, a few men who were trying on blazers as their wives looked on and athletic-looking assistants eager to interest customers in a pair of trainers. Max proceeded to the pet department, which smelled of sawdust and fish food. And there he found a hamster that looked like Blixten, although maybe slightly smaller in size, but he hoped that wouldn't matter. Helen and the kids would probably just think the hamster hadn't had enough to eat while they were away.

By the time Max got home, Katriina had carried their suitcases out to the car. Helen had also arrived.

She was sitting in the kitchen having coffee and looking upset. Max hoped it was because of her grandmother and not something Katriina had said.

Edvard leapt up and down, barking, as Max sneaked into Eva's old room and put the new hamster in the cage with Skorpan.

Max and Katriina were silent for most of the drive, while Helen sat on the back seat and listened to an audio book.

'What are you listening to?' asked Katriina.

'*The Unknown Soldier.*'

Max had talked to Elisabeth, who told him that the situation hadn't changed. Their mother was still in Intensive Care, and it was unclear when, or if, she would be sent to the hospital in Vaasa. There was a hint of anxiety in Elisabeth's voice, an uncertainty, and Max suddenly had the feeling that he hadn't been a very good brother, that there was something he should be doing, something she wanted from him. But how could he know what that was?

Maybe Elisabeth simply needed someone to talk to. Max knew that he should have visited their mother more often over the past few years, but he'd always thought this situation would happen some day far in the future, that he'd have plenty of time with her and they'd be able to establish a closer relationship. He'd always pictured his mother's demise as something quiet and dignified, something slow and thoughtful. He'd never imagined that it would be so stressful.

Now, as Max sat in the car, aware that he was heading for Österbotten to see his mother, who was most likely on her deathbed, he realised that it was too late to make amends.

It occurred to him that Edvard Westermarck had been plagued by guilt in a similar situation. When Westermarck heard that his mother had died, he was on his way to Morocco. He received a telegram from Finland, quite unexpectedly, not long after he'd visited his mother and sister. Westermarck wrote in his memoirs that he wished he'd stayed longer in Finland, as his mother and sister had asked him to do. But he'd been in a hurry to leave and go back to England and Morocco. Max thought he would write something about that, something about Westermarck's relationship to his homeland and what drove him away.

'Eva will come home if there's a funeral,' said Katriina. 'I promised to ring her later today and tell her what's going on.'

It had snowed hard the past few days, but now the snow had stopped. It was a beautiful, crisp winter morning, sunny and bitterly cold. The car seemed to fly along the road, and they kept the radio switched on the whole way. Things almost felt normal. Outside, the sky was blue and the flat, snow-covered landscape was completely indifferent to everything happening in their lives. Max's mobile started vibrating.

'Who is it?' asked Katriina as he took out his phone.

'Just someone from work,' he told her.

It was a text from Matti, wondering how it was going with the book. He wrote that he'd set up an appointment with Laura, and they were hoping he'd be able to come. Max wondered what he really meant by that: whether he'd be able to come. He was talking about the book, right?

Max replied that he'd be out of town for a couple of days, but he'd get back to Matti soon. And he was making progress on the book. Then he sent a text to Laura to say he was on his way to visit his mother in the hospital, and he'd like to discuss his manuscript when she had time.

It occurred to Max that he didn't really know Laura at all. When they'd had sex, he was struck by how cold she felt. Her body temperature was so different from Katriina's. It wasn't unpleasant, just different. And that was interesting.

'Max, I've been wondering about something,' Katriina now said. 'Helen, can you hear me?'

Helen didn't seem to be listening, because she didn't answer.

'If your mother dies, I'd like to sell the summer cottage.'

'Why is that?'

'Because it's yours. And if we get divorced, I want to be able to afford to stay in our flat. You'll have to find another place to live. If we sell Råddon, we'll have some extra cash, both of us will.'

'But why would we get divorced?'

Max was trying to breathe slowly. He wanted to stick with the plan he'd made until there was no other sound but the pulsing of his blood. Set one foot in front of the other and wear down his opponent.

But Katriina was utterly calm.

'I don't know what you and Laura did. I don't give a shit. You can have your little flirtation. But the thing is, you don't really see me any more. When was the last time we had dinner together? When did we last do anything at all together? I'm fifty-five years old, and it's still possible for me to have a whole other life for the next twenty or thirty years. That's what this is about. I'm sick of going around at home, waiting for you to notice me some day.'

Max leaned his head against the cold window. He thought that his normal response would be to protest, to argue. Yet in some perverse way, he wanted to see where Katriina would go with all this.

'But Råddon has been in my family a long time. It wouldn't be fair to Elisabeth if we sold it.'

'Max, for the past thirty years, how much money do you think I've spent on food and shampoo and cleaning supplies? On new clothes for the kids, on furniture and rugs? Don't you realise all of those things cost money? Even though you happen to have a summer cottage in your possession, that doesn't mean you're entitled to keep it.'

Max shivered. Marriage laws. He'd always

353

thought there was something incredibly ugly about the transactions that people negotiated, the trifling calculations upon which they insisted. A power play based on money and property.

He turned to look at Katriina.

'Just listen to us. Listen to how we're carrying on. Do you really want to have this fight? A divorce? Arguing about a summer cottage? How typically Finland–Swedish is it going to get?'

But now Katriina had started crying. She wept as she drove, with the tears running down her cheeks and glistening in the sunlight. She was angry – he could see that – but Max always had a hard time seeing her cry. He wanted to hug her, hold her in his arms until she stopped, as if her despair were based on something that could be repaired if only he held her close enough.

'Max, I just want . . .'

'Katriina, sweetheart, my mother is in the hospital and we need to find a way to make it through the coming weeks. I promise that afterwards everything will be fine again. I promise.'

Now Helen took out her earbuds.

'What is it, Mum?' she asked.

'She's just feeling sad,' said Max. 'We're all sad.'

His mobile began vibrating in his pocket. He took it out and glanced at the display. It was Laura.

'Damn it, Max, WHY CAN'T YOU PUT THAT FUCKING THING AWAY?!'

Katriina grabbed his phone, opened the car window and tossed it out.

CHAPTER 30

U p until now Helen had been immersed in the Väinö Linna novel about the soldiers. She'd finally managed to get into the story. But now she looked up to see her mother throw a phone out of the car window, and then her father clumsily try to fling himself after it, so that Katriina almost lost control of the car. Helen leaned forward to look at her mother's face in the rear-view mirror. Katriina's eyes were filled with tears. And Max was shouting that his mobile had cost four hundred euros.

'What's going on?' asked Helen.

They had passed Björneborg an hour ago and were now about halfway to Kristinestad. Katriina tucked her hair behind her ear and took a firm grip on the steering wheel.

'Your father and I are getting divorced.'

Helen didn't reply for a moment, as she tried to decide what to say. She thought she ought to express surprise – they probably expected her to be upset – but that didn't feel right to her. For as long as she could remember, their marriage had been a rocky relationship, and she'd heard divorce mentioned before. In their family it was always talk, talk, talk – a nonstop babble – and so it was only natural that the topic of Max and Katriina getting a divorce should occasionally crop up in the conversation. Helen could just picture them in a week's time, clinging to each other once again, just as they always did, because in the long run they could only stand to be unhappy together.

'Really? You're getting divorced? Congratulations.'

'This time it's for real. I can't go into all the details, because that's something between your father and me. But this much I can tell you, since you'll find out sooner or later: he's leaving me. He's found someone else.'

This sounds a little more newsworthy, Helen thought. Her father had found someone else? She couldn't imagine who that would be. Was she young or old? Helen realised that she didn't want to know. Not at the moment. She looked out of the car window at the flat landscape, at the barns and fields, and at the low clouds hovering just above the treetops on the horizon, motionless, as if waiting for something, or as if silently following the drama that was unfolding inside the car.

'Grandma is dying. Can't you put your marital crisis aside until later?'

'If we get divorced, we'll have to sell Råddon.'

'Sell Råddon?'

'I'm afraid so.'

For Helen, the summer cottage was a magical place where she'd spent so much of her childhood:

356

near the sea, among the rocks and nettles, inside the house, which always seemed so mute when they moved in for the summer, but which changed and began to breathe once they'd put everything in its proper place. Råddon meant drives to Kristinestad, sugar doughnuts, fresh raspberries and strawberries. But it was also an adventure: being allowed to go out alone to explore the world, to swim and row and take long walks without her parents, to read books late into the night, to squash mosquitoes and leave tiny specks of blood on the wallpaper, to sit outside and breathe in the scent of the green smoke from the coils that were lit to keep mosquitoes away. Pine needles between her toes, dried pine cones under the soles of her feet, the drive from Helsinki, the feeling that she was coming to a foreign place that was nevertheless all her own. The smells of summer, the sunlight, the autumn, rowanberries in August, the stones in the little flowerbed and, if she lifted up the stones, all the ants underneath. And the cottage itself: the linoleum, the potato peeler, an old wood stove, an old tile stove in the small living room, where Max and Katriina always slept. The tiny decorative house that was also a cigarette holder (if you pressed on the chimney, a cigarette would come rolling out).

Above all, Råddon meant Kristinestad and Grandma – her clothes, her thick calves and her wooden clogs. Helen wanted Lukas and Amanda to have a relationship to all of these things. She didn't want to lose the part of herself that was rooted in Österbotten.

'But Råddon belongs to us. I want Lukas and Amanda to be able to go there.'

'But you never spend more than a week out there, tops. Last year you were only there for a few days.'

'I know, but that's only because there's not enough room for all of us. But later on, when you stop going there so often, we'll have more space.'

Now Max jumped into the conversation.

'We're not selling Råddon. At least not now. Not this year or the next. There are a few things that your mother and I need to talk about, but we're not selling the cottage.'

'I'm sorry, but that means the rest of you will have to buy me out. You and your sister. Or your father. However you decide to do it.'

Helen thought Katriina sounded so businesslike.

'Have you talked to Eva about this?'

'We'll talk about it after Eva comes back home.'

Helen had always felt inferior to her mother. One of her earliest memories was of Katriina coming home one day from the hairdresser with her long hair cut short. It was like seeing a complete stranger walk in. She was wearing a knitted yellow jumper, and when she got home she kept looking at herself in the mirror and touching her hair at the nape of her neck, as if to remind herself how short it was. Helen was sitting with Eva at the kitchen table, and she must have been old enough to go to school, because she had homework spread out in front of her. But as she sat there with her sister, Helen looked with surprise at this woman who had come into their flat and claimed to know them. Not only that, she was supposedly their mother! Helen had glanced at Eva, who looked just as astonished as she was.

It was close to three in the afternoon by the time they reached Kristinestad. A light snow was falling, or maybe it was just gusts of wind sending snow-flakes against the car windows. They headed for the hospital where Ebba had been admitted and given a bed in Intensive Care. No one spoke. A melancholy mood had settled over all of them, as if they were approaching a church. Helen thought about the fact that every family experienced similar scenes that had to be endured, other hospitals with ill relatives, other small towns where a grand-mother had suffered a stroke.

Elisabeth was already there when they arrived. She hugged Helen, and then they all sat down in Ebba's room. The whole place smelled of medicine and seemed swathed in a strained, greyish-white air. There was nothing for them to do, nothing to talk about except the formal diagnosis of Ebba's medical condition, which was unchanged. Apparently the effects of the stroke had now lasted so long that the prognosis was very poor. Moving her to the central hospital in Vaasa would not be beneficial. At least not at the moment.

Ebba lay in bed with her eyes open, but she was unable to speak. Helen went over and took her grandmother's hand, which felt dry and lifeless. It was impossible to know whether she recognised Helen. Katriina stood at the end of the bed with her arms crossed. When she started to cry, Max went over to her and put his hand on her shoulder.

An hour later, Helen and Elisabeth were sitting at a table in the small cafeteria. Max and Katriina were still with Ebba.

It was dark outside now, pitch dark, and the hospital was very quiet. The walls in the long, deserted corridors were covered with large photographs of a winter landscape. The small windows were located high up near the ceiling and gave no hint of the world outside. A Christmas tree stood in one corner, adding a patch of light to the hallway.

'You can come over to my place to spend the night,' said Elisabeth. 'I've made up a bed in the living room.'

'Thanks,' said Helen. Neither of them spoke for a moment as they drank their coffee.

'I wish I'd come to visit her more often. When we were kids we saw Grandma and Grandpa every summer.'

'She often talks about you and Eva. She likes to keep up with what you're both doing. She knows a lot more than you'd think.'

'Mum and Dad are having a row. I don't know why they have to carry on like that. Especially today. And Dad refuses to say anything. I have no idea what he's thinking. He must be really upset, since it's his mother, after all.'

Elisabeth looked at her. 'Your father has never been the sort to react emotionally. Who knows what he thinks? Like why did he bring that woman with him yesterday? He didn't even introduce me. Not that it's any of my business.'

Helen stared at Elisabeth. 'Who do you mean?'

'I don't know. I thought maybe she was a younger colleague or something. Suddenly he just turned up here with her. And then she left.'

'What did she look like?'

'I don't know. Dark hair. About your age.'

Helen didn't say a word. A young woman. With dark hair. She refused to think about it. She didn't want the image of her father with a young woman to make it impossible for her to focus on her dying grandmother.

Max and Katriina came into the cafeteria.

'Shall we go?' asked Elisabeth.

'Sure. It's getting late,' Katriina replied.

'I'm staying here tonight,' said Max.

Elisabeth looked at him. Helen didn't say anything, but she picked up her coat from the chair and started walking towards the door.

The drive from Kristinestad to Närpes took a while. Helen sat in the back seat of Elisabeth's car. Katriina sat up front. No one spoke, and Helen thought to herself: I might never say another word. Not now, and not when we get back to Helsinki.

CHAPTER 31

Sarah arrived at Eva's flat half an hour later. She didn't say much, except to ask where Malik was. Then she went to find him in the bathroom, where he was sitting naked in the shower while Russ sprayed him with water. Eva had removed the bed linen, put it in a rubbish sack, and tossed the whole thing into the bin in the back courtyard. The mattress was also damp, so she rolled it up, tied a rope around it and pushed it down the stairs. That, too, ended up in the bin. By then she was sweaty and tired and hardly able to think any more. They had aired out the room, and most of the smell seemed to be gone.

'Are the two of you students of his?' asked Sarah.

'Yes,' said Russ, who looked completely exhausted. 'He phoned and I let him in. Then he collapsed on Eva's bed.'

'He hasn't been like this in a long time. I didn't know things were so bad. He's on medication, you know. We've been going through a rough patch lately. Thanks for phoning me,' she said.

Eva watched as Sarah took over, getting Malik

dressed in the clean clothes that she'd brought along at Eva's request. It was like watching a mother caring for her son. Like getting a glimpse of an entirely different family, a marriage that Eva now realised she knew nothing about. Malik didn't say a word; he still seemed mentally absent, as if he were sleepwalking. And he was shaking, maybe from the cold, maybe from something else.

After Sarah had helped her husband put on his shoes, she sank down on a stool out in the hall.

'Thanks again. I'm sorry you had to see him like this,' she said.

Eva wanted to say something. In some way she felt guilty about the whole situation – because she'd slept with Malik, because she hadn't taken responsibility for what she was doing, even though she was a grown woman. She looked at Sarah and felt like a spoiled teenager in comparison. She'd never had to take care of anyone, never needed to think about anyone but herself. Malik was on his feet now, but clinging to the doorway, still looking as if he might collapse at any moment.

Sarah looked up at Eva. 'Did he say anything?'

'No. About what?'

'About us.'

Eva couldn't look Sarah in the eye. 'No, he just talked about how he could have been one of the three greatest artists . . .'

'Oh, that old subject. He's always saying things like that. It's the biggest trauma of his life. The fact that the world doesn't understand him. Malik was a very talented artist. When we first got together he was the nicest guy you could ever imagine, so polite, so interested in everything. But his home situation was totally fucked up. His whole family is nuts. If I don't look out for him, this is what happens. Or worse.'

Eva was thinking of asking Sarah why she put up with it, why she didn't just leave him. But she felt naive and stupid, like a simple-minded yokel who didn't understand a thing about the real world, who had never been forced to confront anything ugly or difficult. She thought about the phone call from her mother and about her dying grandmother, and suddenly she felt such a longing for Finland – for some sort of pure, childish state that wouldn't require her to deal with these issues, where the mere act of getting up each morning and going over to the nearby convenience shop would provide all the excitement she needed.

Russ was still there when Sarah and Malik left.

'Thanks for all your help,' Eva told him.

'It was nothing. Actually, I don't mean that. I'm completely worn out.'

'Do you want to stay here tonight?'

'Where would I sleep? You don't even have a mattress. Remember? You tossed it into the rubbish bin.'

'Oh, right. I forgot about that.'

Eva realised that her only blanket was in the washing machine, and the only place to sleep was on the hard plywood platform of her bed. Natalia's room was locked.

'I have an idea,' said Russ. 'Have you got any warm clothes?'

The next day, as Eva took the bus to Gatwick Airport, she realised what she wanted to create for the class exhibition at Sarah's gallery. She took her notebook out of her bag and began sketching the piece that had appeared in her mind. It suddenly seemed only natural that she would bring Finland to London. She would get branches from Kristinestad and snow from Helsinki and collect litter from Sibelius Park. She would construct an installation big enough to go inside, enveloping a person on all sides, a place where someone would feel safe, though it resembled the tents outside St Paul's. The sign would say: 'This is none other than the house of God; this is the gate of heaven'. And it would be her paradise. Visitors who went inside her artwork would get a sense of her childhood. In the very back she would display things from her old room, including the cast of her teeth made when she was a kid, that ugly plaster sculpture. Because this was how she was feeling at the moment: she wanted to crawl inside there and never come out. It occurred to her that the installation would work only if she built it with sufficiently sophisticated techniques and really thought through the aesthetic impact. Obviously it had to remind people of the Occupy movement, because what was that whole thing really about other than a protest against an evil world? A dream of a purer social order, a safe place? She also wanted to reclaim the prerogative to interpret the world, the child's sense that she is God, that she has the right to name things.

Eva and Russ had slept in his tent that night, huddled close together inside his sleeping bag. The cathedral bells had woken her up several times, but each time she had turned over and looked at him, feeling the nearness of his body in the dark, and felt strangely safe, even though she could hear all the sounds of London, the collective sounds of a sleeping metropolis, of the late-night carousers and the traffic outside, of the wind and the trees and the ground beneath her.

Only now, as she sat in the plane, did she sink into a deep sleep. When the plane landed she caught a bus and rode home, to Helsinki, and opened the door to an empty flat. Helen, Katriina and Max were in Kristinestad, but it was too late for Eva to go out there now. Instead, she found a box in her parents' wardrobe and began filling it with things from her room. Night fell outside, and soon the whole flat was in darkness. She decided not to turn on any lights, but instead lit a few candles in her room. She wanted to hold on to the feeling as she sat on the floor, arranged the objects she'd chosen and began making sketches. Several cassette tapes, the plaster teeth, papers she'd written in middle school – and now she was glad that her mother had saved everything – and a threadbare flannel shirt that she'd had as a teenager and had never wanted to throw away, since she'd worn it nearly every day in secondary school.

As she sat there in the dark, the only sound was the rustling of the hamsters running in the wheel that spun round and round. She looked at them, wondering what drove them to do that, whether it was a need to flee from some imagined danger, or simply an innate desire to remain in constant motion.

Eva felt like going out. She thought about the friends she'd once had in Helsinki, but she hadn't kept in contact with any of them. She put on her jacket, then went down the stairs and left the building. She headed towards Mannerheimvägen and Hesperia Park. It was snowing. The waters of Töölö Bay swallowed the snowflakes as if in a single, deep inhalation. Eva walked along the road past the Finlandia House, on her way downtown. She took out her mobile to record the sound of the trams driving past. That was something she could use. She kept walking – past Kiasma and the post office and Sokos – with a feeling that she was carrying out a secret mission. No one looked at her, no one had any idea what she was doing. She headed along Mannerheimvägen, past the student building and the Swedish Theatre and up towards Skillnaden Square, past Stora Robertsgatan and the Design Museum and Johanneskyrkan and the hill on Högbergsgatan.

When she came to Maxill's, she decided to go in. This was where her family had eaten Sunday dinners when she was a child, and she wanted to capture some of the sounds, the buzz of conversation in Helsinki. She brushed the snow off her clothes and stomped her feet. The restaurant was packed this evening, with people talking and laughing, but she looked at them as if she were watching extras in a film. She went over to the bar and ordered wine. Then she hung her jacket on a hook and picked up the wine glass with frozen hands. For the first time in ages she felt as if she had some purpose, something that she could build on.

CHAPTER 32

Eva stayed in Helsinki for a week. Katriina had already started talking about making funeral arrangements – she suggested a memorial service with the immediate family in Kristinestad, followed by coffee and *smörgåstårta*, a savoury cake. Elisabeth would help out. But suddenly, after a week, Ebba showed signs of improvement. The doctors decided to keep her in hospital since she was much too weak to be sent back to the nursing home. Ebba had regained feeling in her body and face, so it was now possible to communicate with her. But she seemed confused about the whole situation and kept asking when she could go home.

Max had been staying at Råddon and went into Kristinestad every day, but now he was coming back to Helsinki to fetch some more clothes and spend a few days at work.

Eva had never seen her father cry, and he seemed to be handling everything by talking sensibly about practical matters, about medications and hospital bills, as if he could relate to what was happening only by dealing with concrete tasks.

Helen seemed to be in some sort of emotional state that Eva found a bit disturbing. She talked about memories of their grandmother, about what a warm relationship she'd had with Ebba. Eva didn't comment, but she thought Helen was exaggerating and for some reason trying to claim that she'd had a stronger connection to Kristinestad than her sister. She talked about their grandmother as if she were already dead. Eva loved Ebba too, but she didn't write down improvised speeches intended for future memorial services; she didn't speak with enthusiasm about what an amazing person her grandmother had been. She didn't sit in the kitchen with Max's photo album from his childhood and talk about doing genealogical research. She didn't pretend that her grandmother was suddenly the most important person in her life.

Eva spent the whole week working on her art piece, collecting material and trying to visualise how the whole thing was going to come together from a purely technical point of view. One day when she was in town she suddenly caught sight of Laura Lampela, the journalist who had interviewed Max. She was standing at the tram stop outside of Glaspalatset.

'Laura?'

She was looking at her mobile and didn't react.

'Laura?'

At first she looked puzzled, as if she didn't recognise Eva, or as if she'd forgotten how to respond to a greeting.

'Eva? What are you doing here? I thought you were in London.'

'My grandmother has been ill, so I came home to see her.'

'Oh, right. I heard about that. I'm sorry.'

'Thanks,' said Eva.

For a moment neither of them spoke. Eva wanted to say something. She was happy to see someone she knew. It felt like this might be the right time to reconnect with Helsinki.

When the tram arrived, it turned out they were both heading in the same direction, even though Eva was only going two stops.

'I don't know how much your father has told you,' said Laura. 'But I've read his book. While you've been away in London. I was supposed to help him with the manuscript, but I don't know if that plan is going to work out. This whole situation with your grandmother . . . So how is Max?' said Laura.

Eva had not been allowed to read her father's manuscript. He never talked about his writing at home. It had always been a secret part of his work that he didn't share with the family. She'd read his other books, but only after they were published – and that was when anyone could read them, when they were available to people like Laura and no longer had any special aura about them.

'It's strange about people of your father's generation, don't you think?' said Laura.

'What do you mean?' asked Eva.

'I mean how privileged they are. They build up

a myth about how they've made this great leap in social class, and I guess in some cases they have, but it's really been pretty easy for them. I mean, it's a straight climb up the ladder – they've never had to go through really difficult times.'

'I suppose you're right.'

Eva didn't understand why Laura was talking about this.

'Your father too. That whole generation. In the sixties they were fighting to erase academic hierarchies, to take education out to the people. Now they complain that nobody is getting a classical education any more, that women dominate the university, and that boys can no longer read. It feels like they regret all the changes that brought us to where we are today.'

Eva thought there was something about Laura's analysis that didn't really hold water, a link that was missing, angry rhetoric that lent no real coherence to her argument. But above all, Eva thought this was a strange topic for discussion at the moment. She would have preferred to talk about something else. She sighed.

'I'm sorry,' Laura said. 'I was just thinking out loud. Your grandmother is ill. I'm just so tired of the fact that certain types of people get to decide how things are interpreted in this country. So what are you working on now? Still painting, or what?'

Eva realised that if she told Laura anything about her project, it would wreck her plan and the feeling she had about it, and then she wouldn't be able to finish it. Talking to Laura about her art would sabotage the whole thing. She needed to hold on to the feeling she had, immerse herself in it so it wouldn't slip away. The tram was just now passing the National Museum. Eva was getting off at Hesperia Park.

'We're having an exhibition in March,' she said. 'Want to talk about it?'

Eva looked at Laura. 'Not really.'

'Okay. I understand. I know how it is. You don't want to talk it to death.'

'Exactly,' said Eva.

'If I was going to create a piece of art,' said Laura, 'I'd make something about the academic proletariat, something about temp work and the uncertainty of the job market. Nobody I know has a permanent job.'

Eva wondered how anyone could be so annoying. She was reminded of a classmate named Anna from college who had concealed her competitive nature under a facade of hippie-like love for humanity, when in reality she had dominated the social interaction in the collective where they were both living. Anna had instituted rules about how and when they could have boyfriends over, rules that were suddenly non-existent whenever Anna wanted to bring anyone home and decided to take over the living room for a party. Eva thought that Laura was a little like Anna.

'This is my stop,' she said.

★　　★　　★

373

A couple of days later Katriina had arranged a dinner that would include Helen and Christian and the children. Katriina had organised the whole day, bought the flowers and set the big table in the living room.

It was the first time in ages they were all gathered, the first time no outsiders were present, just the immediate family. Katriina cooked a roast, and Eva made a salad. They began by having a few glasses of wine while they conversed. Helen had already started crying several times. She talked about how close she felt to her grandmother, as if it was something only she understood, as if the other family members were complete strangers. Katriina seemed very taken by Helen's emotional outpouring, and Eva couldn't help feeling left out. She knew what was expected of her, but it wasn't something that came naturally; she couldn't participate fully in this familial fellowship. Instead, she felt like an outside observer. She thought this was similar to how she felt when standing in front of certain paintings. She knew they were masterpieces, and yet she couldn't force herself to have some kind of major, overwhelming response.

She went to her father's study to have a talk with him. Edvard was lying on the floor outside the door and began wagging his tail as soon as she came near. Eva bent down to pet him. She'd never been especially interested in dogs, but right now it was as if she saw Edvard for the first time, as if she really connected with him. He gazed deep into her eyes, and she reciprocated.

'Edvard, what do you think I should do?'

He stared at her and wagged his tail even harder. Apparently he thought she'd asked if he'd like to go out.

She snorted, stood up, and went into her father's room. He was sitting at his desk.

'Hi, Dad.'

She went over and sat down on his lap. Max put his arms around her, and she leaned her head on his shoulder.

'Is dinner ready soon?' he asked.

'I think so.'

'Great. I'm hungry.'

For a moment neither of them spoke. Max smelled good. When Eva was a child and lying in bed, she would notice the scent of his aftershave when he came in to say goodnight. She associated it with his writing. She'd always pictured him sitting at his desk and writing after she'd gone to bed, slipping out of her room to go and work on his books.

'Eva, sweetie. Is everything all right? Are you doing okay in London?'

She pressed her face against his neck.

'I'm doing great, Dad.'

They went into the kitchen, but the food still wasn't ready.

'Could someone make the gravy? There should

be some chanterelles in the freezer,' said Katriina.

Helen opened the freezer and took out two pack-ages. She opened one of them and poured the contents into a bowl. Then she looked at Katriina in surprise.

'What's this?'

CHAPTER 33

Ebba's condition slowly improved, and she was moved to a rehab ward. Max travelled back and forth between Kristinestad and Helsinki. One day in early March he found himself in Matti's big office at the publishing company. He was trying hard not to jump up and strangle his editor. Matti had just told him that his book about Edvard Westermarck was not going to be on the autumn list.

'I don't know, Max. I think it's going to be difficult to fit your book in. The lists have basically already been decided, and you still have a lot of work to do. You have the biographical details more or less under control, but there's still something I'm missing.'

'What do you mean? His moral philosophy?'

'You're the expert. I'm just saying that there's . . . something missing. It needs to be more anchored in the context of the era, or maybe there should be a little more about the fact that he was probably gay. That might be a possible thread to follow. I don't know.'

The tone of Matti's voice hinted that the whole

topic had begun to lose its appeal, and his interest was waning. He seemed restless and kept rearranging the papers on his desk, trying to look pressed for time, as if he wanted to dismiss the whole matter as quickly as possible.

It was Thursday, and Max was taking care of Amanda, since her school was closed for teacher meetings. Max had brought his granddaughter to the publishing company, and right now she was sitting on the sofa next to him, looking bored. Amanda seemed to regard other grown-ups as minor players in her life, and therefore not worthy of attention. She was fiddling with the zipper of her jacket, sliding it up and down, up and down.

'And one more thing,' said Matti. 'It's not really relevant to what we're discussing, but I thought I'd tell you – since it sort of concerns you – that I've been talking with Laura about a book manuscript. She sent me a synopsis that I think sounds tremendously promising. It's partly autobiographical, about how a young woman gets into the patriarchal world of newspaper reporting . . .'

But Max had stopped listening.

When they were back outside, he asked Amanda what she'd like to do.

'Could we go to a café? Please?'

'What would you like to have?'

'A bun.'

They went to the Café Esplanad, and Max ordered buns for both of them. As he sat there, he pondered whether to give up the whole book project. Maybe Matti was right, maybe it just wouldn't interest anyone. Amanda started a running commentary about the way he was eating, like a sports announcer doing a play-by-play of a football match.

'Now Max Paul takes another bite of the bun. Hey, that piece was a little too big, but he gulps down some water, and now he seems to have swallowed it.'

Max looked at her. When she saw his surprised expression, she continued with even greater enthusiasm.

'Max Paul has had a tough day. He's been to see his publisher and received some bad news. His book isn't going to come out this autumn. There was no room for it on the list.'

Max was amazed that Amanda had paid such close attention. In Matti's office she had seemed bored, staring off into space. The café was packed with people, and now Amanda had started her spiel over, looking even more eager.

'Max Paul has had a very, very tough day.'

'Amanda, could you stop that?'

But that just seemed to encourage her.

'Now Max Paul is getting annoyed. He asks his granddaughter to stop. He picks up his coffee cup and raises it to his lips. He swallows some coffee. For Max Paul, life seems to be causing him a lot of trouble. And the newspapers print nothing but stupid articles.'

'Come on, Amanda, could you please stop?'

People in the café were looking at them. Max took Amanda's hand and leaned close to whisper, 'I'm not really in the mood for this at the moment. You need to stop.'

But his words only seemed to spur Amanda on to push the boundaries. She saw how uncomfortable he looked and sensed the power she had over him. Now she was sitting across from him, with her arms folded.

'Max Paul is a great writer. But his new book isn't going to be published. Max Paul is sitting in a café, brooding about life. What should someone do when he gets old? Now Max Paul takes another sip of coffee. Now his face is red. Now he almost drops the cup . . .'

'Shut up, Amanda!'

The words flew out of his mouth much louder than he'd planned. His hand was shaking, and he spilled some of the coffee on the table.

Everyone nearby was staring at Max. A young father who was there with his family got up and came over to the table.

'Is there a problem here?'

Amanda looked up at the man, but didn't say a word. She was both fascinated and amused. Max could feel himself sliding down on the bench, wanting to explain, but realising how stupid any explanation would sound. He looked around and realised that now everyone in the café was staring at them.

'No, there's no problem,' he said.

'You let me know if there's a problem, okay?' said the young father to Amanda.

She just looked at him, her eyes wide, delighted by the chain of events that she'd started. Max stood up, gathered their coats and took Amanda by the hand. Then they left.

That evening, after Katriina had driven Amanda home, Helen rang, sounding very upset. She hadn't spoken to her parents in two weeks. She phoned Max on his mobile.

'Amanda says that you told her to shut up in a café today. Is that right, Dad?'

'Well, er . . . you know, I was having a really bad day. And she kept on teasing me. It wasn't as bad as it sounds.'

'Kept on teasing you? Are you ten years old, or what? Apparently it was bad enough for a complete stranger to come over and talk to you.'

'Okay, okay. But she just wouldn't stop . . .'

'So now you're blaming Amanda? A nine-year-old?'

'No, no, but . . . you know how kids can be.'

'Let me talk to Mum.'

Max handed the phone to Katriina. They'd been conducting a silent form of trench warfare all week. Max had a feeling that Katriina was watching every step he took to see what he was doing and where he was going. Max had responded by retreating to his study to sleep and surf the forums on the web. Eva had gone back to London, taking along a big box of branches and sticks and other materials, but she refused to say what they were for.

When Katriina had finished talking to Helen on the phone, she turned to her husband and said, 'Max. Two things. I want a divorce. And we have to sell Råddon.'

The next day Katriina handed him a printout of several emails. Apparently she'd been in touch with a lawyer. Max read phrases such as: 'Concerning the previously shared residence, there is a statute in the marriage laws that makes it possible for the party who is viewed as having a greater need for the property to be allowed to stay there until a legal settlement has been reached and instituted, although for no more than two years.'

'What does all this mean?'

'It means I want the flat. You'll have to move out.'

'But I have nowhere to go.'

'You should have thought of that before you started having an affair with a twenty-five-year-old.'

'Twenty-nine,' Max corrected her, but Katriina wasn't listening.

'Because you didn't think about the conse-quences, did you? You should have realised that this would happen, sooner or later. Or weren't you planning on telling me?'

Max hadn't told her a thing, but somehow

Katriina had known all along. Max missed the quarrels they used to have. He would have preferred to get everything out in the open once and for all.

That night he was sitting at the computer in his study, and he Googled Laura's name. There turned out to be an entire thread about her on the discussion site Hommaforum. Lots of comments about her appearance and her newspaper columns. Someone had written that she was a 'typical politically correct journalist who took up space bemoaning the fact that she couldn't get laid'. Somebody else wrote that *Iltasanomat* was being taken over by 'leftist feminists who hate the nuclear family and their native country'. A third person said that Laura 'looks like she has nice boobs'.

Max got up and closed the door to his study.

He could hear Katriina in the kitchen. She'd started putting all the plates and other dishes into boxes, after informing him that it was time to redo the kitchen. Max had seen the plans that she'd commissioned, but had merely nodded without comment and then retreated to his room.

Now he poured himself a whisky and again opened the browser on his computer.

Then he started writing.

CHAPTER 34

Helen and Christian did not have a summer cottage of their own. The one that belonged to Christian's family was located almost on the Russian border, and it wasn't really a cottage. It was more of an old farmstead, the place where his paternal grandmother had grown up. He spoke nostalgically about the house and had suggested many times that they ought to start using it, since none of his relatives ever spent more than a couple of nights there each year. But Helen thought it was much too remote to stay at the place for any length of time. And it wasn't on the water. It was just a shady plot of land filled with mosquitoes and tall grass at the end of a tractor path with a huge rock that they almost always ran into when they went there. In reality, Helen had gone out there only twice: once when Amanda was a toddler – the first thing they'd had to do was clear away all the mouse droppings and dead mice – and once last summer. That was when they'd had a free weekend and Christian had persuaded his family to drive out to the cottage.

'Mum, I don't want to go to that place. I want to drive to Flamingo,' Amanda had complained.

For Christian, the summer place was a personal obsession, and he talked about it the way someone might tell an old family story that just got funnier the more often it was repeated and enhanced. Christian had so many memories linked to that place, although they seemed inexplicably boring whenever he tried to talk about them to anyone else. His biggest dream was for his children to develop a similar emotional attachment to the cottage the way he had done, or the way Helen had grown fond of Sideby.

On a Saturday morning in June they had driven out to the cottage. The drive took three and a half hours, which really wasn't that long, through the beautiful landscape of eastern Finland. Helen actually caught herself thinking that it wasn't so bad – maybe the house had potential, maybe she would change her opinion once she saw it again.

They certainly couldn't afford to renovate an old family farm, since any extra money went towards work on their own house. But maybe the place only needed a few basic repairs.

When they arrived, they discovered that it was impossible to drive into the yard because the grass was two metres high. They had to get out and wade through the grass to reach the front steps. As Helen was walking, she pictured a snake biting her. Amanda shrieked and said she could feel ticks jumping on her legs.

'Why did we have to come out here to this damn house?' asked Lukas.

Christian found the keys under a rock and opened the door. The whole place smelled of mould. Helen noticed it at once. There was nothing really wrong with the house itself. It was spacious, with high ceilings, and the floor was covered in a lovely linoleum from the early 1900s. But everything looked worn, lifeless and crude, with visible damage from moisture. This time there were no dead mice or voles lying about, but the air smelled foul and dead, like an old doper's den that just happened to have furniture from the 1930s. Christian quickly stepped inside to give an enthusiastic tour to his extremely sceptical audience. He showed them everything – from the kitschy painting depicting an old fence to a little suitcase which he claimed had come from America. He spoke about everything as if they were magical objects, as if they possessed powers that only he could see.

'When can we leave?' asked Lukas, and Amanda nodded that she, too, wanted to know.

'We don't have to stay long, do we?' she asked.

'We could spend the night,' suggested Christian. 'There must be some bed linen in the cupboard.'

Helen gave him a stern look.

Half an hour later, when they were back in the car, Lukas solemnly declared that the house 'was worse than I ever imagined'. Amanda, who was always

386

trying to be the dutiful daughter and who liked to side with her father, said, 'It was sort of yucky, but I'm sure it was nice enough, *in its own way*.'

As they drove home, Helen attempted to be diplomatic. 'Looks like it needs a bit more than a coat of paint on the outside,' she said as they entered the motorway and saw the sign for Helsinki. 'There's a lot of mould.'

'How do you know that?' asked Christian.

'I just do. I could feel it,' she replied.

For a few minutes Christian didn't say anything, as if considering whether to drop the subject.

Then he said, 'Okay. Let's say that you're right. There might very well be mould in the house. But I just wonder how you know that. Because of the smell? No one has lived there for years, and that's the way old houses always smell. Or do you have some special ability to distinguish the smell of mould?'

'Maybe I have,' said Helen.

'All right. But it's strange how everybody has been talking about mould lately. Nobody did in the seventies. It's like the subject of lactose intolerance. Suddenly nobody can drink milk. And suddenly all old houses have moisture damage.'

They hadn't gone back since then, and Helen was afraid the topic might pop up again if Max and Katriina really did sell Råddon.

Helen had found it hard to concentrate on her work ever since Ebba ended up in hospital. She felt weighed down, sad about something that seemed to be slipping away, not just Ebba, but some part of herself, the way she had once been. She thought that there were certain facets of her character that Christian would never understand, but which might be more important than she wanted to admit. They had to do with her whole view of life. Or maybe what she was feeling was a sense that something important was missing, something that she'd had in the past.

She tried all week to put this feeling into words, just for herself. When Friday arrived, Christian said that he was going to the gym and then to a pub with Michael.

'We'll probably have a bite to eat, so you don't have to make any dinner for me.'

'You're going out? But you went out last week.'

Christian and Michael had been out twice since the dinner party at their place.

'So? Does it matter? We're just having a couple of beers. He told me that he doesn't know the city very well.'

'And you do? You haven't gone out on the town in years.'

'But I do know a few good pubs. And at work I keep hearing about all the trendy places. I was thinking we'd try that new restaurant near Skillnaden. They're supposed to have good food.'

'Okay,' said Helen.

When she got home she put some fish fingers and chips in the oven and let the kids eat in front of the TV. Then she stretched out on the bed and tried not to think about what Christian and Michael might talk about together. She went into the living room and ate the leftover food from the kids' plates, looking at her children for a long time as they watched TV.

Christian didn't come home until four in the morning. She knew what time it was because she woke up when he practically fell into bed. He was awake by eight, but at breakfast he seemed drunk, telling an incoherent story about what he and Michael had done. They'd ended up at a nightclub and then had to wait an hour for a cab. Finally, Helen suggested it might be better if he went back to bed.

Christian didn't get up again until noon and still seemed tired and sluggish as he sat down at his computer.

'I was thinking of taking the kids sledging over at the hill,' she told him as she came into the living room.

Christian was hunched over his mobile. Who was he sending a text message to? Michael?

'Did you guys have fun last night?'

'Yeah. It was great.'

'Is that who you're texting? Michael?'

'Uh-huh. We were planning to meet at the gym today.'

'Oh,' said Helen. 'Sounds like you've really become good friends.'

'I don't know. It's just the gym.'

She couldn't believe this was the same Christian who so recently had insisted that they take their own sandwiches on the ferry boat, who always chose the familiar over the unfamiliar, who never really let loose. What was it about Michael that made him suddenly behave this way? Was it some sort of early midlife crisis? Was he trying to make up for those lost years of his childhood?

That evening she asked him if they could make love. They were lying in bed and had just watched a DVD. The kids were already asleep in their own beds. He responded at once, turning over to lie on top of her. He pulled off his shorts and her knickers, and the whole thing was over in less than ten minutes.

'Thanks,' he said. 'That was great.'

'Yes, it was. We should have sex more often.'

'Uh-huh. We should.'

For a while neither of them spoke. Helen was just about to doze off when he suddenly started talking.

'There's something I've been thinking about,' he said.

'Mmmm.'

'The thing is we don't really know each other. I mean, we do know each other, but we never talked much about our lives before we had chil-

390

dren. We met and we had the kids and that's when our life together began, but we don't know anything about before. It's like my whole life before Amanda and Lukas belonged to another person, not to me.'

'You mean like all the music that you've started listening to lately?'

'Sure . . . but not just that. Or rather, that too. I had to stop everything I used to do because I thought that was required, that I needed to leave everything behind.'

'But I've never asked you to do that.'

'I know, I know. I don't really understand why I did that. But I've been talking a lot about this with Michael, and that's what made me realise that I haven't really been myself. He didn't change anything just because he had a child.'

'No, but his wife is dead. And how do you know he didn't change?'

'Because that's what he says.'

'Huh. So what do you want to do? Join a rock band? Is that what you mean?'

'Maybe. For example.'

Neither of them spoke for a while.

'He seems to know a hell of a lot. He's got an amazing knowledge of all sorts of things.'

'Who? Michael?'

'Yeah.'

'It sounds like you really admire him.'

'I don't know about that,' said Christian dismissively. 'I just meant that he knows a lot.'

Silence settled over them, and Helen almost fell

asleep, but she managed to stop herself and refocus her attention on the room and one more thing she wanted to say.

'Christian?'

'What?'

'I think I'll go up to Kristinestad and visit Grandma.'

'When?'

'Soon. Maybe next weekend.'

'Sure. Go ahead.'

She lay in bed thinking about that. She decided to take a day off from school and drive up to Kristinestad.

CHAPTER 35

Eva was sitting in the dark, inside her art installation. It was the thirteenth of March. Over the past few days the weather had turned warmer in London, so that people could sit outside in the sunshine to have their coffee and take long walks along the river without freezing. It was almost possible to feel that life was tolerable, that something was just around the corner and it was worth waiting for.

She had put together her art piece in two weeks. Sarah had given her a big space in the gallery. Eva went over there every morning to ponder and plan. Sometimes she would forget to eat, and Sarah would surprise her with a plate of food. Some days she kept working until she discovered that it was two in the morning and time to go home. The other students worked on their pieces at the school, but Eva had been given permission to construct hers on-site. She used a power hammer and steel wires, and Sarah helped her to measure angles and dimensions. The most time-consuming part was weaving the whole structure of the hut she was building. For that she used some of the branches that she'd brought back from Kristinestad. The rest she'd gathered in the nearby woods that she and Russ had located on Google Maps. Then she carted them over to the gallery in three big boxes from IKEA. She decided to have the Bible quote from St Paul's Cathedral in both Swedish and English. She'd post them on the wall next to some crocheted doilies that were an Österbotten tradition.

Now she was almost finished, she just had to arrange the lighting inside the hut. There was a small TV in the back, showing a film that she'd made with Helen's help. Clips from movies that Max had taken of the two sisters when they were kids. Eva thought there was something so immediate and aesthetic about Super 8 films with no sound.

Sarah crawled inside and looked around.

'I like it. It has such a harmonious feeling. Most artists who show their work in our gallery have some sort of ugly but interesting aesthetic. It's rare that anyone dares embrace beauty in such a natural way.'

Eva was pleased to hear her words of praise. Lately she'd been thinking a lot about the word 'love'. Maybe it wasn't bad to make something out of love. Maybe everything didn't have to be so trendy. There was a reason for not creating a layer of irony between the viewer and the artist.

'Let me say again that I'm sorry about what

happened with Malik. I haven't seen him in such a bad state in a long time. But that's how it is when someone's bipolar. Sooner or later the manic period ends and he hits the wall. Don't tell anyone, but I think it was because of some girl at your school that he'd fallen in love with. When she rejected him, he flipped out.'

Eva didn't know what to say. 'But doesn't that bother you? I mean, since you're married and all?'

Sarah laughed. She gave Eva a look that suddenly reminded her of Katriina, the way she simply dismissed the whole issue.

'We haven't had a functioning marriage for ten years. I don't even know if I like the man any more. But I can't just . . . Someone has to take care of him. Someone has to make sure he seeks help when he needs it. Usually he manages to lead a more-or-less normal life. As I already told you, his family is really fucked up. It's hereditary, you know.'

When Eva went home that evening, she took the route past St Paul's and sat down on the steps. The Occupy encampment had been cleared away at the end of February, and many had given up. Some had moved their tents to nearby Finsbury Square, but the movement as a whole had largely dispersed. Now tourists crowded the square in front of the cathedral, as if nothing had changed, or as if everything was back to normal and life was inexorably continuing on. She thought it was sad. The fact that there was such a thin line between the two options: world-wide revolution or total oblivion. A warm gust of wind seeped through her jumper. She got up and walked home.

JUNE

CHAPTER 36

Max felt as if he'd spent his whole adult life waiting for this moment. He straightened his back, squared his shoulders, and looked down at his notes.

He was about to give a speech on the occasion of his younger daughter's wedding, and he was so excited that he hardly knew where to begin.

He'd given a speech at Helen's wedding, but that was different. When Eva was born, he'd played a greater role as father. On countless evenings he'd rocked her to sleep, holding her in his arms as he listened to Rachmaninov, whose work he'd been obsessed with during that autumn in the early eighties. How sublime that had been. And the whole time he had imagined Eva all grown up and the day when he would give this speech for her and say these words. As if their entire relationship was defined by this moment when she was leaving him, and he could say: this is how you were. This is what it was like. This is what our life together looked like. This is what I did.

It didn't matter that he didn't really know Russ. He seemed nice, and Max thought everything would be fine. Because what was the alternative? Life went on its merry way. People got divorced, others got married.

Now he was standing at the table in the banquet room of Roddstadion, clinking a knife against the side of his wine glass until he had everyone's attention.

Everything was green outside, the light green of early summer, when all the blossoms hadn't yet faded, a time of thousands of promises and endless possibilities. It was no wonder that the older he got the more he treasured the springtime – it was tangible proof that life was reborn each year, that there was still time.

Max had written out his speech on a piece of paper that was sweaty and crumpled, but he smoothed it out and placed it on the table in front of him. He had on his reading glasses, but he could probably speak without referring to his notes, since he'd already read the speech so many times.

He cleared his throat, smiled at Eva – she wore a pale yellow dress – smiled at Russ – he'd had a haircut and trimmed his moustache – and then he began:

'My dear friends. For a Finnish sociologist, it seems unthinkable to give a wedding speech without mentioning Edvard Westermarck. What we most often remember Westermarck for today, aside from his criticism of Freud, is his pioneering work on the history of marriage. There is a deluxe

Swedish edition of his text in which we learn a great deal about marriage rituals in large parts of the world. Of course, Westermarck wrote during the late nineteenth century, and the anthropological findings of his day were without a doubt marked by a colonial outlook. Quite a few of the stories are based on Westermarck's interviews with missionaries. Nonetheless, it might be interesting to take a look at what the good Edvard had to say about marriage as an institution. I'd like to read you a passage from his notes.'

Max again cleared his throat.

'"Before a young man of the Macusi Indian tribe in British Guiana can take a wife, he must demonstrate that he is a man and is capable of carrying out a man's work. Without flinching he must endure having his flesh sliced open, or allow himself to be sewn into a hammock filled with fire ants, or display his courage through other similar tests."'

The wedding guests laughed.

Max made eye contact with Katriina who was drinking from a glass that she now set down on the table. Her smile was strained, almost contemptuous. Max shifted his gaze to look at his sister. The hall was brightly lit, but the birch trees outside the windows cast shadows over the walls. Elisabeth was looking at him as she always had, with a slightly amused expression, as if she was the only person in the world who knew that he was actually playing a role. That it was all theatre.

Eva was translating for Russ, who made an effort to join in the laughter.

Max continued.

'Dear Russ, you should be glad that you're getting married in the twenty-first century. If this were the late 1800s, it might not have been as simple. In Siberia the prospective father-in-law went into the woods and chopped down the tree with the thickest trunk that he could find. The son-in-law was then forced to carry that tree all the way back to town. Only if he managed to do so was he considered a worthy husband.'

More laughter. Max thought that he could risk one more example. And besides, he was just getting warmed up.

'Now I'm going to quote directly from Westermarck.'

Max picked up the book, an edition from 1923, and began reading aloud.

' "Among the Wapokomo in British East Africa, young people were prevented from marrying too early because of the requirement that a young man could only marry after he had killed a crocodile and presented the woman with some of the meat to eat. And among various southeast Asian tribes who practised headhunting, it is said that no man was allowed to marry unless he could present at least one human head as a sign of his courage." '

Max again caught Katriina's eye. She looked bored as she stared back down at her wine glass.

'But of course marriage is not about these kinds of tests of strength but about completely different trials. Anybody can prepare a shrunken head or kill a crocodile . . .'

His audience roared with laughter.

'What's really difficult, and what you two will soon discover, is not to lose sight of each other, to find a way to live through the other person instead of through yourself. This was something that Westermarck also said. Westermarck himself never married, and today it's generally thought that he was a homosexual. But he focussed attention on one interesting detail: people seldom talk about happy marriages. As he writes: "Those are not the ones on which theatres, biographies and novelists build their dramas." That said, I am convinced that the two of you have more sense than Eva's mother and I did. We managed to stay together for a very long time, as all of you know, but shit happens.'

There was no response from his audience or from Katriina. He looked at Helen. She looked horrified. Again he cleared his throat.

'Russ! We don't yet know each other very well, but from what I've been able to observe, you make my daughter tremendously happy. We'll just have to ignore the fact that you are from London – a city that Westermarck described, by the way, as a place that needs "its fog in order to conceal the hideous architecture". Now let's all drink a toast to the newlyweds!'

Everyone toasted the couple, including Katriina, who was now looking at Max with a different expression, as if she intended to stand up at any minute and say something extremely sarcastic.

Max had taken time off from his job so he could travel to London to see Eva's art exhibit. He stayed for a week in a much too expensive hotel right near Hyde Park, ate dinner with Eva and Russ when they had time, and took long walks through the city that was in full springtime bloom. One evening he was having dinner alone and almost started talking to two men who sat next to him and were telling each other stories from the Second World War. Max would have liked to join in the conversation. He could have told them that he was from Finland and said something about the Winter War – the two men seemed as though they would have been impressed, and it would have been great to talk to someone his own age. But each time he tried to make eye contact, he failed. So he just sat there listening for an hour or two while the men got more and more boisterous and finally ended up quarrelling. Max left the restaurant with a feeling that London was a place he would need considerably more time to understand. When he went to the British Museum the following day, he was disappointed to discover that the Reading Room where Westermarck had done his research was closed because the museum was installing a new exhibition. He went into the gift shop, thinking that he would buy a small set of bookends in the shape of the god Anubis, but when he stepped over to the cashier, he suddenly remembered that all of his books were packed in boxes. And he no longer had a study.

Max was still standing in front of the wedding guests.

'Well, that's all I really wanted to say. Or . . . wait, there's one more thing. While I'm standing here I want to be sure to say that I'm so proud of both of you. My two daughters. You make your father very happy. So keep on doing that.'

He looked around the room. At Katriina, at Eva, at Helen and Christian and his grandchildren. Russ was sitting next to Eva, looking like a man who had just won the lottery. Elisabeth was there too, and Ebba, sitting in her wheelchair. The strange thing was that his mother looked better than she had in years. Maybe she would outlive them all.

After the applause Max went over to Eva and kissed her on the forehead.

Elisabeth called out to him. 'Great speech. You really know how to bullshit,' she said.

Risto came up and patted him on the shoulder, wanting to offer his congratulations. Then someone started up the music, a Beach Boys tune that poured out of the loudspeakers, filling the whole room. People were out on the balcony, talking. Max looked around the room and met Eva's eye. She was standing in the doorway to the dining room in her pale yellow linen dress.

★　　★　　★

Max went over to Helen. She was holding Lukas on her lap. He had turned six just a week ago. Amanda, wearing a blue dress, had a balloon that she tossed into the air and then caught, over and over.

'Aren't you going to say hi to Grandpa?' asked Helen.

'Hi, Grandpa,' said Amanda.

'How long do we have to stay at this damn wedding?' said Lukas, clinging to his mother.

'What did we tell you about using that word?'

Almost two hundred guests had been invited to the wedding. Twenty of them came from England. They had formed a little clique in one corner of the room, and Max had the feeling that most of them were friends with both Russ and Eva. As far as Russ's family was concerned, only his mother had come, along with his sister and her children. Max and Katriina had been introduced to them, very briefly, and he wondered whether they'd ever get to know each other better. Or maybe this would be the first and last time he ever saw his daughter's mother-in-law.

He found Katriina out on the balcony. She was sitting on a bench having a smoke. She looked so beautiful, and Max hated himself for thinking so.

'Not a bad wedding.'

'No, it's quite lovely,' she replied.

'Have you talked to Russ's mother?'

'Just a little. She seems nice. Have you?'

'No, not at all. His sister is awfully young.'

'Not much younger than I was when I had Helen.'

'Maybe not.'

Max sat there, with the midsummer sun high in the sky, feeling the warm air – with no mosquitoes in sight – and it was almost as if nothing had changed. He could have leaned towards Katriina, put his arm around her, and sat there all night.

'What are you staring at?' she asked.

'Well, um . . . I'm not. Staring, I mean.'

'We should go in. I don't want people to get the wrong idea. There's no going back for us, you know.'

'No, I know.' Max said.